TROUBLE
MAKING
TOYS

TROUBLE MAKING TOYS

A. M. Pyle

Walker and Company
New York

Copyright © 1985 by Albert Pyle

First published in the United States of America
in 1985 by the Walker Publishing Company, Inc.

Published simultaneously in Canada by John Wiley & Sons
Canada, Limited, Rexdale, Ontario.

Library of Congress Cataloging in Publication Data

Pyle, A. M. (Albert M.)
   Trouble making toys.

   I. Title.
PS3566.Y53T7   1985   813′.54   84-29162
ISBN 0-8027-5610-7

Printed in the United States of America

Book Design by Teresa M. Carboni

10 9 8 7 6 5 4 3 2 1

1

"Every little girl in your life wants a Denver Doll, no matter how old she is."

Banner Strathmore's voice was rich with promise, husky but pert. She parted her lips in an equally promising smile, revealing nearly eighteen inches of absolutely perfect teeth, then turned to face her tiny duplicate, prettily changing her expression to one of prepubescent longing. The Banner Strathmore/Cassie Brooks doll remained silent, but her voluptuous image promised every bit as much as the real Banner had, and she was available. $4.98 plus tax.

The screen went dark.

"No boobs. I can't believe it." Irving Golden hit the light switch and glared all the way around the table. "That broad cost me *$45,000*. That's four-five-zero-zero-zero. *My dollars*. And for one reason I say okay spend $45,000 and that one reason is her two breasts and they don't even show up in your commercial. Where are my TITS?"

There was no immediate answer. Eleven people stared at him, adjusting to the light as well as to his outburst.

"What have I got, a roomful of owls? Where are the most expensive tits in America? I want to know."

Six throats cleared, but it was Phillip Bennett, owner and president of The Bennett Agency, who finally spoke. "Irv, it wouldn't be right."

"Whattaya mean wouldn't be right? Those are the most famous . . ."

"Irving, believe me. There are just too many problems. Above all, there is the problem of the FTC. The total Banner Strathmore is, quite simply, too much woman for a child's product. Wait, please, let me finish. We *tried* shooting a version including her breasts but they completely overwhelmed the product. They dwarfed the doll. I'm afraid the effect was obscene."

"Of course it was obscene. *She's* obscene. Why do you suppose she's a star? Talent? Come on! Who shot this garbage, the Limey?"

The Limey, Evelyn Osborne spoke. "Who else could breathe such life into thirty seconds, Irving? You know it was I."

"And you couldn't get her jugs on camera without a problem? I thought you were the technical genius."

"I am Irving, there can be no doubt. But I must admit I have never faced the problem of such . . ." he paused stagily, "of such an exu-

1

berant bosom. I don't know how many times she toppled her little doppelganger while inhaling."

"Did you get it on tape?"

"You have it on your cassette, Irving."

"Set it up before you leave."

"With pleasure."

"There's something else—oh yeah, how come the doll's in pants?" Irving reached into his shirt pocket and pulled out one of the little dolls. This example was wearing silver stretch lamé. "What happened to the cocktail dress that shows the boobs off? The pants look like shit." The momentary calm had ended.

"Irving, that's your prototype. You know we tested—"

"Please, Mr. Bennett," Marianne Kelly spoke for the first time since the meeting began, "Mr. Golden, that was my decision."

"*Your* decision? What is this, Phil? You're letting twenty-two-year-old bulldykes make the decisions now? Is that what you think about my account?" Golden ignored Marianne's gasp of outrage and continued to address Phillip Bennett. "You know, every time I turn on the news they've got a bunch of lesbian liberators investigating Pogue's cans and complaining because there's no urinals in the ladies and there she is right in the middle, shooting her mouth off, and you're letting her decide how to dress my dolls."

"Irving—"

"Please, Mr. Bennett." Marianne was scarlet, and her voice shook slightly, but her yoga paid off. "Mr. Golden, we researched those outfits for months and—"

"And your research told you lesbian dolls were going to be the—"

"And our research showed that the doll in pants, Levis, actually, looked the most like the Cassie Brooks character to girls eight to twelve who watched 'Denver.' If you watched the show you would know that Banner, or rather Cassie Brooks, almost always wears pants, usually Levis, and—"

"Honey, don't get smart with me. I watch the show and I know what I watch is her boobs, and I know that any other guy watching is watching the same thing."

"But we're selling to little girls."

"And those little girls are gonna turn into little truck drivers if you have your way, right? Right."

"Now, just a minute!"

"Shut up, kid. I know what I'm talking about and I want that doll in a dress."

Jack Squires, Bennett's Group Executive for Toys stepped into the fray. "Irv, can we get back to the commercial?" Squires' New Zealand accent, usually under control, got thicker with stress. "You know what a reshoot would cost and I don't even know if we could get Banner

2

back for another take. So it's really important to take a fair look at the one we've got. Frankly, I think the Levis are pretty sexy, don't you, Evelyn?"

"I think they're positively lewd."

"But you're right, of course, Irv. The woman really has a splendid bosom," Jack was back in form. "And I must say your techs have done their usual terrific job scaling them down without losing any flamboyance. And if you think about it, the Levis really show them off. Here, look." Jack picked up one of the several tiny dolls that were scattered around the conference table. "Joe, your boys really outdid themselves." Joseph Enneking, Production Manager for Golden Time Toys, nodded.

"I mean, look how that tiny waist nips in, Irv. And see how those marvelous Sri Lankans have done the elastic at the top of the trouser. You really can't miss the boobs, Irving. Honestly. Let's run the tape again, shall we? Or have you seen enough?"

"I think we've seen enough, Irving. It's getting late."

"Shut up, Fred. Roll it, Osborne."

Frederick Golden's fury at his brother's rudeness disappeared into the dark as Irving hit his personal dimmer. All eyes turned to the giant video projection screen to feast again on the luscious Miss Strathmore. "Denver" theme music filled the room.

Tom Cleary let himself feel an immodest thrill as his own copy oozed from Banner Strathmore's luscious lips.

"It's a dream come true! It makes me feel like a little girl again! The Cassie Brooks Denver Doll is just like me! She's adorable! And so tiny! She's irresistible and—"

"CUT!"

"What's wrong, Irv?"

"Phil, who wrote this *awful* copy?"

"Irving, you approved the copy personally last month."

"Bennett, there is no way I would approve copy like *that*. Who wrote it?

Tom's pleasant moment was past, "I did, Mr. Golden."

"Name?"

"Tom Cleary, Mr. Golden."

"Well, Tom Cleary, what the fuck gives you the nerve to call that doll *tiny*?"

"Tiny?"

"You heard it. You wrote it. Or can't you remember what you wrote?"

"I remember, sir."

"Do you know what this doll lists for?"

"$4.98, sir."

"Right, brainchild, $4.98. And for $4.98 you don't want *tiny*. You feel stupid shelling out that kind of money for something that's *tiny*. Maybe you don't feel stupid. Maybe Bennett pays you so much that you don't know what $4.98 is anymore."

"Sir, I know we've priced this carefully. I *do* know the value, but in all the pretests *every* test girl said the Denver Dolls were tiny. But they *loved* them. They like tiny things. They think they're dear."

"Well, *dear* Mr. Cleary. I am very terribly sorry, but your copy stinks. I hate it. I hate the whole goddamned ad. '*Tiny*.' Jesus."

Frederick Golden tried again. "Irving, really, it's after five. The ad is fine."

"Frederick, shut up. If you've got to take a leak, go take a leak. If you've got a hot date, go take a hot date, but I'm trying to do *business* and we will stay here until I've done my business, all right? Christ, I hope Mom appreciates the crap I take from you, I really do."

"Irving, do we want to resume?"

"Yeah, we want to resume, don't we guys? Play it, Osborne."

Before Evelyn could restart the Betamax there was a violent clatter as a door opened and various parts of a vacuum cleaner fell through.

"Donna, for crying out *loud*. We're busy."

Donna Creech followed her tools into the room.

"Oh, Mr. Golden. I'm sorry. I thought it was empty. Hi, Miz Meynell. Oh, you've got the Denver Dolls. Aren't they cute?" She gasped, "Oooh, they look *just* like Banner Strathmore. Oh, Mr. G., Stacey's gonna love this." She sat down and began to pose one of the little dolls.

"Donna, we're having a meeting."

"Oh, I'm sorry. Here I am sittin' down when I'm supposed to be cleanin'. Mr. G., I tried to do your washroom, but it's locked. Can I get your keys?"

"They're on the desk. Be sure you put them back."

"Oh, ha ha, I won't forget again, Mr. G."

"And leave the doll, Donna."

"Oops! It's just so cute, Mr. G. Tiny, don't you know?" She returned her attachments and clanked through to Mr. G.'s office at the end of the conference room. Conversation was impossible.

"Rosemary, make sure those keys make it back to the desk, will you? And bring a cigar."

Rosemary Meynell, Irving's secretary, deftly changed the cassette in her recorder and followed Donna into the office.

"Oh, hon, I'm so embarrassed. I didn't know you were still—"

"That's all right, Donna. Let's just get through here," and she pulled the door shut behind them.

There had been many, many hours spent in debate at The Bennett Agency over the mystery of Donna Creech. More precisely, over Irving Golden's tolerance of Donna Creech. In the entire city only Mr. Bennett's own building supervisor, Ted Harris, approached her inability to clean an office. Absolutely no one could touch her ability to fawn, lie, and slander in a single sentence. She was not even good looking. A lifetime diet of bologna and Mountain Dew had left her with grey skin and a full set of false teeth.

The theories ranged from the criminal (she supplied Irving with marijuana that she got from her black boyfriends) to the lewd (Irving had found her in Hamburg in the company of well-trained beasts of burden) to the uncharitable (she reminded Irving of himself as a lad). Not even Rosemary Meynell, the best secretary in three states, could settle the matter.

Tom Cleary was silently formulating a new theory (Irving's unnatural daughter out of an Appalachian snake-handling priestess), when the phone rang. Rosemary picked it up.

"I'm sorry, sir." Rosemary's English accent was at its frostiest. "I can't connect you with Mr. Golden if you won't tell me . . . I'm very sorry, sir, but 'He'll know' just won't—"

"Gimme that!" Golden snatched the phone from her. "Yeah? Yeah . . . damn . . . yeah . . . when? . . . SHIT . . . you're sure? No . . . yeah . . . well, how much *did* you find out? . . . not tomorrow . . . bring it by the house tonight . . . yeah . . . I don't care, just bring it."

Irving slammed the phone into the hook and when it bounced out, slammed it in again. "YOU STUPID BUNCH OF SCHMUCKS." He banged his fist on the table. "I CAN'T BELIEVE I'VE GOT THE STUPIDEST AD AGENCY IN THE WHOLE STINKING WORLD." He banged his fist again, this time catching the toe of his little doll, thereby causing her to flip gracefully into the ashtray where she perched on a cigar butt.

"What is it now, Irving?" Bennett was nearly as grey as Donna Creech.

"What is it now? I'll tell you what it is. What it is is Whizbang is bringing out, four weeks from today, a complete line of Boston Babes."

"Irving, we knew that they were going to do that."

"Let me *finish*, Bennett. They're going to have nipples *and* knees." Absolute silence.

"What's the matter? Nothing to say? Hunh? Well, I've got plenty. Bennett, you *swore* I'd have a riot with nipples. I told you Denver Dolls had to have 'em. Wouldn't be right without 'em, but you, you talked me out of it. 'Not in good taste' you said. And didn't I tell you where American taste was? And didn't you say Whizbang wouldn't do nipples, that they would realize they couldn't get away with it? And, Enneking, didn't you tell me my knees were cheesy? Didn't you tell me they would break down and didn't you tell me Whizbang would have the same problem if they tried doing knees and didn't you both say 'Don't worry, Irving'? And now we've got Denver Dolls with stiff legs and no nipples up against Boston Babes with real knees *and* real nipples."

Bob Atwood cut in "Irv, Irv, Irv, don't *worry*."

"Don't worry?" Golden glared at Phillip Bennett's right-hand man.

"No. Listen, Irv, the Boston Babes are skags. Real dogs. We've got the winners without knees."

"You've seen them?"

"What? Sure. I watch the show. Believe me. I'll bet you 'Boston' doesn't last through the season. Really. The girls on that show are pigs next to 'Denver.' Besides, ABC's putting 'Tank Saga' in that slot. 'Boston's' going to get creamed."

"You better pray you're right, Atwood."

"Trust me."

"Trust you? You think I trust any one of you idiots? After this ad? After you let Punk City sign with Kiddy Town? After the FTC hits us for 'misleading' the world about kid-proof crayons? After Whizbang comes out with *my* knees and nipples? Give me one good reason why I should trust any of you. One good reason."

There was another long silence until Phillip Bennett took a deep and audible breath.

"Irving, please. I am deeply sorry if you are unhappy. I do think we were right about the nipples. I don't think America is ready yet, but I may be mistaken. I also think Joe was right about the knees. We really can't take another beating on defective features. I think the ad is sound. It's a good ad. It says all the right things. I think we should go with it. Please. Sleep on it. We'll get together tomorrow morning."

"Maybe we will. Maybe we won't." Golden imitated Bennett's deep and tired tones, then reverted to his own rasp. "Maybe I have had it with two-bit local agencies. Maybe it's time I talked to the big time. Maybe it's time I got rid of my house Nazi and maybe it's time I told the board what my brother does with *his* time, and . . . SHIT!" Irving had knocked over his coffee. "Rosemary! Get in here and clean this up."

Rosemary emerged from the office with Donna hot on her heels.

"Let me clean that up, hon. I'll just get the Kleenex." Donna pulled out fifty Puffs from a box on the bookshelf and sopped up the coffee, palming Irving's doll, a Pentel, and a Bic lighter in the process.

"Thank you, Donna." Rosemary grasped Donna firmly at the elbow and steered her away from the table. "Your cigar, Mr. Golden."

Golden snatched the cigar and barked his dismissal. "Everybody out. I want everybody out of here. I got to think."

There was an indecently hasty scramble to be the first out.

"Oh! Wait everybody! Just a minute! Mr. G., can they go out through your office? The floor's still wet in the hall . . ."

6

"Sure, sure. Just get out. Osborne, you got that cassette in? The good one?"

"It's ready to go, Irving. Push the little 'Play' button."

"Out."

Joe Enneking and Frederick Golden were the last out. They carefully sidestepped the lethally slippery compound that Donna had slathered in the hall, retrieved their coats and cases, and tiptoed through Irving's office.

"Nite, Mr. Enneking. Nite, Mr. Fred."

"Good night, Donna," in chorus.

Frederick Golden looked over his shoulder on the way out. Peering through to the conference room he could make out one enormous breast on the screen and, as he turned to leave, he heard his brother's famous growl.

No one had left the parking lot. Despite the late hour and the bitter wind, the Denver Dolls Task Force had reassembled in two groups. Joe Enneking and Frederick Golden had joined Phillip Bennett, Rosemary Meynell, Bob Atwood, and Evelyn Osborne in the lee of Irving Golden's Cadillac.

Jack Squires and Tom Cleary stood in the center of the nearly empty lot with their backs to the wind, facing a furious Marianne Kelly.

"Bulldyke. He called me a bulldyke. Me! And I *let* him. God! What a jerk."

Tom Cleary tried to comfort her.

"He's not worth it, Kelly. He's a jerk. Forget it."

"Oh, sure. Forget it." She was still furious. "How can you be so stupid? He ought to be *locked up*. God, I wish I could turn him in. And *you* were a big help. You sat there and let him dump on you and me and didn't say a damned thing. Not a damned thing."

"Marianne, I—"

"You're a coward. So am I, but you're a bigger one. And *no* one, *no* one helped poor Mr. Bennett. He must be disgusted with all of us. Jack, why didn't *you* tell him off?"

"I can't do that, love. You know that."

"I can't do that, love," she mimicked.

"Stop it, Kelly." Tom was embarrassed.

"It's all right, mate. Let her steam it out. She's right, you know. He was a perfect shit. I wish I could have said something."

"Well, why couldn't you?" Marianne wailed. "Why couldn't anybody say *anything*?"

"Come on, love. You know why. You can't say anything to him when he's like that."

"But he's like that *all* the time."

"Well, he was particularly nasty today. And you did the right thing. You stuck to business. And I think he'll respect that. That was good."

"Good? He called me a bulldyke, a *bulldyke*. God, I wish I *was* a bulldyke. I'd get a bunch of bulldykes and kick the shit out of him."

It was too much for Tom. The image of Marianne Kelly, five foot two, in her blue suit and pumps surrounded by a phalanx of leather ladies hit him the wrong way and he laughed.

"You *creep!* You think it's funny, don't you? You would. You probably like him. You probably think he's neat, don't you? God. You're such a . . . such a *milquetoast*. Well, he was right about one thing, Cleary. Your copy stinks. It *stinks*."

"Ease up, love, please. Phillip can hear you." Jack put his arm around her.

"Don't *touch* me. Don't *ever* touch me."

"All right, all right. Just keep it down."

Conversation in the group that had gathered around Mr. Bennett had indeed stopped. All eyes were on Marianne.

"All right, I'm calm. I'm through. For tonight. But I want out of your group, Jack. I want to get off dolls tomorrow. For sure. I am never, never having anything to do with that bastard or his dippy dolls ever again. You understand? Off. Tomorrow. First thing." And Marianne wheeled around and headed out of the lot.

"Oooh, dear, she's got a lot to learn."

"I'm really sorry, Jack."

"What for? She's not your account exec.—she's mine. I'm the one charged with civilizing her."

"I know, but . . . Well, she's *from* here and you're not and you really put up with a lot from her. You shouldn't have to."

"Thanks," said Squires, "Goes with the job. As long as I've got a job."

"Are you worried? Was he serious?"

"About firing the agency?" Jack paused and looked over to the other group. "It's possible, Tom. I talked to an old mate from London in New York last week. Apparently Irv's had some meetings with J. F. Bean up there and they were very, very nice to him."

"Oh, God, Bean." Tom was pained.

"Yes, Bean. And I don't know if Phillip can hold on to him. I mean look at him. The poor devil can barely stand up, he's so sick. He wasn't even supposed to get out of bed until next week."

"I didn't know he was that sick."

"Oh, he's not going to die, I don't think. But he's barely got a stomach. All that crap he's taken and all the charm he's served up to meet the crap. He really is a kind man, you know. I've never met anyone to touch him."

"I do know, Jack. Who else would have hired me?"

8

"Oh, you're good, Tom. You know you are."

"Enough, enough. You want to go get a drink?"

"Thanks, mate, but it's late. You need a ride?"

"No, thanks, I think I'll stop in at Arnold's. I've got my car."

"Goodnight, then."

"Goodnight."

Tom headed for Arnold's and Jack headed for the other group.

"Anybody need a ride?"

Phillip Bennett checked the circle of faces. "No, thanks, Jack. See you tomorrow." And Jack left.

"Not if I have anything to say about it, Phil," Frederick Golden resumed as Squires left the parking lot. "He's a fool to talk to any other agency. An absolute fool. You've been loyal. You've been good. You've made the company, for heaven's sake."

Enneking unusually agreed. "He would be a fool. Believe me, my father would never, never have treated you like that."

"Joe, please," said Frederick, "your father never even advertised."

"Fortunate man," said Osborne.

"Evelyn, really." Rosemary was not only bitterly cold, she was angry about Evelyn's outtakes. There was no need to indulge Irving's prurience.

"Phillip," said Evelyn, "you are not to worry. Not to worry. I am absolutely certain that my little collection of film snips will so calm the man that he will have forgotten his ugly little threat by the end of the tape. No, I think distract is the word. I did a bit of editing."

"Oh, God, Evelyn, you are revolting."

"Rosemary, dear, I may have saved everyone's ass. What is revolting about that?"

"Mr. Bennett, I apologize for Evelyn. I'm afraid he's been particularly tasteless."

"What did you do, Oz?" asked Bob Atwood.

"Forgive me, Phillip. What I did, Bob, was a slight enhancement of the already titillating outtakes. I grafted some artfully matched close-ups from an adult film in sequence with dear Miss Strathmore's occasional accidents."

"Accidents?"

"Her bosom fell out, Bob. Several times. Aren't you sorry you're too busy for production work these days?"

Phillip Bennett leaned against the Cadillac. "Mr. Bennett, are you all right?"

"I'm fine, Rosemary. Just tired. Bob, Evelyn, let's get together with Jack first thing tomorrow and see if we can't sort it out. I don't think there's any point working tonight. All right? Rosemary, Fred, Joe, goodnight. Sorry about the way things went."

"Phil, please don't worry. I'm going to take care of it."

"I'll be fine, Fred. Thanks." Phillip Bennett picked up his briefcase, smiled wearily, and left.

"Well, anyone for drinks?" said Evelyn.

"Not I, thank you, and not you either, dear," said Rosemary. "I'm starved and frozen and I would like to go home."

"You're quite certain."

"I'm quite certain. Say goodnight."

"Goodnight."

Bob Atwood, Frederick Golden, and Joe Enneking stood alone.

"Jeez, I wish she'd take me home," said Atwood as he watched the departing Rosemary.

"If she did, you would be sure to have Mr. Osborne as voyeur, no doubt recording and directing the proceedings. He is not jealous, but he could be critical." It was as close as Enneking came to humor.

"I'd do it." Atwood grinned.

"You probably would," said Frederick Golden. "Goodnight."

"Asshole," muttered Atwood, but Enneking had slipped away.

"Goodnight, guys," and Atwood headed for the alley leading to the Ninth Street offices of The Bennett Agency.

The parking lot was empty.

2

"LIST ALL PROGRAM goals. Goals must be quantifiable and relate directly to the benchmarks for measurement in Column C. Do not include goals for which there will be no measurable benchmarks."

Cesar Franck read the instructions again. They were as unclear to him as they had been the first and second times he had read them that evening and the five or six times he had read them last week and the ten or twelve times he had read them last year. He tried to remember the directions as they had been put out by the slick little twerp from Research, Evaluation and Budget at the mandatory Orientation Training for the Cincinnati Program Budget. He could remember the twerp exactly: five eight, a hundred and forty, blond, chewed fingernails, blue pinstripe, red tie, yellow shirt, Johnston & Murphy tassel wing tips. Cesar wondered if the J&M's were standard issue from REB supplies. Then he thought about the black guy who had done the orientation the year before. He wore the same outfit, only it must have come from another supply depot. Dino's? You could always tell the difference, but you couldn't explain it. Except the shoes. The black guys at REB wore Bally instead of Johnston & Murphy. They were all twerps, and Cesar hated them whenever he had to deal with them. He dealt with them as little as possible.

As far as he was concerned, this Program Budget Narrative Form was the perfect example of REB bullshit. If they never did any other thing in their entire existence, Cesar would give them top bullshit honors (Bullshit Hall of Fame) for the Program Budget Narrative Form. Any idiot could tell that this was a gotcha form.

1. It was designed to make everybody who ever had to fill it out feel stupider than the dumbest Management Analyst in Research, Evaluation and Budget. Nobody in the Police Division, and there were some smart guys, knew how to fill it out right. Gotcha.
2. Except Cesar. Last year Cesar's attempt was the first time the Homicide Squad Program Budget Narrative had not come back for a rewrite, which was why Lieutenant Tieves assigned it to him again. Gotcha, gotcha.
3. When all the Narratives from all the Divisions and Departments got put in a big budget book and the REB Director dumped

it on the City Manager and City Council, they all thought it was wonderful because it weighed as much as a Pontiac and none of them could read it so they all thought REB had slaved their asses off and were worth more than the entire Police Division. Gotcha.

Cesar had only one comfort looking as his uncompleted, unstarted Budget Narrative Form. The REB twerp had explained to him and the other poor jerks getting oriented that REB and City Council would use all these Program Budgets to decide which parts of city government were going to stay oiled and which were going to get shut down. The REB twerp said it was going to be a lean year and some programs would have to get the axe. Cesar's comfort came from knowing that even if he and every other Narrative Bullshit Artist in the Police Division filled out their forms in Swahili and said that their goal and objectives were to make every REB twerp march down to the Metropolitan Sewer District ponds and jump in, the Division would get its funds. Every survey that REB ever sent out came back with police the number one city priority. Cincinnati loved its cops.

But. REB could still get you. If you filled out the form in Swahili, even if you filled it out in perfect English but they didn't like it, they would send over a twerp in tasseled wing tips to explain to you just how stupid you were and to make your supervisor make sure that you got it right.

Christ. It was a Chinese torture.

GOAL: The goal of the Homicide Squad is to find out who killed citizens of Cincinnati and get them locked up so they don't kill any more citizens of Cincinnati.

Cesar checked the instruction manual. He had not written quantifiable goals. Shit. He looked at last year's effort.

GOAL: The Homicide Squad's goal is to reduce the number of unsolved murders by 27 percent.

That was quantifiable. Now, how to say the same thing without looking like he did. The orientator twerp said they would not accept cut and paste. Any numerical goals had to show improvement.

GOAL: The Homicide Squad's goal is to increase the number of solved murders by 30 percent.

Right? Wrong. It sort of looked like they were going to go out and murder a few extra to make a quota.

The phone rang.

"Homicide. Detective Franck speaking."

"Just a minute, I'm writin' this down."

"Okay, ma'am." Cesar waited.

"That's Detective Franck, right?"

"Right. F-R-A-N-C-K."

"Oh, okay. I didn't know about that C. I've got it now."

"Can I help you, ma'am?"

"Yes. This is Mrs. Donna Creech callin'. I'm at the Golden Time Toy Company executive offices at 220 East Eighth Street and I'm callin' to report a murder."

Cesar reached for an incident report.

"Ma'am, could you—"

"Hold on just a minute. Is he dead? Ohhh, be careful."

"Ma'am, is someone there with you?"

"Yes, I called the Rescue Squad because he wasn't quite dead yet when I found him, but I'm pretty sure he's dyin'. He's hurt real bad, Detective Franck."

Cesar recorded the time. 9:20 P.M.

"Your name again, please ma'am."

"It's Mrs. Creech. C-R-E-E-C-H."

"Okay, Mrs. Creech, and can you give me the name of the injured party?"

"Yes. It's Mr. Irving Golden. He's the president of Golden Time Toys."

"Ma'am, are there any police officers there or on the way?"

"I don't think so. I just called the Rescue Squad and then I called you direct 'cause I thought the Homicide Squad would want to be here in case he died, don't you know."

"Okay, listen, ma'am, there should be an officer over in a couple of minutes. They're supposed to meet the Rescue Squad, but I'm going to put you on hold while I check on that."

Cesar checked. The area patrol was on its way.

"Mrs. Creech, there's an officer on his way up. He'll be taking a statement from you. Can you tell me why you believe there's been a homicide?"

"Well, like I said, Mr. Golden's not quite dead yet, but I don't think he's goin' to live much longer. He's hurt real bad. It looks like someone smashed his head in, and I think I know how they did it."

Nature of incident: Assault.

"Are you writin' this down?"

"Yes, ma'am."

"All right, I'll go a little slower. I used to be a secretary and I know it's hard to write if you go too fast."

"Thanks, I'm getting it, ma'am."

"I do the cleanin' now. That's how I found Mr. Golden. Oh, wait a minute. Sir? Sir? You can take him out through the office if you're in the lot. I'll show you. Detective Franck?"

"Yes, ma'am."

"I'm going to show them how to get out. I'll call you right back."

"I'll hold."

"No. I've got your number and I've got to go to the ladies room. I'll get right back to you." She hung up.

Cesar stared at his incomplete Incident Report Form. He pushed it aside and looked at his incomplete Program Budget Narrative Form. Thursday nights were supposed to be slow. Freezing cold nights were almost guaranteed slow. He wanted Irving Golden to stay alive. Please. How was he supposed to get the Budget Narrative done and Lt. Tieves off his back if he had a major case? And if Irving Golden died it was going to be major for sure.

Cesar remembered his mother and her opinion of the Golden Time Toy Company and particularly of Irving Golden. When Cesar's father died, Mrs. Franck found herself with two children and a pension that did not cover Christmas. She answered an ad for seasonal employment with Golden. Cesar remembered how she would come home looking whipped after a day spent packing toys and riding buses. She would collapse in her chair in the living room and say the same thing every day. "No Golden Time Toys for you kids this year or ever. I hope Irving Golden roasts in hell." She wouldn't explain, and Cesar and his sister didn't try to make her. They felt bad enough that she was working for their Christmas. That was a bad year for everybody.

By the next Christmas Mrs. Franck had taken a bookkeeping course and gone to work at Shillito's. She stuck to her word. There never were any Golden Time Toys under the tree; not for her children, not for her nieces and nephews. Mrs. Franck wasn't going to lose any sleep over Irving Golden's assault. Or murder. Whichever.

Why hadn't Donna Creech called back? How long did it take to go to the toilet? Give her some time.

Cesar wandered out of the squad office and into the hall. Quiet. He wandered out into the lobby. Quiet there, too. How come he had the only action? No fair. At least the lab guys would have to go out. Should he call Donna Creech back? Should he work on Goals and Objectives? Could he work on Goals and Objectives? Donna Creech sounded like a real pain in the neck. Was she worse than or better than a Narrative Form? He dragged back to the squad office and dug out a phone book. Anything was better than the budget. He dialed Golden Time Toys.

"Officer Freihofer speaking."

"Hey, Dick. What are you doing answering?"

"Cesar?"

"Yeah. Is Mrs. Creech out of the can?"

"Who?"

"The cleaning lady. She called me."

"She's gone. Left just before I got here."

"Oh, for Christ's sake. I knew she was gonna be funny. Is anyone there?"

"Security. Lab's on the way."

"Ask the security guy where she went. Dumb bitch."

"He says she's on her way over to see you."

"Detective Franck?" Cesar had company.

"Never mind, Dick. She's here."

"Have fun, Ceez."

"Yeah. Did Golden make it?"

"Unh-unh, DOA."

"Great. Later."

Cesar hung up. He put the Narrative Form on the edge of his desk and centered the incident report.

"Have a seat, ma'am."

"I'm Donna Creech. I called you about Mr. Golden."

"I figured. I thought you were going to wait for the area patrol."

"I know I said I would, but I got this real bad headache so I just thought I'd get out and buy some Stanback and then I thought I should just come over and see you and save a call."

Save a call, sure. What she wanted to do was snoop. New snoopy adventure, Cesar was sure. She had taken in everything on his desk and she was about to pop her eyes out trying to read the incident report upside down. Cesar took a minute to snoop around her. She looked like Loretta Lynn without the money. Kentucky for sure. Hillbilly for sure. Bad feet. Good teeth, so they were probably fake. K-Mart pants. K-Mart sweater. Not too clean. Fake fur coat. She pulled out a pack of Kool kings. When she pulled a cigarette from the bottom of the pack, Cesar groaned to himself. The only guys he knew who kept up the old Vietnam habit of opening their cigarettes, particularly Kools, from the bottom were Bad Dudes. Mrs. Creech was into Bad Dudes. Cesar would bet on it. She lit up. The matches were from the Top Hat, that cinched it. The Top Hat was strictly Bad Dudes. If he hadn't swapped night duty with Henry, Henry would be sitting here right now and he would have her in complete control. Henry could be a Bad Dude. Cesar couldn't.

"Is there a pop machine around?"

"Sure. What'll you have?"

"Mountain Dew. How much are they?"

"My treat."

"I'll take Pepsi if they don't have Mountain Dew."

Cesar took his time. He figured she would read everything on the desk and then maybe she'd be able to concentrate on the job. She was on the phone when he got back but hung up fast.

"I hope you don't mind. I had to tell my kids where I was."

"It's okay."

"Oh, Detective Franck. I'll bet I wasn't supposed to leave."

And I'll bet you knew that and I'll also bet you came looking for "Hill Street Blues" and you're going to spend a week talking about your night on the grill.

"No problem. I'll get your statement now and if I need anything more I'll talk to you tomorrow."

"You've got duty tomorrow, too?"

"Yes, ma'am."

"That's terrible. You're gonna be so tired."

"I'll be all right, ma'am. Now, what happened?" You're on, lady. This is your big chance.

"Well, I was cleanin' up in Mr. G.'s office."

"What time was it?" Cesar was taking notes.

"Let me see. I believe it was about seven-thirty. Anyway, I was cleaning up and I found his Tina on the floor so I picked it up—"

"Tina?"

"Oh, that's his big award. It's like an Oscar only it's from the toy industry and it's real heavy. It's got this cute gold statue of a baby. He was real proud of it 'cause he got it for Patty Raccoon, don't you know. He made up Patty Raccoon."

"Oh."

"Anyway, I just thought he'd knocked it off his desk only I don't think he'd do that but it was kind of wet so I thought maybe he'd spilled some coffee on it so I used some Glass Plus on it and got it clean, but now I'm thinkin' it might have been blood. Oooh." She made a face and took a hit on her Mountain Dew. "I guess I shouldn't have cleant it off, but I didn't know. I just knew Mr. G. would want that Tina nice and clean."

"Right."

"Anyway, I heard this kind of crying noise from the conference room. Well, I nearly jumped out of my skin since I thought I was by myself and I hung onto that Tina in case it was a burglar and I turned on the light in there. Mr. G's got a switch by his desk. Well, there was Mr. G. all slumped over the conference table so I went in to see what was wrong and I'll tell you, Detective Franck, it was pitiful. Just pitiful. Someone had bashed him hard in the head. Am I going too fast?"

"No, you're doing fine."

"Do you know Calvin McFarland?"

"Sure."

"He goes with my cousin Linda. He's real nice. Is he still in the vice squad?"

"Yeah."

16

"Well, he hasn't been over to see Linda for a week and if you see him, tell him I'm after him. She's too proud to call him."

"I'll tell him."

"Anyway, I took a pillow off one of the arm chairs and put it under his head and I thought about getting an ice pack only he really looked bad. Like an ice pack wouldn't help. So I had Leonard call the Rescue Squad."

"Who's Leonard?"

"Leonard Cassidy. He's the security guard."

"Were you and this guard the only people in the office?"

"In the building. Yes. And Mr. Golden."

"Right."

"I'm real worried about him, you know. I mean his head looked awful bad."

"He didn't make it. I'm sorry."

There was a pause while Donna's eyes filled with tears. "Detective Franck, that's terrible. It really is terrible. I know a lot of people hated Mr. Golden, but he was always real nice to me. A lot of men don't understand me, but he would always listen and I think he always wanted to see me do better. Do you have a Kleenex?" She blew her nose. "This is gonna tear my kids up. They thought the world of him 'cause he was always sendin' home toys for them 'cause he knew I couldn't buy them too much. I'm divorced, you know. And their daddy's not too good about sendin' that support. But Mr. G. was always thinkin' about them even though he was real busy. But he wasn't stuck up, you know, like his brother. He was real nice."

She paused again to think about how nice he was. Cesar thought about his mother and how she cursed the nice Mr. Golden regularly. He couldn't think of anybody else she had ever cursed. Regularly or not.

"Well, he was murdered, Detective Franck. I just know it."

Good guess, ma'am. We don't see a lot of citizens clubbing themselves with toy awards and flinging the blunt instruments into the next room.

"How's that, ma'am?"

"Oh, hon, just call me Donna. I'm just as old as you are." Cesar was thirty. Donna looked at least forty. Cesar split the difference and decided she was thirty-five.

"Well, how do you figure he was murdered, Donna?"

"Well, I was thinkin' after I had Leonard call the Rescue Squad. And I thought somebody got in here and beat up Mr. G. and I tried to think how they did it and who it could have been 'cause there wasn't anyone there but me and Leonard. Oh," she stopped and stared at him. "Hon, it wasn't me or Leonard. I swear. You must be thinkin' we're suspects, but we didn't do it. I swear. I hadn't even thought about that."

Maybe. Maybe not.

"We haven't even thought about suspects yet, Donna."

"Well, I didn't do it. And I know Leonard didn't either. He wouldn't."

"So you figure someone else got in the building."

"Yes. But they didn't come through the front 'cause Leonard didn't let anybody in and he has to. They've got a double lock."

"Window, maybe."

"Wait, hon. That's what I'm telling you. You see, Mr. G.'s real big on security. That's why he keeps Leonard. He had the windows all bricked up, and all the outside doors except in front and the back door to his office. And you can't get in that building after five unless Leonard lets you in."

"What about the other door? The back one."

"Well, that's what I'm tryin' to tell you. There's only one way you can get in that door and that's with Mr. G's key. He had a special lock from Israel put on that door. He was real proud of it 'cause he got it from the president."

Ron gave him a lock? "What president?"

"The president of Israel. He used to go there all the time, don't you know, and the president gave him this lock. And it's the only lock like that in town. You can't even get keys made for it."

"How do you know?"

"Well, he lost the key once and he called Stan the Key Man and he couldn't get in and he told Mr. G. he'd have to call Israel if he didn't want to cut the door off. And he did. He called Israel and they had the number from the lock and they sent him a new key."

"So you think someone else got that key."

"No. He found it before the one from Israel got here. It was in his chest of drawers at home. So he put the new one in his safe deposit box. He didn't want to call Israel again, you know."

"So how did whoever get in?"

"They got in through that door. They got his keys. And I think I know who it was."

"Who was it?"

"Well, it had to be one of the people at the meetin'."

Is this going to be easy? Big meeting? Small meeting? How do you lift keys off a toy company president? "Meeting?"

"There was a meeting, and those keys were in his office. I know they were on his desk 'cause I had to clean his bathroom and I had to get the keys and put them back so I know one of the people at the meeting must have taken them when they went out."

"Who was at the meeting?"

"Well, I've been trying to think 'cause I'm *sure* one of them did it. Hon, they was fightin' in there!"

"Bad meeting?"

That called for another sip of Mountain Dew. She could really nurse a soda. Must be warm by now. Wait for a Kool. Come on, lady.

"Mr. G. was yellin'. He's got kind of a temper only he never did once yell at me. And when I went in—they were having a meeting about the Denver Dolls—everybody looked real upset."

"Denver Dolls?"

"Oh, they're real cute. They're copies of the stars from 'Denver.' On TV. I know they're gonna be real popular. My daughter loves hers. They're new."

"You mean like Banner Strathmore?"

"Just like her. It's amazin'. And Rita and Sallyanne, too. And, hon, they've got little outfits and they're gonna have little cars."

"Just like on the show."

"Just like 'em."

"And that's what they were talking about?"

"I think they were talking about the new commercials 'cause the people from Bennett—that's their advertising agency—they were there and they had the big screen and the Betamax out, but I think Mr. G. didn't like the commercial."

When did this lady clean?

"And everybody knew those keys were on the desk 'cause he told me to put them there so any one of them could have just picked them up when they went out the door."

"From his office?"

"I asked Mr. G. couldn't they go out that way since I was moppin' the floor in the hall and I didn't want anybody slippin' and gettin' hurt. That's supposed to be Mr. G's door. It goes right to his parking place. Everybody else is supposed to use the front door. Even his brother."

"And you think one of them came back in the same way?"

"That's the only way they could have come in. Leonard didn't let nobody, anybody, back in."

"What about the factory? Does everybody from there go out the front?"

"Yes, but they're all gone by four-thirty."

"That's a lot of people. How do you know they were all gone?"

"Hon, Leonard's only got one real job and he's not too bright, but he gets it right. It's not real hard."

"What?"

"He checks everybody out. You got to turn in your I.D. to Leonard before you go out or he won't let you go. And Leonard checks every single I.D.—he looks at the picture and looks at your face to make sure they're the same. He's real careful."

"He keeps pretty tight security."

"Well, Mr. Golden, he's always afraid someone's gonna steal one of his new toys, don't you know."

"Okay, so someone came in the back door and assaulted the deceased."

"Not just someone, someone from that meetin'."

"Was there any sign of a fight? Anything knocked over besides that Oscar?"

"Tina. No, unh-unh. I don't even think he heard whoever it was 'cause he had the Betamax on. Anyway he was watchin' it when I went downstairs to talk to Leonard and when I found him the lights were still off."

Cesar looked at his incident report and his notes and then he looked at Donna Creech. She was looking pretty smug. She was a mess, but, you had to admit it, she wasn't dumb. It made sense to Cesar. It was possible, at any rate. Did she say she was a secretary once? What was she doing cleaning offices? She probably didn't look enough like a secretary. She sure didn't look like any secretary he knew.

"Did you notice anything else?"

She paused. "I can't think of anything."

That didn't sound quite right.

"Well, I think I know who it was."

"Who?"

"I don't think I'd better say 'cause it's just my opinion and I don't want to get anybody in trouble."

"You're just guessing?"

"Oh, I'm pretty sure but I'm gonna think about it before I say anything."

Okay, lady. You think about it.

"That's fine, ma'am, but—"

"Now, you're supposed to call me Donna, remember?"

"Right."

"Now, I've got to get back and finish that cleanin' and get my kids to bed. I don't like for them to be up too late, you know."

Cesar couldn't think of any reason to keep her. He got her home number and address. Millvale—Jesus. She really did like to live dangerously. She collected her Mountain Dew, still unfinished, and her purse and stood up.

"Would you mind doin' me a favor, hon?"

"What do you need?"

"Well, my car's been actin' just a little funny. It doesn't always start. And I wondered if you'd follow me out and make sure I get it goin'. I don't like sittin' in this neighborhood if I've got car trouble."

Lady, you're surrounded by cops here and anyway you live in Millvale which makes the West End look like Westwood.

20

"Sure, Donna. Tell you what, I'll follow you over."

"Oh, hon, would you? That's real nice."

Well, why not? He could get a look at the place. Besides, he'd get away from the Budget Narrative Form. If he played this right he might get taken off the budget. Duty tomorrow. He was going to get this case for sure since he was already on it. Maybe he could talk Sgt. Evans into putting Carole Griesel on the budget. Perfect. He checked out with the desk and switched his phone over. They went out through the front lobby. Christ, it was cold. Lincoln Park–Ezzard Charles Drive was deserted. Not a rapist in sight. Not even any cops on the steps.

Donna's ten-year-old 98 Regency Brougham started right up. "Now wouldn't you know that? If you hadn't been here I would have cranked that battery down to nothin'." She drove him to the lot so he could pick up the squad car. He followed her around Central Parkway to Sycamore where she turned on to Eighth and halfway down the block into the Golden Time parking lot. The lab truck and a patrol car were still there. She waited for him.

"Now, see that door? That's the one. It goes right up to his office." Cesar flashed his light on the lock. It didn't look forced, but it would have to be checked. He followed her around to the front. Arnold's Bar next door was the first sign of life he'd seen since he left Central Station. Donna beat on the door even though there was a buzzer.

The security guard let them in. "Leonard, this is Detective Franck. He's gonna investigate."

"Can I see your I.D.?" Cesar flashed. He started to put his shield away. "Can I see it again? I have to write down your number."

"Now, didn't I tell you Leonard was careful?" They started upstairs to the offices.

"Wait a minute, sir. You can't go up there without a visitor's tag." Oh, brother. Cesar was going to argue, but Donna had been right. Leonard didn't look too bright—maybe even a little retarded. No point in making him cry. Cesar put on a visitor's tag.

Dick Freihofer was upstairs in the hall watching the lab wizards working over the conference room.

"Oh, Lord, what a mess! How'm I s'posed to get this clean tonight?"

"Dick, this is the cleaning lady who was going to wait for you. Mrs. Creech. Donna, this is Officer Freihofer."

"Are they gonna be cleanin' this up? 'Cause if they're not I don't know what I'm gonna do. I've *got* to get my kids to bed."

"Ma'am, I'm going to have to get a statement from you."

"It's okay, Dick. I got one."

"You sure?"

"I'm sure. Donna, these guys are going to be here a while and they'll probably seal it off."

"Well, I'm supposed to clean it."

"Look, if there's any trouble about it, I'll tell them I told you not to do it, all right?"

You're probably thrilled to get out of doing it anyway.

"Did you tell them to check that Tina there? For fingerprints? 'Cause mine are probably on it." Donna pointed to the office.

"It's a statue, Dick. Looks like an Oscar."

"I'll show you. It's right in here." Donna led them into Irving Golden's office.

Cheap office. It looked like the same paneling all the Cincinnati criminal lawyers and bail bondsmen used. In fact, it was the same stuff in every office north of Seventh Street. There must be one guy who does all the offices. "Now, you haven't ever been in here, have you? Well, that's the Tina and all those pictures, they're Mr. G. with a lot of real famous people."

"Donna says that was the weapon, Dick."

"Only I cleant all the blood off."

Dick Freihofer took the Tina over to the conference room door for the lab while Cesar looked at Irv-with-the-Famous.

They were pretty famous, too. Irv with Menachem Begin had the place of honor. There was Irv with Golda Meir and Irv with Richard Nixon and Irv with Governor Rhodes. And Pat Boone, and Billy Graham, and Soupy Sales, and the last five mayors, and Senator Taft, and Senator Metzenbaum, and Senator Glenn, and Monty Hall, and Ruth Lyons. No pope, though, and no queen. No matter who he was with, Irving always wore a short sleeved shirt and no coat. He was built tough, with a heavy duty bald head. It looked like most of the people were having their picture taken with him instead of the other way around. All the pictures were on one wall. On the adjoining wall there was a display case full of toys.

"Now, see, there's Patty Raccoon. The one I was tellin' you about that he got the Tina for. All these toys here, they're the big sellers and the ones he thought up. Now that's the Glo-Ball there, and there's Baby Trudy. I used to want a Baby Trudy real bad when I was little. I still think she's so cute. And see down there? Those are Color Bangs. They're crayons that when you get halfway down they pop. They never did make them 'cause the government wouldn't let them but Mr. G. thought they would have been real popular. I know my little boy would like them. Ohhh! I'd better call them. Can I use the phone now? My fingerprints are already on it from when I called you, but I can use a Kleenex."

"No, go ahead."

Cesar turned back to the display case while she talked to her kids. He had seen some of the toys on TV and at other kids' houses, but his mother had stuck to her guns. She even checked their old toys and threw out anything from Golden Time.

Donna sure wasn't June Cleaver. "Stacey, you better have those dishes done when I get home or you're gettin' a whippin' . . . well, Mitch doesn't have to, he did them last night . . . I'm tellin' you you better do them . . . remember last time? . . . pretty soon, so you better get your butt in the kitchen."

Cesar looked at his watch. 11:45. How old were these kids?

"Look, why don't you get on home? I've got your number if I need you."

"You sure? 'Cause I can stay . . ."

"No. Go on home. Put your kids to bed."

"Okay, I'll do that. And listen, hon, anything you want to know, you just call me or else come on over while I'm cleanin'. I sure do want to catch whoever kilt poor Mr. G. I really do."

"Thanks, Donna, I'll do that. You've already helped a lot."

"Goodnight, everybody!" She stuck her head into the conference room. "You be real careful with that Betamax! That's real expensive." The officer stared at her.

Cesar and Dick watched her until she hit the lobby at the bottom of the stairs. "Knows all, sees all," said Cesar.

"Hey, some of these cleaning ladies know more about what's going on than the guys they clean for."

"Yeah. Listen, I'm going to talk to our ace security guard down here. I'll catch you when you get off."

"Right. Later."

You had to watch it with Freihofer. He could talk your arm off if he got started.

Cesar reached the lobby just as Donna Creech was leaving. He checked out Leonard Cassidy again. No doubt about it, Leonard was dedicated. Clean shave. Shined shoes. Creases. Hat square. No books in evidence. No TV. And he was wide awake. Leonard checked Cesar out. Cesar could tell that Leonard didn't trust him. Policemen wore police uniforms. Cesar didn't wear a uniform so he couldn't really be a policeman. "I'm a detective, Mr. Cassidy. We're not supposed to wear our uniforms when we're detecting." Leonard still scowled. "Like Kojack." Ahh! That turned the lights on.

Cesar got Leonard's version of the story; it agreed with Donna's. Leonard had been at his post since 4:30. He hadn't left once, not even when Donna found Irving Golden. Leonard Cassidy had amazing bladder control. Cesar figured that if Leonard Cassidy said everyone was out of the building you could count on it. He thanked Leonard and headed for the door.

"Sir? Your visitor's pass, I've got to have that back."

Cesar undid the clip.

"You better find the guy that killed Mr. Golden."

"That's my job, Mr. Cassidy."

"I liked Mr. Golden. He gaved me this job and I never had one before. He said I did good work."

"I'll do my best."

Cesar stepped to the sidewalk. Jeez. It was getting colder. He glanced through the steamed-up window of Arnold's Bar. Somebody was playing the piano and it looked warm, but he'd never been in there before and he hated being new to a bar. He got in the car and pulled out into Eighth. As he passed the entrance to Golden Time he saw Leonard Cassidy standing at parade rest and staring at the street through the glass door.

3

CESAR STARED AT the thermometer while he rinsed out his coffee cup. Five above. "Mom, let me give you a ride this morning. You're gonna freeze at the bus stop."

"What is it?"

"Five above, for crying out loud."

"No, I'll take the bus, Gus."

Gus. For Auguste. Cesar Auguste Franck. The late Mr. Franck, a man who had not insisted on much in his life, had insisted on naming his only son after his collateral and distant relative, the composer. His wife was not crazy about "Cesar," associating the name with the Latin movie star, but Mrs. Franck, who had been a Fletemeyer, thought Auguste was okay, even with the extra "e." Her older brother was named August. Cesar's dad had called him Cesar, his mother called him Gus, cops called him Ceez. Cesar considered it a real fringe benefit of his job that he could introduce himself as Detective Franck.

"Mom, I'll take you right to the door."

"No, I don't think so."

"It won't make me late. I got time."

"Did the paper come?"

"Yeah, the paper came."

"I don't know about that new paperboy. He doesn't like to deliver when it gets too cold."

"Yeah, well, he's got more sense than old ladies that stand out freezing waiting for a bus when they could ride with their sons. Look, I'll even warm the car up before you get in."

"No. Don't do that. I'm taking the bus. I want to take the bus. Don't argue with me."

"Well, Ma, I sincerely hope that Queen City Metro appreciates your loyalty. They oughta name the bus route for you."

"Not bad, Gus. I missed out on the B49's."

"The number Nine Lillian Franck."

"I like it."

Cesar watched his mother pull on her Shillito's stadium boots. He held her Shillito's Better Coat for her. She swaddled her face in a Shillito's scarf and squeezed her Shillito's perm into a nice warm Shillito's knit hat. The power of the employee discount.

"Mom, I'm going to park by the bus stop and sit there with the motor on and the heater running and you're gonna feel stupid standing there."

"Stupid? I'll tell you what's stupid. Working all night, sleeping two hours, and then going back to work at eight in the morning. Don't talk to me about stupid."

"I forgot. You got your wish. Irving Golden's dead. He got murdered last night."

"What do you mean 'my wish'?"

"Don't you remember? When you worked at Golden Time? You came home every night and cursed him good."

Lillian looked at her son for a moment.

"God. The things kids remember. I shouldn't have said that."

"Well, that was pretty rough on you."

"It was a terrible job. The other girls and I worked like dogs. Mr. Golden used to come through and yell. He had lousy toilets and he didn't pay. But I shouldn't have said that."

"Well, he's dead. You didn't do it."

"No. But I'm ashamed anyway. I gotta go. I'm gonna be late."

Cesar watched her as far as the corner. She was really going to be in trouble if the city gave up on Metro. She had ridden buses so long and so often that Cesar was pretty sure she was afraid of cars. He knew she hated his Camaro. The only time she would get in it was when they went to see Kathy and Fred who weren't on the bus line. Those trips were crazy. She'd flinch every time she saw a truck, convinced the low-slung Camaro was particularly vulnerable to swerving semis. As soon as they would get to Kathy and Fred's she would point to Fred's mammoth Buick and say, "Gus, that's a safe machine. You should get one." Anytime the *Enquirer* had a picture of a wrecked Camaro he could count on finding it on his plate at supper.

Cesar pulled on his U.S. Navy foul weather parka (no employee discount—he had swiped it) and locked up the house. When he got to Harrison Avenue, Mrs. Franck was still waiting. He honked but she ignored him. Crazy woman. He turned onto Harrison and headed for town. When he saw the bus in the rear view mirror he picked up speed.

An hour later Cesar was seated across from Rosemary Meynell in an office adjoining the late Irv's.

He had been right in guessing that he would be assigned the case. He had been wrong in thinking he could dump the Program Narrative Budget Form on Detective Carole Griesel. Carole had radar. Sonar, maybe. Cesar had just barely started to outline his proposed shift of duties when Carole came in like a banshee. "No way, Sergeant. I just did the Safety Committee report. He's not gonna slide that off on me. I'm not taking it." Sgt. Evans stared at her. He didn't know what she was talking about and he didn't know what Cesar wanted. He had one way of dealing with Detective Griesel.

"Okay, Carole."

She flipped Cesar the bird behind her back before she slipped out of the squad office. Real nice girl.

"Boy, that supervisor training really pays off, Sarge. I mean I wouldn't have known how to deal with that so fast."

"Cesar."

"Sergeant?"

"Go play with Golden Time Toys."

So here he was in Rosemary Meynell's office counting her many admirable qualities as she dealt with a flood of telephone calls.

First admirable quality: Miss Meynell was beautiful. Not cute, not pretty, but beautiful. He wasn't sure he had ever seen anyone in real life who looked like her. Cesar went to his mental movie file and came up with Jean Simmons and Dana Wynter. Pretty close.

Second admirable quality: no junk on the desk. Miss Meynell didn't go in for kittycat postcards or Garfield planters. There were no happy-faces, no fake flowers, no spider plants, no cartoon coffee mugs. In fact, looking around the room, Cesar couldn't find anything that wasn't strictly business except for a small picture on the wall to the left of her desk. There was the same cheap paneling he had seen in Irv's office but she somehow made it look expensive.

Third admirable quality: Miss Meynell was to the telephone as Dave Concepcion was to shortstop. She was very good. There must have been ten calls in the short time he had been sitting there. Every caller was looking for news about the murder or trying to find out what was going to happen to Golden Time Toys. Miss Meynell was so polite and so friendly that Cesar knew it wasn't until they hung up that the callers realized she hadn't given any information at all. This lady was in control. Cesar thought about bringing Detective Carole Griesel in here. Detective Griesel had a habit of dumping on secretaries as empty-headed traitors to sharp career women like herself. He'd bet anything that this lady could put Griesel in her place in about fifteen seconds. He dropped the fantasy to listen to her dealing with a clearly different caller.

"No . . . no . . . that's not funny . . . stop . . . stop. You're being an ass . . . no . . . bugger off." She slapped the caller's button and reached the switchboard. "Jean, don't let him through again . . . no, just take a message . . . don't listen to him . . . no, he won't be angry with you, and Jean, I hate to do this to you but you're going to have to hold the calls for a while. There's a gentleman to see me . . . yes. I'll let you know."

She smiled at Cesar, "I'm so sorry to keep you waiting. It's been an absolute madhouse all morning."

"I'll bet."

"I'm sorry I didn't get your name."

"I'm Detective Franck." He fished for a card. She glanced at it and did an elegant double take.

"Is the C. A. for Cesar Auguste?" He had seldom had that reaction. Cousin Cesar was not up there with Barry Manilow or Paul Anka in the public consciousness.

"Caesar August. That's how I say it."

"Well. Welcome, Detective Franck. What may I do for you?"

Cesar concentrated. He was going to have to be careful not to be so charmed that he wound up being interviewed and out the door in two minutes.

"Basically, ma'am, I'd like to go over the events just prior to the assault on your employer." Cop talk. "I've been given some information by some other employees. If you would give me your version . . ."

"Other employees?" She wanted names.

"Yes." He wasn't naming names.

"I must guess them. You will have had a chat with our char, Mrs. Creech. Well, then, you must have had an earful."

Cesar was sure he was stonefaced, but she laughed, "Delightful, isn't she? Such a fine mind. She's truly wasted in her present position." Miss Meynell stared pointedly at a very grubby windowsill. At least she kept Tina clean.

"You were going to tell me about what happened yesterday afternoon, ma'am."

Predictably, her account of the events was perfectly organized, brief, and unadorned. Cesar didn't learn anything he hadn't heard from Donna Creech. He wrote in his notebook anyway, and kept writing after she finished talking. How the hell was he going to get her to loosen up a little?

"Ma'am, can we go over who all was at that meeting? I'm going to need to get that straight."

"Why don't I do a list?"

"Sure."

"Have you had coffee? Would you like some?"

"Sure. Where is it?"

"Right through there," she pointed to Irv's office.

By the time he got back she had a roster with names and titles, separated into Golden Time and Bennett staffs. By that time, Cesar could have typed two, maybe three, names.

"Will that help?"

"Yes, ma'am." Jesus, he was back on the defensive again. Retreat to the list. Some of the names he knew already from Donna—Irv, Frederick Golden, Bennett. He knew Rosemary now. Tom Cleary? It said he was a copywriter.

"Tom Cleary, is he about thirty—glasses? Kind of heavyset?"

"Do you know him?"

"I knew a Tom Cleary in school."

"Perhaps he's your friend."

"Might be."

She was still handling him. Try again.

"This is everyone who was at the meeting. Is that right, ma'am?"

"With the exception of Mrs. Creech, yes."

"Mrs. Creech says that everyone cleared out right after the meeting, is that right?"

She nodded.

"Did you leave last? Is that how you know?"

"No, but everyone reassembled more or less in the parking lot. I saw them all."

"Who was last out?"

"Just a minute . . . Frederick Golden and Mr. Enneking were last out. They came out together."

"Did Irving Golden come out while you were in the parking lot?"

"No."

"Did anyone go back into the building?"

"No."

"Mrs. Creech says there's a special lock on the door to the parking lot and that there's only one key."

"There are two."

"But one's in Mr. Golden's safe-deposit box."

"That's right."

"She said she had the keys but she put them back on the desk. Did you see them there?"

"Yes."

"Were they there when you left?"

"I assume they were. I didn't check. Are they missing?"

"They didn't turn up last night."

"Oh." She understood.

"Miss Meynell, Mrs. Creech also said that things got a little hot at the meeting. You didn't mention that."

"Detective Franck, I think there are a few things you need to know about Donna Creech. You do know already that she is almost professionally observant. She is also capable of certain exaggerations. Beyond that she is a liar."

Oh. Surprise.

"Was she exaggerating or lying about the meeting?"

Miss Meynell paused only briefly.

"There was a certain amount of friction."

"A lot?"

"It was not excessive."

"Donna Creech said Mr. Golden was yelling. Was he abusing anyone?"

"Mr. Golden could be . . . severe."

"Was he 'severe' yesterday?"

"Yes."

"With anyone in particular?"

"If your question is whether or not he could have provoked someone to the point of murder, the answer is no."

"She also said a lot of people hated Mr. Golden. Was she right about that?"

Rosemary looked at him. She stood up and walked over to close the door. She walked like a queen. When she got back to her desk she had made up her mind.

"You will hear many things about Irving Golden as you investigate this matter. Many people did not like Mr. Golden; many of those thought that he had hurt them deliberately. He was not particularly tactful. I've told you he could be severe. But he built a business, a very strong business. He has made a number of people wealthy and he has employed many people who needed work and couldn't find it elsewhere." Lillian Franck, for example?

"How were his employee relations?"

That brought a very cool stare.

"I suspect you think you know the answer to that." She was right. More than once Cesar had been handed leaflets outside the department stores. Those leaflets charged Golden Time as well as Mr. Golden with union busting.

"I will tell you my experience. I hope you will think about it.

"Mr. Golden hired me ten years ago. I found him abrasive and boorish and was certain that he had hired me as a status symbol. English secretaries were in vogue. As it happens, I had rather good training. I put his office in order, giving him, in effect, two or three more business hours each day. He did not become less abrasive; he didn't change any habits or behavior. However, after one month and without comment he doubled my salary. I have received substantial raises since then and have never had to ask. I must also point out that he was never sexually offensive. I came to respect Irving Golden. I am still ashamed of my first reaction."

Her telephone buzzed politely, as if it were trained to wait until she was ready. It was for Cesar. Sgt. Evans.

"Cesar, I don't know what you had planned, but you're going out to Amberley to see Mrs. Golden."

What Cesar had planned was to spend more time here and then go over to The Bennett Agency. "Now?" he asked.

"Yeah, now. She's called the mayor and the manager and the chief and she wants, and I quote, 'My husband's detective' at her house immediately. Says she has things to say."

"Oh. Okay." What could he say?

"Are you getting anywhere there? You want Henry over there to help out?"

"No, not yet. Give me the address." He wrote it down. "You got any idea what she wants to say?"

"Nope. Have fun." Cesar hung up. Apparently they trained English secretaries to read upside down without their eyes popping out like Donna Creech's.

"Would you like directions? It's a little confusing to find."

Yes, he would, thank you, ma'am.

"Will we see you again, Detective Franck?"

"Probably. Maybe not today."

"We're closed Saturday. Will you need to see anyone at home?"

"I might. I don't know."

"Here's my number. If you do need to reach anyone, call me. I do have staff addresses and numbers."

I'm sure you do.

"Thanks. That'll be a help."

Cesar stood up and fought an urge to bow. "Thanks again."

"Not at all."

4

WHAT TO DO? Eat and drive? Skyline Chili at the counter? Look pitifully hungry at the Golden's and hope for a snack? He chose to eat and drive, having mastered that technique years ago. He hadn't dropped tartar sauce on himself since he was twenty-three.

The same Mill Creek Expressway that terrified his mother relaxed Cesar. He knew it so well that he was on auto-pilot, free to juggle his Frisch's Big Boy triple decker, large Coke, and his thoughts. Did he know what he was doing yet? Was he in charge or was he just following the direction Donna Creech had pointed? Donna Creech was a liar. Rosemary Meynell said so. How could he argue with Rosemary Meynell? How could anybody? But everything she had told him checked out with Leonard Cassidy and Rosemary Meynell. He was already assuming Donna's theory, though. Was that right to do? She was a snoop, a Bad Dude Groupie, an exaggerator, a liar. But she wasn't dumb. According to the lab guys, a hefty bonk with a Tina would do anyone in. Irv's back door was the only way to get in without going past Loyal Leonard. Rosemary Meynell said that everyone left the building except Donna, Irv, and Leonard. He could check that out. He was going to have to check out Leonard and Donna, but he wasn't going to spend a lot of time on them. Why not? Well, they both needed jobs and they were pretty near unemployable. Why would they kill the only man in Cincinnati nice enough to keep them on?

Nice? Irving Golden "nice"? Irving Golden exploited housewives, including Cesar's favorite housewife, Lillian. Labor said he was a union buster. Rosemary Meynell said he was a great boss. No, she said he was fair to her. And he kept his hands off. He must have been tempted. Was he a bad guy or a nice guy? Who were the last people out of the building? Cesar fished for a napkin in the Frisch's bag and carefully cleaned all traces of grease off his hands. He got Miss Meynell's list out of his coat pocket. He had underlined Joseph Enneking and Frederick Golden and written "last out" in the margin. Did they swing the Tina jointly? Possible, but not likely. Had Irv given them a rough time at the meeting? Miss Rosemary Meynell made that meeting sound like a quiet day at the convent. Did she have to be so discreet? Her boss was dead. Who got the use of her terrific discretion now? Did she still have a job? Was this Section Road coming up?

32

Time to get off and pay attention. Cesar did not know Amberley. He ticked off Miss Meynell's directions in his head. Right on Kingsway. Left on Fairway, left again on Bon Air to 7843. It was dumb not to write them down but he had to do something to impress her. When he got to Bon Air it was full of parked cars, so he had to go a block past 7843 and park. The aged, motor-pool Hornet looked worse than usual, surrounded as it was by so many very clean, very slick, and very foreign cars. Seventy-eight forty-three was a large ranch house. Cesar's ring was answered by a middle-aged woman.

"Mrs. Golden?"

"No, I'm her sister."

"I'm Detective Franck, Cincinnati Homicide Squad. Mrs. Golden asked to see me."

"Oh. Come in."

The Golden house may have been plain ranch house outside, but inside it was plain money. Cesar stepped into an entry hall as big as a movie lobby. He was pretty sure he was standing on polished marble. Columns to the right of him, columns to the left of him, and the marble flowed both ways. Take away the crowd and there would be plenty of room for Dorothy Hamill. But there was a crowd; more fur hats than Cesar had ever seen under one roof. There was clearly a connection with the nice sedans outside. Lots of diamonds, too. Mrs. Golden's sister steered him through the entry hall, under an arch and into the land of bedrooms. She tapped on a door and opened it.

Mr. and Mrs. Golden's bedroom was different from his mother's. It was also different from Irv's office. Cesar did a quick mental check for recent encounters with dog turds, came up negative, and stepped into the white wool carpet. Even with the curtains closed there was a glare. White walls, white spread, white chaise lounge, white armchairs, white marble fireplace, white curtains. There was a large portrait over the fireplace showing a very pretty blonde lady with her arms around two pretty kids, seven and eight maybe. Both of them had lots of brown curls. Cesar looked to his left. The pretty lady in the picture was sitting on a stool, flanked by a man and a woman, both about Cesar's age. If they were the kids in the picture, they had changed a lot more than their mother. Both still had brown curls, but the girl had acquired a spectacular figure. The boy wore glasses and a beard. All three were in black.

"Irene, this is Detective Franck. Detective Franck, this is Mrs. Golden." Mrs. Golden's sister went back to the skating rink.

"Louie, get a chair for Mr. Franck." Louie brought one of the white armchairs and set it opposite his mother. "Thank you, dear, and now I want to talk to Mr. Franck alone." Both children kissed their mother and left.

Irene Golden looked at her shoes so Cesar did too. Black high heels. He looked back up. She had her back to a big makeup table. Cesar saw three Irenes and three Cesars in the hinged mirror. She looked terrific but he began to wonder if he should have worn something besides his red pants and black-checked sport coat. Mrs. Golden lifted her head and Cesar got his first good look at her face. She showed a few of the years since the portrait, but not many. Even with her eyes swollen from crying, she was a beautiful woman. She was also very different from Cesar's usual widows. The bulk of his business was couples stabbing each other or drug-related shootouts. The stabbing widows were usually poor and frantic. The drug widows went in for tattoos. He waited for Irene Golden to speak.

"Mr. Franck."

"Yes, ma'am."

"You have to arrest my husband's murderer."

"I'm certainly going to do my best, ma'am." He waited for a response but there wasn't any. "Ma'am, the chief said you had some information for me."

"Yes, I do." She stood up and walked across the room. She had very nice legs. There was a picture of Irv on the bedside table. She picked it up and looked at it fondly, moving it closer and closer to her face. Should she be wearing glasses? She turned to Cesar.

"My husband was a wonderful man." She recrossed the room, put the picture at the end of her dressing table, and sat down. "He was a wonderful husband and father and a wonderful son. Did you know his mother is alive? She's very old." She paused. Cesar couldn't see any pictures of old ladies anywhere. "He was a wonderful brother, too. Did you know he has a brother?"

"Yes, ma'am."

"I don't know how to say this. It's so awful. I think Frederick, his brother . . . I think Frederick killed my husband." She stopped and stared at him, opening her very large grey eyes as wide as she could. Cesar wondered if he should move in closer so she could see. He could see fine.

"You do?"

"I know. It's awful, horrible to think about. That a brother could do something so . . . so brutal. But you don't know."

"Ma'am?"

"Frederick was horribly jealous of Irving. Irving was so smart. He had so much talent. And he was so handsome." Cesar looked at the picture. Same Irv. "They shared the business, you know. But it should have been Irving's. He *made* the business. He was such a good son. It belongs to Mrs. Golden, all of it."

"The toy company?"

"Yes. Irv's father left it to her. I don't know why. He should have left it to Irving. But it's hers. Irving would have taken care of Frederick, you know. He would never have hurt his brother. And now Frederick has done *this*!" Tears rolled from her eyes.

Oh, nuts.

"Mrs. Golden, I realize this has been very . . . tough for you." What was he supposed to say? "You think your brother-in-law is responsible for your husband's death?"

"I'm sure he is."

"I'm going to need a little more information to follow up on this."

"What do you mean?"

"Well, did they have a fight? Did your husband's brother ever threaten your husband? In front of witnesses?"

"Oh, they had terrible fights. I couldn't stand to watch them."

"Were they . . . did they become violent?"

"They were horrible. Frederick would come here and Irving would take him into his den so I wouldn't have to hear. Frederick could be so ugly."

"Was there any physical violence?"

"I don't know. Irving didn't tell me what went on. I always came in here."

"Do you know if there were ever any threats?"

"Threats? Oh, I'm sure there were. Frederick always thought Irving was threatening, but Irving would never have hurt him."

"No, what I meant was, did your brother-in-law threaten your husband?"

"Oh. I don't know. He must have. I mean he was always so loud when they would fight."

"Mrs. Golden, I have to say I'm a little confused. You seem to be pretty sure your brother-in-law is responsible for your husband's death, but I don't see that I've got anything to go on. A lot of brothers fight, ma'am. They just do."

"But you don't understand, Mr. Franck."

"Ma'am?"

"Frederick wanted the business."

"He wanted to run it?"

"No. Oh, no. He could never do that, not without Irving. He wants to sell it. He wants the money. Frederick hates the toy business. Irving said so. Frederick is a snob."

It was Cesar's turn to stare at Mrs. Golden. Was he supposed to go back to Central Station and report a dangerous snob? A killer snob?

"You don't understand, do you?"

No, lady, I do not.

"We're Jewish, Mr. Franck. Are you?"

"No, ma'am."

"Frederick likes to think he's not. You'll see that when you meet him. He thought Irving was too Jewish. It embarrassed him. And Golden Time Toys embarrasses him. Isn't that ridiculous? But he hated it."

"Do you know why?" Cesar didn't think toys were Jewish, but he wasn't really sure what was and what wasn't.

"Mr. Golden, Irving's father, used to work there, you know. He bought it from the Ennekings during the Depression when they went bankrupt. He saved the business really. And he lived for toys. He wanted the boys to live for toys, too. And Irving did. But Frederick was a snob even then. He wanted to be like his school friends, Irving says. He never worked in the factory after school. He never even went there. So, of course, now he doesn't know the business. Irving just kept him on out of duty. He even wanted Irving to change the name back to Queen City Toys, so people wouldn't connect him with toys. He was furious about the new dolls."

"The Denver Dolls?"

"Yes! Can you imagine? He said they were tasteless. I think they're adorable. Have you seen them?"

"Not yet."

"Irving says they're going to be very popular. Every one watches 'Denver.' Well, Frederick says *he* doesn't, of course."

"And the dolls made him angry?"

"He tried to make Irving kill the project. He even went to Mrs. Golden, but she loves 'Denver.'"

"Oh."

"Well, don't you see? They're going to be a national fad. *Everyone* will have them. And they'll be Golden . . . and there Frederick will be at the Symmes Club knowing that everyone connects him with dolls instead of machine tools. He'll hate it. But Irving would have been proud."

That called for another fond look in Irving's direction. Cesar still wanted to know what was Jewish about toys, but how was he supposed to ask?

"And the last fight they had was about the dolls. So I *know* that's why Frederick did it."

"Ma'am, I'm certainly going to look into this conflict as part of my ongoing investigation and I certainly appreciate your bringing it to my attention."

"Just be sure you talk to Mrs. Golden quickly. Before Frederick has her completely in control. Please. That's so important."

"Ma'am?"

"She's so vacillating. She loved both of them. I don't know why."

"I guess you know how it is with mothers, Mrs. Golden."

"Most mothers don't have a murderer for a son."

Cesar guessed not. Was he supposed to go now?

"I'm very tired, Mr. Franck."

"Oh, gosh. I didn't realize I'd kept you so long. I'm sorry, ma'am."

"Not at all. Thank you so much for coming. You'll let me know when I have to testify? I will testify, you know."

"Sure, ma'am. I'll just let myself out. You get some rest. And, please, I'm very sorry about your husband."

"Thank you, Mr. Franck."

Cesar eased out into the hall. He was headed for the front door when Louie Golden grabbed his elbow. "Can we talk, officer? For a minute?"

"I'm supposed to be getting back."

"I really do only want to talk for a minute."

"Uh. Okay."

Louie Golden steered Cesar back toward the land of bedrooms, but his sister intercepted them under the arch.

"What are you doing, Louis?"

"The detective and I need to talk for a minute, Grace. Excuse us."

"No."

"Grace!"

"Not alone, you're not."

There was a tense little moment. Cesar looked at them both, bet on Grace, and won.

"We'll talk in my room, officer."

"It's Detective Franck."

"Of course."

Louie Golden's bedroom looked like a rich high school athlete's bedroom, but Louie was long out of high school.

"I know. It's amazing. Irene keeps it as sort of a shrine. She keeps hoping I'll come back."

"Don't, Louie," said Grace.

Cesar was with Grace. You shouldn't make fun of your mother when there's been a death in the house. Especially when it's your father who's dead.

"Just say whatever you think is so important and let Detective Franck go home."

Cesar thought Grace was very pretty. Was Grace a married lady? Did she go out on dates?

"Detective Franck, I suspect my mother has been telling you her pet theory about my father's murderer. Am I right?" Louie gave a coaxing smile.

"We were discussing certain aspects of the case."

"Yes. Well. In this case the aspect is Uncle Fred, isn't it? Come on, I know I'm right."

"Mr. Golden . . ."

"Please. It's Louie."

"Mr. Golden, I was talking to your mother in confidence. If there's something you need to tell me, go ahead."

"Well, I think you should know that my mother is not exactly rational about Uncle Fred or his family. That's putting it mildly, really. I mean she would blame him for the *Holocaust* if he hadn't been in Cincinnati when it happened."

"Louie, stop being a shit."

"Grace, *please*. Detective Frank will think you're coarse.

Grace turned red.

"At any rate, Detective Franck, I wanted you to know, before you clamp him in irons, that Uncle Frederick, tiresome as he may be, is not a murderer. Even Irene will admit that when she's less upset. Uncle Fred is a bore, a philistine, a womanizer, and an anti-Semite, but he's not a murderer. Now if you want a truly logical suspect I would suspect Joe Enneking."

"Louie!"

"Why not? You do know who Joe Enneking is, Detective Franck?"

"He was one of your father's employees."

"Oh, much more than that. Much more. I mean, yes, he is the Production Manager, but he's also the son of Karl Enneking."

"So?" said Cesar.

"Karl Enneking was the man who lost the Queen City Toy Company to my grandfather. Of course, Grandpa bought it, but Joe . . . Joe thinks Karl was tricked. Well, probably Joe thinks of it as *usurped*. Joe is the lost prince."

"Louie, please."

"He thinks he's Hamlet. Schlegel, of course."

Hamlet Schlegel?

"My brother wants you to know that he's been to lots of schools, Detective Franck. That's what he does. Schlegel translated Hamlet into German."

"My sister is cruel. But you'll notice she doesn't disagree. Oh, and she's been to a few schools herself."

But she doesn't rub it in.

"Are you through, Louie?"

"Nearly, nearly. I just want to be sure that Detective Franck is curious enough to call on Joe at Schloss Enneking. He really must see it. Have you been there yet?" he asked Cesar.

"No, sir."

"It is truly grim. I know you'll be fascinated."

Mrs. Golden's sister opened the door. "Louie, Irene wants you."

"Tell her I'll be right there. The Hun, Detective Franck. Seek out the Hun." Louie left.

"Please excuse my brother, Detective Franck."

"Sure."

"Has anyone offered you anything? Coffee? Or a drink?"

"No, but that's all right."

"Please. You must have something."

"Well, coffee would be fine. Black."

"Sit down, please. I'll be right back."

Cesar sat down in a recliner. Jeez. Louie had his own recliner in his bedroom in high school. Cesar's mother hadn't had hers very long and it was in the living room. Louie had lots of tennis trophies. Che Guevara was still hanging on the wall. And there was a bong on the table beside him. Was he allowed to smoke dope in high school? What a life. He was a snot, though. Rich creep. Cesar liked Grace and wondered why she wasn't a creep like her brother. She came back with the coffee and sat on the end of Louie's bed.

"I really appreciate this, Miss Golden."

"Oh, it's nice to get out of there for a while."

"I'm sorry about your father."

"Thank you."

They drank coffee and didn't talk for a while. Finally Grace said, "I'm sorry you had to come all the way out here. I know Mother called the mayor."

"No, it's all right."

"You must have a terrible impression of the family."

"No, I . . ."

"Please. I know. Mother's in a state and Louie's being a perfect shit. They can both do much better. I hope you'll forget it."

"Well, it's a hard time . . ." Cesar didn't know what to say. She was right. Mrs. Golden seemed pretty dizzy to him. Louie was probably anti-cop.

"My mother's not an airhead. Not always. She's spoiled. Daddy wanted to spoil her and she let him. I'm afraid she's rather confused now. But she's a very kind person, and generous. And she loved my father."

"She seems like a very nice lady."

"And my brother can be nice, too. He doesn't always show off."

I hope he appreciates what a nice sister he's got.

"Now," Grace continued, "my mother probably told you that Frederick was jealous of Daddy and that he wasn't much help to the company. Is that right?" Cesar started to clear his threat but Grace went on. "Oh! I'm putting you on the spot, aren't I? You can't tell me what she said. But I can guess. Did she tell you he wants to sell the business?"

"Yes."

"Did she explain that my grandmother actually owns Golden Time? Yes? And I'm sure she told you that Daddy and Frederick didn't get along. So you have something of a picture. What she probably didn't tell you is that my uncle is a very weak and very silly man. He's been very angry at my father off and on all his life, but he's never done anything about it. I think, when Mother's calmed down, she will agree. No matter how silly he is, he's family. Daddy was his brother. Would you like more coffee?''

"No, thanks. This is fine.''

"Will you be talking to him? Uncle Frederick?''

"I'll be talking to all of the people who saw your father yesterday.''

"I think you'll see what I mean.''

Cesar thought about whether he should ask her any more questions. This was a wake, after all, or whatever the Jewish custom was. But it was nice talking to her, and she didn't seem to have any axes to grind.

"Your brother was talking about Mr. Enneking.''

"My father's production manager.''

"Yes. Did he and your father get along?''

She thought about that. "He's not really someone you get along with. But then I don't suppose my father was either. They weren't alike. I don't mean that. But I think they both just worked.''

"Please?''

"I guess I mean that when they went to work they worked. They didn't work for status or to be with people. Joe goes to work to make toys. Daddy went to work to sell toys. And I think they respected each other because of that.''

"Your brother was saying that Mr. Enneking might have resented your father.''

"Oh, that's just Louie. I told you he was showing off. I've never seen any resentment. No. He's a very good production manager. I certainly intend to keep him on.''

"Oh. Do you work there, too?''

"No. But I'm going to. I always wanted to. And now I'm going to.''

"What will you do?''

"I'm going to run it.''

"As president?''

"That's who runs it.''

"Wow!''

"Are you surprised?''

"Sort of.''

"Why?''

"I don't know. You're young, I guess.''

"And female.''

"No, not that. Well, maybe. What will your uncle do?''

"He'll probably run to Grandma and try to get her to stop me.''

"Will she?''

"If she does, I'll get tough with her. Like Daddy did. She likes that. And Frederick will cave in. I'll have to keep him on, of course."

Cesar was impressed. He was disappointed, too. The longer he talked to Grace the more he thought about asking her out. She was smart and pretty and she wasn't stuck-up. But now she was going to be a president, and he didn't think presidents went out with cops. Oh, well.

"Well, good luck to you."

"You don't look very happy about it."

"No, I mean it. It's a lot of work."

"It is. I know that. And I'll need good luck. I'm going to have to stir things up and do them my way and I'm going to have people mad at me pretty fast."

"Not too mad, I hope."

She stared at him. Oh, Christ. He had forgotten about Irving.

"I'm sorry. I didn't mean—"

"My father. I didn't mean that either. But I suppose I should think about it. I'm probably going to fire The Bennett Agency."

"Is that a big deal?"

"It's a very big deal. For many reasons. They've had our business for years. We're their biggest account. And I have a lot of friends there."

"That's pretty heavy. Do you have to do it? Right away?"

"I think so. If I don't do it right away, I might not do it. And it's time. I think they've gotten comfortable over the years and I need an agency that's hungry. And healthy."

"Healthy?"

"Do you know Phillip Bennett?"

"No."

"He's sick. Daddy told me. And it shows. The agency's sick. It's pretty much his show still. When he's sick, the agency's sick. I think Daddy was ready to fire them, too. They may have known that. I'm sure Phillip Bennett knows."

"What's wrong with him?"

"I don't know. I don't think Daddy knew."

"You don't think he'll get better?"

"No. And I don't think the agency will either."

Cesar had watched her as she talked about the agency. It seemed to him that the problem with Bennett was a pretty big deal to her, maybe not just business. Either that or she was too emotional for his idea of the corporate world. But before she talked about Bennett she seemed pretty tough. Cesar didn't know much about advertising agencies.

"Miss Golden, thanks a lot for the coffee. I need to get back downtown now. Unless there's anything else you need to tell me. Or ask about."

"No, that's all. Thank you. Thank you for coming out."

"You or your mother can call me any time if you think of anything else."

"Thank you."

"When will you start to work?"

"Monday."

"Good luck. I'll probably see you there."

"Let me show you out."

"I can get out."

"It's crowded. Come on." When they got back to the entry he was glad she came. It really was crowded, but everyone backed off for Grace. The gossip noise which was pretty loud dimmed a little and changed to sympathy noise. She followed him out the front door.

"I wish I didn't have to go back in," she said.

"There's a lot of people."

"I'm going to have to talk to every single one."

He started down the driveway.

"Detective Franck?"

"Yes, ma'am."

"Can you hot-wire a car?"

"I can try."

"Daddy's car. It's in the lot and we need it. We can't find any keys."

"We'll get it out here."

"Thanks."

Great. Terrific. Cesar's Hornet was trapped between a Seville and a Jaguar with about twelve inches of maneuvering room. He thought for a minute about going back to find the owners to see if they would show a little mercy. No. If he asked for the owners of a Seville and a Jaguar he'd nearly empty the place. It took twelve passes to get out. Someday, someway he would find the tightwad in Purchasing who thought power steering was a luxury and he would . . . Cesar stopped to glare at an Amberley cop who was glaring at him. The nice snug feeling he had had from talking with Grace and drinking her coffee was gone.

42

5

CESAR GOT BACK to the squad office at 3:00. His desk was littered with pink message slips. No reason why people couldn't put them in a nice neat stack. Cesar always did. He sat down and tuned into Henry Chapman's phone conversation at the desk behind his. One of the many lady friends. He tuned out and went through the messages.

"Donna Creech called, please call."
"Donna Creech called, will call back."
"Donna Creech called, will call back."
"Lieutenant Tieves called, wants to see you."
"Mrs. Franck called, please call, wants to know about supper."
"Leon Wilson (*Enquirer*) called, please call (called twice)."
"Donna Creech called, wants to see you, can't be reached. Has something *important* to tell you. Will be at the Top Hat tonight (changing your image?)"

Henry had taken that last message and most of the others. Damn. He never put the time down. Or the date. Cesar always did for him. Lt. Tieves would want to know about the Budget Narrative first and the Golden case second. Cesar called his mother and left a message telling her not to wait for him. He tried twice for Donna Creech. He wanted to talk to Henry before he saw Lt. Tieves, but it might be five o'clock before he got off the phone. Cesar went to see Lt. Tieves.

Lt. Tieves' office never failed to impress Cesar. It was at least as clean as an operating room and considerably neater. All of the lieutenants and captains went in for terrifically clean, neat, and bare offices. Henry, who understood these things better, had explained it as a tactic used in the eternal war against the City Hall boys. In the upper levels over at Plum Street they went in for carpets, artwork, and lots of furniture and, like corporate hotshots, they fought over space and corners. The lieutenants loved to have the management analysts, finance bullies, and even the councilmen over to visit. Five minutes of sitting in a plain steel chair in one of those featureless offices would usually reduce the pinstripe boys to a state of panic. Fear of dentist. Fear of doctor. Fear of cop. Lt. Tieves' office was shinier and barer than any other lieutenant's in Central Station. He had a blotter on his desk and that was it. Cesar wondered if he paid someone to come in and Simonize the ceramic bricks on the wall. Maybe he did it himself on weekends. Only Lillian's bathroom could equal Lt. Tieves' office.

Lt. Tieves was pretty impressive himself. When Cesar looked in a mirror he saw someone who looked like most of the cops he knew. Blond hair, getting a little thin, moustache, roundish face, a frame that was starting to show the effect of thousands of Frisch's Big Boys. But Lt. Tieves was different from the other cops. He was tall, steel-jawed, clean-shaven, and clearly stayed away from Frisch's. His squad was certain he was on the way to the top.

"Cesar, come on in." He even had a winner's voice. Loud, deep, and clear. "Did you see Mrs. Golden?"

"Yes, sir."

"Did she have anything?"

"Not much. She seems to think her brother-in-law is involved. No proof. Nothing to follow. Nothing solid anyway."

"Sorry you had to go out there. She's got friends. I'll send somebody else if she calls again. Now, what have you got?"

Not much. Not much at all. Cesar had thought all the way back from Amberley about how he was going to tell Lt. Tieves that he didn't have anything solid for him. He had a murder weapon and that was it. He didn't even have a theory. Well, he had a theory, but when your theory is that one of ten people at a meeting was a murderer it isn't much of a theory.

But Cesar wasn't dumb. And he knew Lt. Tieves. Lt. Tieves was going to be talking to the City Manager and he wanted something meaty to present, something that sounded like detecting. He also knew that the lieutenant didn't want details. Lt. Tieves thought of himself as a manager. If there were useful details he would get those from Sgt. Evans. So Cesar gave him what he wanted. Donna Creech's screwed-up visit to the office became "an interview with a key employee within minutes of the incident." The total lack of any concrete lead became the "elimination of robbery as a motive," and the various accusations of Irene and Louie Golden became "the revelation of several key aspects of the case by close family members." It was the best he could do and it seemed to satisfy Lt. Tieves, who sent him to Sgt. Evans for his real grilling.

Cesar was ready for that, too. He found Sgt. Evans outside the toilet and hit him with a preemptive strike. "Sergeant, look. I haven't gotten anywhere on this case. It's nearly four and I've talked to exactly one person who gave me anything to go on and that's Golden's daughter. I haven't seen any of the guys who were with Golden at that meeting, and they're all gonna be gone for the weekend if I don't get over there. I've seen Tieves. He's happy. I want to get on over to this advertising agency right now. What do you say?"

"I say you're gonna work on this tomorrow. You're gonna go see people at their homes if you have to. Henry is gonna help you. You're also going to call me at home twice a day and fill me in completely. You talked to reporters?"

"No. Leon Wilson called."

"I'll call him back, the little shit. You know you've got about two more days before we start taking a load from the media."

"I know, Sergeant."

"What you don't have here is a friendly stabbing over a game of Tonk."

"Right. I know that."

"Also, Lieutenant Tieves asked me to do something about your clothes if you're going to be calling on anyone in Hyde Park or anyplace like that."

"What's that mean?"

"It means he doesn't want his squad to look like cops when they call on his future friends and supporters. No red pants."

"Terrific. Does he want me to buy a pair of penny loafers?"

"I don't know, for Christ's sake. Just try to look a little collegiate, all right?"

"Sure, Sergeant." Cesar was not a little miffed. He wore red pants to college, and he wasn't the only one who did.

"You can go."

Cesar went back to his desk.

"Ceez, bay-bee." Amazing. Henry was off the phone. "There is a lady who likes you a whole lot. She *really* wants to talk to you."

"Yeah, I know."

"And, Cesar! The Top Hat! Hey, bay-bee, the Top Hat is a Bad club. You and your lady are in for a very big time. *Very* cool."

"Henry, you're coming with me."

"Cesar, you don't understand, the Top Hat is BAD. Too bad for me. The Brothers at the Top Hat take guys like me and feed them to their dogs, man. No, I've got other plans. But listen, you have a *good* time."

"Henry, shut up. Donna Creech is a lead in the Golden case, all right? Can you meet me out there?"

"No, man. I got plans."

"So did I."

"Those guys are *mean*, Cesar."

"Sergeant Evans informed me that I am to have your assistance."

"He did?"

"I request your assistance. I am scared to go to the Top Hat without the accompaniment of a minority police officer. I will see you at the Top Hat Lounge at nine o'clock."

"When are you going to understand that People don't party until late, Cesar? I will meet you at twelve-thirty if I meet you."

"Twelve-thirty?"

"Twelve-thirty and we'll be early. Believe me."

"Jesus, I'm glad I'm not black. I couldn't take the hours."

"You'll love it."

Bashing magnates in a conference room,
Tycoons dropping off like flies.
Irving Golden has gone to his doom
And humbugs start to eulogize.
Everybody tries to speak of him as 'quite a guy,'
No one speaks ill of the dead.
Since he was so grand then I want to know why
Some fiend has battered in his head.

The music was Mel Torme's, and Evelyn Osborne had spent the entire day writing the new lyrics. It did not seem to bother him that only his assistant Gretel Tenbosch paid any attention. Evelyn was obviously fond of his own voice and wit. Gretel was a dear, but she was clearly wrecked and unlikely to understand just how truly clever his little rewrite was. He and Gretel were at the piano in the room upstairs at Arnold's Bar. The room was filled with employees of The Bennett Agency, all officially still at work since it was not yet five o'clock.

Mary Cunningham, the upstairs waitress, stood at the dumbwaiter, pretending to straighten out the ropes, eavesdropping for all she was worth. There was only one topic of conversation today and it was red hot, Irving Golden. More precisely, Irving Golden's murder. Right now, for instance, she was tuning into Marianne Kelly and Bob Atwood.

"Why do you have to say a man did it?" Marianne's face was flushed with bad temper and light beer. "Why do you assume a man did it?"

"Right. Right. I'm discriminating. Sorry."

"Well, you are discriminating. You always discriminate. It's really a pain."

Mary noticed that Marianne's pain was not enough to make her remove Bob's hand from her leg. "Do you actually think you have to be a man to kill a jerk like that? I'll bet there are plenty of women who hate him enough to do it. They're strong enough, too."

"Hated."

"Hated. I mean he was really unfair to women. You saw what he did to me."

"Ah! But you didn't kill him."

"How do you know? Do you *know* I didn't?"

Mary nearly dropped a beer bottle down the dumbwaiter. Bob and Marianne glared at her so she moved over to the door and pretended to add up checks. From that spot she could hear Evelyn Osborne, who had abandoned his song and turned his back on the piano. Gretel still faced the piano as if she expected it to finish the song. Evelyn was addressing the nearest table.

"Absolutely without doubt. It was Herr Enneking and it was a crime of *passion*. Grand passion. Grand Teutonic passion."

Of his audience only Crystal Morris, Queen of Accounting, had drunk enough to encourage him. "Whaddya mean, Eve?"

"Thank you, dear lady. I mean that Herr Enneking had formed a holy passion for Miss Banner Strathmore. He worshipped her. His little dollies were teensy ikons, wee objects of veneration. And when Irving made unchaste reference to the bosom of Our Lady of Denver, well— it was too much for the Hun. Something snapped and . . ."

Gretel pulled at his elbow. "Sing your song, Evelyn. It's beautiful." Evelyn obliged.

Tom Cleary and Jack Squires were alone at a table in the corner farthest from the door.

"God, we're a heartless lot," said Jack. "When you think of it, Irving's put bread on our tables for years and look at us. Not a wet eye in the house. Me mum would be shocked."

"Are you upset?"

"Over Irving? Personally? I don't know." Jack thought for a minute. "I didn't like him. Who did? But it's a sordid way to go, isn't it?"

Tom nodded.

"And I know they don't mean any harm laughing about it, but I feel a little bit spooked. I don't like it. I guess I hate to think of dying and knowing that there might be a session like this where everybody jokes about me. Depressing."

"Don't worry, Jack. We'd miss you. We wouldn't joke."

"Thanks, mate."

They settled back to drink. It was becoming too noisy for conversation. Suddenly the noise level dropped. Tom looked around. Everyone's eyes were on the door, where a stranger stood. The stranger was searching the crowd until his eyes lit on Tom. Tom stared back. Should he know him? Did he know anybody who wore red pants? The stranger spoke to him, "Are you Tom Cleary?"

"Yes?" Tom stood up.

"We used to know each other. You remember?"

"No, I'm sorry."

"I'm Cesar, Cesar Franck."

"Cesar! Sure!" Tom paused and then it slipped out, "But you're a cop!" The room went completely quiet and Cesar blushed. It was Gretel Tenbosch who broke the silence.

"I'm so *confused*. I thought Cesar Franck was dead."

6

CONVERSATIONS RESUMED AFTER Cesar crossed the room and settled in at Jack and Tom's table, but Cesar could feel a lot of eyes on his back.

"I'm sorry I didn't recognize you, Cesar. It's been a long time."

"Don't feel bad. I knew who I was looking for. You didn't expect me. So. How've you been?"

"Fine. How about yourself? You want a drink?"

"No, thanks. Maybe later."

"Was I right? About you being a cop?"

"Yeah. Still a cop."

"How do you like it?"

"Being a cop? Okay. It gets weird sometimes, but it's pretty interesting. I'm Cesar Franck." He stuck his hand out for Jack.

"Oh, Jeez. I'm sorry. Cesar, this is Jack Squires. He works with me."

"How'd you do? I didn't know Tom had any respectable friends. This is a pleasure."

"Why? Are you hanging around with hoods these days?" Cesar asked Tom.

Tom waved his arm at the room, "Bums, not hoods."

"They look pretty nice to me."

"Wait until you know them, Mr. Franck. They're heathens, all of them," said Jack.

"Well, tell me about yourself. What are you doing here?"

"I'm on duty, actually, Tom. I'm investigating Irving Golden's death."

"Oh! Are you a detective?"

Cesar nodded.

"But that's pretty good, isn't it? Better than being a regular cop?"

The hubbub eased for a few seconds and then resumed when the sharper agency ears heard the word "detective." Cesar's ears were sharp enough that he heard the word "detective" bouncing around the room for minutes.

"It's pretty interesting."

"And you're on the Golden case?"

"Right."

48

"Well."

Cesar and Tom looked at each other. It was an awkward reunion.

"How do you two know each other—school?" asked Jack.

"We grew up together—same block," said Tom.

"Different high schools," said Cesar.

Walnut Hills for Tom, Western Hills for Cesar. Cesar remembered the estrangement he had felt when Tom told him that he was taking the test for Walnut Hills, the city's college prep school. Tom would be gone, as surely as if he were joining the priesthood. The separation was, in fact, sure and final. The years spent on bicycles, patrolling Westwood, were over. There was no fight, no discussion, no attempt to stay friends. Tom went to Walnut Hills and became a person who did not go to Western Hills, the neighborhood high school. And here he was, an advertising man. Cesar didn't know any other advertising people. Rosemary Meynell's roster said that Tom was a copywriter. What did they do? Everyone knew what detectives did.

"How's your mom?" asked Tom.

"Fine. Same as ever."

"He's got a really nice mom," Tom told Jack. "I'd like to see her again."

"She's still at Shillito's."

Cesar wished he could have a beer.

"You said you were on the Golden case," said Jack. "I suppose you know we're all pretty interested in it. Nasty business."

"Is that what you do? Homicide?" asked Tom.

Cesar nodded.

"This is a pretty wild one, isn't it? For Cincinnati?"

"For anywhere, I guess. You knew him? Mr. Golden?"

"Sort of. Jack actually worked a lot closer with him."

"But you both were at the meeting yesterday?"

Jack and Tom stared at him.

"That's right." Jack finally spoke. "How did you know? Wait, that's silly, isn't it? That's your job."

"I talked to Mr. Golden's secretary this morning. She told me."

"So you met The Best Secretary in Ohio. She's something, isn't she?"

"She seemed like a nice lady."

"Did you know she actually is one?" asked Jack.

"What do you mean?"

"She's a Lady. Lady Rosemary. Her dad's an earl."

"Oh."

"She's very posh. I'm sure you picked up on that."

"I don't know about posh. She sure can type."

"Discreet, too. I'll bet you didn't get much out of her, did you?"

"We talked. She gave me this list." Cesar pulled out the typewritten sheet. "It seems most of the people at the meeting were from your office."

"We like to send a full team," said Jack. "Safety in numbers."

"I went to your office first."

"Oh, then you met Renée."

"Is she the receptionist?"

"Mr. Bennett says she is."

"She's kind of hard to understand," said Cesar.

"No kidding. She's Haitian. Another one of Phillip's good works. I'm surprised you understood her enough to find us."

"She didn't tell me. A guy did. Older guy."

"Grey hair? Glasses? Skinny?" asked Tom. "Milt. He loves to rat on us. I mean we're supposed to be at work. But Bob's the boss and he's here. So. Tough luck, Milt."

Cesar looked at his list. "Who's the boss? I've got Mr. Bennett's name as Phillip."

"Atwood. Over there. Nuzzling Miss Dress for Success."

Cesar turned around to look for the nuzzler. He saw a balding man in grey pinstripes talking into the ear of a young woman in grey pinstripes. The young woman glared at Cesar.

"Looks vaguely incestuous, doesn't it?" asked Jack.

"Who's she?" asked Cesar.

"Marianne Kelly," said Tom. "She should be on your list. If she's not, she'll sue."

"Are they friends?" What a dumb question.

"They're office pals, as far as we know. There's a Mrs. Atwood tucked away in Terrace Park. Two Baby Atwoods. Doggy Atwood. Kitty Atwood."

"He's the boss?"

"Might as well be," said Tom. "He's the heir apparent. Senior vice-president. Phillip's choice. Phillip's sick."

Cesar looked his question. Crazy or flu?

Jack answered. "Mr. Bennett's been pretty sick for a year. He hasn't told us what's wrong."

Cesar looked back at the list. He had at least sighted everyone on his list from the agency except for Phillip Bennett and Evelyn Osborne.

"Is Ms. Osborne here?"

Jack laughed. "It's Mr. Osborne. As in Waugh."

Cesar looked blank.

"Eeeve-lin. At the piano."

When Cesar turned around, the man at the piano blew him a kiss. Cesar blushed.

"Is he—?"

"Gay? No," said Tom. "He likes to have people think he is, though. They get annoyed. He'll behave better shortly, Rosemary's due any minute."

"Mr. Golden's secretary?"

"And Evelyn's keeper. And there she is. Perfectly punctual."

Perfectly punctual, perfectly groomed, and perfectly imposing. Cesar felt the room settle down as she stepped in. The noise fell to a polite level; someone's voice changed from a cackle to a normal sound in midlaugh. Atwood and Kelly separated to a more tactful distance. Cesar felt his own back straighten and was not surprised to see others, including Jack and Tom, come to attention. Rosemary commanded respect.

"Watch Evelyn," Tom muttered, and Cesar saw Evelyn somehow transform himself from an apparent degenerate to a gentleman in a split second. Neat trick. Rosemary crooked her finger and Osborne left the piano to join her at a table.

"One does not give Rosemary shit," said Tom.

"I guess not," said Cesar.

"What did she tell you about the meeting?"

"Not too much. Would you mind giving me your versions? That's what I came over for."

Tom looked at Jack who looked around the room. Cesar was still attracting a lot of interest.

"You want to go downstairs?" asked Cesar.

"It would be quieter, wouldn't it? Good idea," said Jack. They stood.

"Off to get grilled, mates! Pray for us." There were nervous waves from the agency staff as they left. Jack, Tom, and Cesar carefully groped their way down Arnold's horrible stairs. "Never fails to thrill, does it? Always have to pee when I make it down." Jack headed for the men's room and Tom found them a booth.

"Been here before?" asked Tom. Cesar shook his head no. He leaned back in the booth and looked around.

"It's Cincinnati's answer to Sardi's," said Tom. "And a few other places. Something for everybody. You like jazz?"

"Not much."

"Oh. I don't either, but it's supposed to be great here. The courtyard's nice in the summer. I guess the crowd's what I like best."

Cesar, who had cased the clients and found downtown execs, a couple of punk musicians, several reporters, an old lady communist, some leftover hippies, and a huddle of antique alcoholics, agreed that the crowd was interesting. The restaurant itself was not much different from some of the old bars in the Over-the-Rhine, the district serving double duty as skid row and Bedford-Stuyvesant. The furniture was old, dark, and wooden, the bar was old, the beer signs on the wall were old. In fact, Cesar could find very few of the usual twentieth-century touches he would expect even in an Over-the-Rhine. No cigarette machine, no Pac Man, no Jerry Lewis Muscular Dystrophy collection cans. Not a bad place, he decided.

He returned his attention to Tom. "Is he from England?" asked Cesar, pointing to Jack Squires' unfilled seat.

"New Zealand."

"But Miss Meynell's from England?"

"Right. She and Evelyn."

"What are they doing here?"

"Money. They can't make money over there."

"How do they like it?"

"Jack loves it. I think Evelyn wants to go back."

"She doesn't?"

"Rosemary goes where Evelyn goes."

"Are they married?"

"He is. She isn't."

"What about you?"

"Nope. You?"

"Not yet."

They were silent for a moment. Then Cesar asked, "Where do you live now?"

"Madison Road."

"Hyde Park?"

"Walnut Hills. You still with your mom?"

"Still with my mom."

"You like it? Being in the police?"

"Sure."

"It's what you always wanted to be."

"Right."

Conversation ran out. Cesar was a little depressed. He'd been kind of excited when he saw Tom's name on Rosemary's list. Tom was the only kid he knew who could ride his bike as long as Cesar when they were ten. Now he didn't know anything about Tom except that he lived on the east side and wrote copy. Foreign territory.

Jack came back from the men's room. "Ready to grill me? Did anyone take your order? Wouldn't you like some coffee? Prudence, my love!" He waved to a waitress across the room. "Coffee and two more." He pointed at their glasses. Prudence seemed to understand the order.

"If it's all right with Tom, I'd like to spill my guts first. I'm definitely due home by six-thirty. Okay, Tom?"

"Fine."

"What do you need to know?"

"I need to know about the meeting?"

"You think one of us did it, do you?"

"No, no. I haven't got that far. It just seems you people at the meeting were the last to see Irving Golden before he died. We need to know what went on and what happened afterward. Anything you saw."

Jack Squires' story squared with Donna Creech's. He didn't tell it the same way. Who could? But he didn't tell much more about fighting than Rosemary Meynell had. Cesar didn't tell him he had talked to Donna. He asked if the meeting had been controversial.

"Controversial? Well." Squires thought for a couple of seconds. "Do you mean did anyone want to kill Irving? Everyone always wanted to kill Irving. Figuratively, of course. But no one threatened him. He does—he did, I should say—more or less control our livelihood. You did know that? It was a tense meeting. They usually are. I guess it was tenser than usual. But not *murderous*."

"How about after the meeting?"

"Everyone went home."

"No one stayed late?"

"We talked awhile in the parking lot, but that was it."

"Everybody?"

"I think so. Let's see." He thought a minute. "I'm pretty sure everyone came out."

"No one went back in?"

"Couldn't. The door locks after you leave. I suppose someone could have gone 'round the front. There's a guard there."

"Do you remember who came out last?"

"That would be Golden people. Frederick Golden and Joe Enneking. Right, Tom?"

Tom nodded.

"Did you see anybody hanging around the parking lot while you were talking?"

"No. It was freezing."

"How about in the building?"

"No. Just Golden people."

"How long did you stay in the parking lot?"

"Not long. Enough for a quick postmortem. It was too cold to chat."

"What do you mean 'postmortem'?"

"Freudian slip, what? Wrap up. We just talked about the meeting."

"Everybody?"

"Except Irving."

"Just people from your office?"

"No. The gents from Golden were there, too."

"Mr. Squires, I talked to the cleaning lady who was in the building yesterday. She seemed to think that the meeting got pretty hot."

"Ahhh! Mrs. Creech. She did pop in, didn't she?"

"She seemed to think people were upset."

"I suppose it may have looked that way to her. Irving can get testy. Maybe even a bit offensive. Peoples' feelings got hurt from time to time. But I told you, no fisticuffs. We're a gentle lot. Really we are."

"Testy." Miss Meynell said he was "severe." What was it with these people? Was Golden a son-of-a-bitch or not? Why was everyone being so *nice?*

"Mr. Squires, I've heard that Irving Golden was a pretty tough guy. Maybe he wasn't so bad yesterday, but maybe yesterday was the last straw for somebody. Did he get on anyone's case in particular?"

"Any one person? No. As a matter of fact he was pretty fair . . . slapped wrists all around you might say."

Cesar looked at Tom. He was fiddling with his beer coaster. He hadn't said anything since Squires got back from the men's room. Cesar couldn't tell whether Tom agreed with Squires or not. It was clear that Squires wasn't going to help much. Maybe Tom could loosen up when Squires was gone.

"You need to get home, don't you?" Cesar said to Jack. Jack looked at his watch.

"Thanks for reminding me. You're right. Can I go?"

"Sure. I'm sorry I kept you so long. Listen, it was nice meeting you."

"Nice meeting you, too. Sorry I don't know too much. Maybe if you put Tom here in thumbscrews he'll sing. Right, Tom?"

"See you tomorrow Jack."

"Goodnight. Goodnight, Cesar."

The New Zealander worked his way out, clapping men on the back, winking at women.

"Nice guy," said Cesar.

"He really is. Probably the nicest guy in the office."

Tom looked down into his beer. Cesar wanted him to talk. What kind of guy was he now? Could they be friends again? Did he hate cops? He didn't know any cops who had been at Walnut Hills. What did they learn over there? What did Tom know about Irving Golden?

Cesar even had to wonder if Tom had changed enough to murder someone. That made him think about Tom as a kid. Tom and Cesar always had their hair cut down to nothing in the summer and Tom's ears always looked huge. His ears were half covered now. Jesus, he even had a little grey in his sideburns. His bike buddy going grey. Speak to me, bike buddy.

"What's the food like here?" he asked Tom.

"Not bad. Modified hippy. You want to eat?"

"Sure. Is it expensive?"

"No. The pasta's cheap. Try it."

They ordered mostaccioli with sausage sauce. Cesar broke down and asked for beer. They filled each other in while they waited for supper.

It seemed to Cesar that Tom was feeling the same way he was, a little sad. You never thought when you were ten that your friends would stop being your friends. You didn't even think much about being friends. Being friends was normal.

Finally Tom said, "This is crazy."

"What's crazy?"

"Talking like this. Meeting over a murder."

"Yeah, it is."

"You remember when I told you I wasn't going to go to West High? You know what you did? You got on your bike and rode away. You didn't say anything. I felt like a turd."

"You did?"

"Completely."

"Yeah? Well. I didn't know what to say. I didn't even know what Walnut Hills High School was then."

"You could have gone, too, you know. You're smart."

"I told you, I didn't know what it was. Nobody ever told me."

Prudence brought the mostaccioli.

"I was pissed off at you for years," said Tom.

"How come?"

"You just rode off on your bike. Like I had the plague."

"Boy, I'm sorry."

"Why'd you do that?"

"Jeez, I don't know. I guess I thought you were going to be real different."

Tom chewed mostaccioli for a minute.

"Am I different?" he asked.

"I don't know. I haven't seen you for years. Yeah. I guess so. You're in advertising. You're the only kid I know who grew up and works in advertising."

"What's everybody else doing?" asked Tom.

"Cops. Firemen. Insurance. Couple of teachers. Lawyers."

"A lot of them still around? In Westwood?"

"Yeah."

"You should have gone to Walnut Hills. You would have liked it."

"I liked West High okay. But I'll tell you where I should have gone is Elder."

"Why? You're not Catholic."

"It helps when you're with the city."

"Does West High hurt you?"

"No. But Elder helps."

"You're the only cop I know, Cesar."

"So?"

"You said I was the only advertising guy you know."

"I didn't insult you, did I?"

"No."

"Listen. I'm sorry about the way I acted . . . when I rode off on my bike. Okay?"

"You're forgiven."

They ate some more. Cesar felt better. He figured Tom was still a nice guy. He hoped he was nice enough to give him some real information about Irving Golden. Was it going to piss him off? Asking about it?

"You know," said Cesar. "I've got to admit I'm not doing too well on this case."

"How's that?"

And Cesar decided. Tom wasn't a murderer. If he was, Cesar was not a detective.

"I do have suspects. I think someone who was in that meeting, for some reason, killed Golden. I know about when. I know how. I don't know why. But you're not on the list."

"Why not?"

"I've got reasons."

Tom laughed. Cesar asked, "What's so funny?"

"You looked just like you used to when you said that. Like when we'd try to stand off big kids. Only you've got a moustache now."

"Yeah, well." Cesar laughed, too. It worried him, though. That was supposed to be his poker face. "But I need help. No kidding. I'm running into this very polite wall, I can tell."

"Cesar," Tom began and then stopped to think. "Cesar, you have to know people like us are scared of people like you."

"Me?"

"Well, not *me*. I know you. But them, they all think you've got magic powers. They've all got old parking tickets in their glove compartments, so they're scared of any cop, and now they think you're going to charge them with murder."

"You got parking tickets?"

"Maybe."

"Pay up."

"You can't fix them?"

"This is Cincinnati, boy."

"I'll pay."

"They ought to be scared. Murder stinks."

"What do you want to know?"

"Well, first off, you could tell me what happened at that meeting. It was bad, wasn't it?"

And Tom told him. Cesar listened carefully and he was sure he was getting the complete version as far as Tom remembered it. It was about time.

"So Squires was right. Golden managed to piss off everyone in the room."

"Except Rosemary."

"Had that ever happened before?"

"Sure, but this was worse than usual."

"How come?"

"Are you like a priest?"

"What are you talking about?"

"Is this like confession? Can you keep a secret?"

"Hell, no. I'm investigating."

"That's what I thought."

"Secret from who?" asked Cesar.

"Newspapers, I guess. It's supposed to be confidential."

"I don't talk to reporters. I'm not allowed."

"Can you be careful with what I tell you? I mean you'll probably find out sooner or later and you ought to know."

"Tom, you can trust me. I don't spill business secrets."

Tom looked around him and then leaned over the table.

"Everybody thinks Mr. Bennett's selling the agency."

"That's the secret?"

"No. The secret is that it's true. Jack told me. Mr. Bennett told him."

"You guys keep real tight security. It sounds like everybody knows."

"They do. Or they *think* they do. But it's not supposed to get to the newspapers. Or to Golden Time."

"So what does that have to do with the meeting yesterday? You said it was about dolls."

"It was, but think. In the first place, everyone at Bennett is on edge. No one knows who's buying the agency. No one knows who's going to stay and who's going to go, but everyone knows there'll be house-cleaning. Mr. Bennett's been lax. He hasn't fired anyone for years. So everyone's just plain jumpy. In the second place, the Golden Time account is far and away the biggest we've got. It pays the bills and it makes the agency valuable. Irving has been threatening for years to go with a national agency, and the threats have been escalating. Yesterday he sounded really serious to me. I was scared."

"What would happen?" asked Cesar.

"If he fired the agency?" asked Tom. Cesar nodded. "At best we'd have to lay off half the staff. It could be the agency would fold. These are tough times. It would be really bad for Mr. Bennett. He'd lose his buyer."

"Does he have to sell?"

"You mean financially? I don't know. I do know he's sick and he's tired and he wants to get out while he's still alive. He's a nice man, Cesar. If anyone earned a cushy retirement, he has."

"Is he the only owner?"

"Yep. He built it up from scratch. Started it with himself and his wife. And as far as I'm concerned, he's the one who made Golden Times . . . at least as much as Irving Golden. He's very smart. And he cares about his people. You can bet he'll work some deal to see that the new owners don't lay off the good people."

"So everyone was scared of Golden."

"Terrified. Even Mr. Bennett. He's kept Irving in line for years, but he was losing his grip. What's sad is that everybody thinks they're out of the woods with Irving gone. That's why they were so crazy upstairs. They were celebrating. They all think Brother Fred is going to run Golden Times."

"He's a nicer guy?"

"He's supposed to be a pushover. But I don't think he's going to be the boss."

"Who is?"

"Not Frederick."

"Why not?"

"I just don't think so."

For the first time since he had started talking about the meeting, Tom got vague. Cesar wondered what was up. Grace had told him she was going to take over. Did Tom know that or was there another candidate? Did he know Grace Golden? Did she date Tom? Damn.

"What about Marianne Kelly?" he asked Tom.

"What do you mean?"

"It sounds like she really got it from Mr. Golden. Worse than anybody else."

"Marianne as murderer?" Tom laughed. "You should tell her that. It'll make her day."

"Well, he was rough with her."

"Oh, he was. Very nasty. She had every right to blow up. And she was furious. We really got it afterwards."

"Why you?"

"*We failed to defend her.* You have to understand her. She's rabidly feminist, dying to succeed in business, dressing her way to success, bad-tempered, smart, thin-skinned, and a bully. She's completely inconsistent. One minute you're supposed to treat her like an executive, next minute like a nun. She's crazy."

"Must make you crazy, too."

"It does. I put up with it only because she's a fellow immigrant. She's from Price Hill. Went to Seton. Trying to live as a Hyde Park native and it's driving her 'round the bend."

"She's kind of cute."

"I suppose so. Atwood thinks she is."

Tom made a face.

"You don't like Atwood?"

"He's a jerk."

"But he's going to be boss?"

"He's going to be boss."

"I don't remember what Golden got on him about."

"Nothing. That's Atwood's skill. He is never in trouble. Of course, he never does anything with advertising. He manages the money, thank God."

"Hunh?"

"Well, if we didn't have him we'd probably be bankrupt. Mr. Bennett does not understand money. Atwood does."

"Would he get fired if you lost the Golden Time business?"

"Bob? Are you kidding? That's not in his plans. Are you looking for a motive?"

"I'm just trying to sort things out."

"Oh, God, wouldn't it be *terrific* if it were Atwood. That would be too much."

"Why would he?"

"He wouldn't. I just wish he had."

"Okay. Why wouldn't he?"

"Not cool. Murder's not on the success track. Managers—and he's a manager—do it with finesse, not blunt instruments."

"How did he get along with Golden?"

"Fine. It made me sick. Golden dumped on Jack weekly. But Bob was his boy."

"Okay. What about Osborne?"

"Not your man."

"No?"

"No. Irving respected Evelyn. And, goofy as Evelyn is, he's respectable. He does terrific filmwork. He also refuses—refused to take any of Irving's abuse. If Irving tried to get tough, Evelyn would just walk away. Singing something."

"Would he get fired?"

"I doubt it. He's too valuable. He also wouldn't care if he *were* fired. He can get a better job any time. He stays here to please Rosemary. She likes him where she can keep an eye on him."

"What about your friend Squires? Would he get fired?"

Tom looked at his plate for a moment and then answered, "Yes."

"What are you worried about?"

"You. And Jack."

"Why?"

"Because you're going to take a close look at him. You'll have to."

"What's wrong with that?"

"What's wrong is that you're probably going to put him on your short list."

"Why?"

"Because if I didn't know him, he'd be on mine."

"Just because he'd be fired?"

"That. He'd be the first—he's senior AE . . . sorry, account executive . . . and they're always sacrificed. And he's got problems. Money and family."

"Such as."

"Such as he hasn't got any sense about money. Charges like a fool. He just bought a big house. Let a real estate salesman talk him into thinking he couldn't afford not to buy a place. And he's crazy about gadgets."

"Like . . . "

"Like a home computer, a Betamax, Atari games, a Cuisinart—whatever's going."

"So he's broke."

"Constantly."

"And the family?"

"They have one son. He's severely retarded."

"That's too bad."

"It's too bad and it's expensive. Jack's crazy about him. Buys him everything any kid could want. The kid can't figure out how to use half the stuff he's got. And he sends him to a private school—says the public schools don't treat him right. His wife sits at home and wishes she were back in New Zealand. She's no help, but that's the way he wants it. Jack loves to be a hero. He was, too."

"A hero?"

"Before he got fat, before he got into advertising, he was a commando. Served in Vietnam."

"For us?"

"For New Zealand."

"Is he your boss?"

"No. But I like him better than anyone else at the agency. There isn't anyone nicer."

"Do you think he could have killed Mr. Golden?"

"No. But listen, Cesar. I don't think *anyone* could have. That's my problem."

"Somebody did, buddy."

"I know. I know. But no one from Bennett. I *know* them. There's nobody crazy enough. We're all chicken anyway."

"Except for Squires."

Tom looked at Cesar.

"Jack didn't do it."

"You know that for sure?"

"I don't know anything for sure except that I didn't and Jack wouldn't."

"Okay, what about the guys from Golden Time?"

"Frederick and Joe Enneking? Hm. I've been worrying about *us*. Not them."

"Do you know anything about them?"

"We joke a lot about Enneking. Usually Nazi jokes. Teutonic efficiency. That sort of thing. Nobody knows him real well. He's production, not marketing. We're probably not fair . . ." He trailed off.

"Not fair?" Cesar prodded.

"What? Oh, I wasn't thinking about that. I was thinking about Evelyn. He did one of his songs about Enneking being a former concentration camp administrator with an eye on Golden. Golden was Jewish, you know. It was in wretched taste, of course, but funny."

"But Enneking's from Cincinnati."

"Sure. He couldn't be a Nazi—I told you it was just our joke. He just strikes everyone at Bennett as sort of menacing. You can tell he thinks we're a waste of money. Money that might be going into production. But, like I told you, I don't really know him."

"What about Frederick Golden?"

"Ah, yes. Fred. Fred I know a little better. Fred was Irving's cross to bear. And vice versa. That's bad imagery, but I don't know the Jewish equivalent of a cross to bear. They were both ashamed of each other and they both resented each other. You know that Irving lacked charm. Well, Frederick is Mr. Charming Cincinnati. Very polished. Very clubby. As Episcopalian as you can be and still be Jewish.

"Irving thought Frederick was worthless, but that wasn't quite fair. Frederick's job was to clean up after Irving—smooth things over, and he did. He also did the United Appeal and the Fine Arts Fund and the Hospital Board. Irving thought that was goofing off, but somebody's got to do it—it's part of doing business here. Irving thought Frederick was pretentious and Frederick thought Irving was a philistine and they were both right. It was fun to watch."

"How come you know so much about them?"

"Well, we've been their agency for years, so everybody knows a lot about them. And I know Irving's daughter."

"Grace?"

"Have you met her?"

"I talked to her today."

"How'd you like her?"

"I liked her."

"Did you meet Irene?" Tom asked with a grin.

"Yes."

"Different, aren't they?"

"They sure are. How come you know them?"

"I went to school with Louie. He's Grace's brother."

"I met him, too."

"You didn't like him, did you?"

"I don't know. He was a little snobbish maybe. I didn't talk to him very long."

"We were pretty good friends," said Tom. "I guess we still are. But I know what you mean. I thought he was a creep at first. He's extremely smart and spoiled rotten."

"Sounds like a prince."

"I told you. I thought he was a creep. But he can be very funny and he's very generous. And loyal."

"What about Grace?"

"She's . . . I used to date her."

"I can see why."

"We talked a lot about the family. Used to. Remember when I said Frederick wouldn't take over the business? Unless Grace has changed her mind, and she doesn't . . . change it . . . not often . . . she'll be the next president. She's a very tough little girl."

"Tough, maybe. She didn't seem like a little girl to me."

"She's not. I know. She's a big girl."

"You don't date anymore?"

"No. Not since she went to New York. Not even before that. Not much."

"What's she do in New York?" Cesar asked.

"Works for her great-uncle. Runs his fur business for him."

Cesar thought Tom looked a little angry. What happened? Did he dump her? She dump him? Was he still interested? Cesar couldn't blame him. She was going to be a very popular company president. Cesar didn't know much about advertising, but he guessed Tom wasn't on any fast track to the top.

Life isn't fair. Twenty years ago you could count on a girl's not turning out to be a big shot when you fell in love with her.

"About Frederick. You said he didn't like his brother a lot?"

"Despised him. They were blind about each other. Frederick thought Irving was coarse. And he hated the toy business. At least the cheap toy business—and that's what Golden Time is. Frederick would no more go into a discount store to see a Golden Time display than he would go into a porno house. He wanted Minnie to sell out."

"Who's Minnie?"

"His mother."

"I heard about her from Grace," said Cesar.

"So she told you something about the family. Why'd you ask me?"

"I have to check."

"Listen, if Grace tells you something, that's the way it is."

Tom looked bitter again. Did he know about Grace wanting to fire the agency or was he just burned?

"So, what do you think, Tom? If you don't think anyone at your office could get tough, kill somebody, what about those two?"

"Don't ask me, Cesar. I don't really believe anybody could kill anybody else."

"They do. I can prove it."

"I know. I know. But I always think of murder as something that doesn't really happen, even when it does. So I can't finger anyone, Cesar. I really can't."

"I don't want you to finger anyone."

"Okay."

"I just want a little help."

"Why don't you . . . Why are you looking here? Why does it have to be someone from that meeting? Whatever happened to drug-crazed hippies?"

"We've still got them."

"Well?"

"They kill each other."

"Maybe Irving sold coke on the side."

"Maybe he did."

"But you're not looking for hippies."

"No."

"Punk rockers?"

"Nope."

"So you know about the keys."

"What about the keys?"

"Irving's keys. Come on, Cesar. You're as smart as I am. I'm as smart as you are. Even Marianne figured out the keys. We all know about them—where they were. Irving showed everybody his fabulous lock. That's the other reason why everybody was so jumpy upstairs. We've all figured out that one of us swiped the keys off his desk. You did know that, didn't you?"

"Yeah."

"I thought so. No one was going to tell you. They all think they're smarter than the police."

"Maybe they are."

"I doubt it."

"We've got some dummies on the force."

"But you're not one of them."

"I hope not." Cesar was never *completely* sure.

"You want any dessert?"

"No."

"You figure out who did it?"

"No."

"Where do you go from here?"

"Home. What about you? Have you figured out who did it?"

"No." Tom laughed.

"Any opinion?"

"No."

"You sure?"

"I'm sure I have no opinion."

"Will you call me if you get one?"

Tom stared at Cesar.

"I just want you to call." said Cesar. "I need ideas. Or if you think of anything. Can't you do that?"

"Yeah. I can do that. I was just thinking about who should get my loyalty. For what *that's* worth. My grown-up friends or my old buddy."

"Well, your old buddy needs help."

"So do they."

"Tom, the murderer is not your friend. Murderers are bad guys."

"But I don't think the bad guys did it."

"Believe me. I know what I'm talking about. I'm not asking you to rat on anyone. Just think. Okay?"

"Okay. I'll think."

Cesar stood up. Tom looked at him from the booth and said, "Make your poker face again." So Cesar made his poker face. "See you later."

"Later."

7

CESAR PAID FOR his mostaccioli and went outside. He walked past Golden Time Toys. Loyal Leonard was on the job. When he got to the parking lot he cringed. Irving's Cadillac was still there. He was supposed to have impressed Grace by having that in her driveway eight hours ago. First thing tomorrow for sure.

First thing tomorrow was going to be the rendezvous with Donna Creech in five and a half hours. Cesar felt his customary panic at the thought of less than a full night's sleep. He climbed into the city Hornet and cranked. If it didn't start in this cold he was going to feel full-fledged panic, but the engine caught and he began to lumber westward. No chance to sleep in tomorrow either. Up with the birds to go interview the higher-ups from Golden Time and Bennett. He turned on to Central and headed for the parking lot. The light caught him at Ninth. He could feel the weight of City Hall to his right. Somewhere in there was a big chart covered with Plexiglass and the Plexiglass was covered with a grid of little squares and the little squares had grease pencil X's to show where Budget Narrative Forms had been completed by Divisions and Departments and His Wasn't Done. No X for Cesar. More panic. The light changed and he floored the accelerator. The Hornet died. He got it started again and coughed his way to the police parking lot.

Cesar felt much better in his own Camaro. He had Central Parkway nearly to himself. The panic had lifted by the time he turned onto the Western Hills viaduct. He let the Camaro take over the driving and began to think about Tom Cleary.

He wasn't going to check out Tom, not unless things got really screwy. Tom might have—no, he *had* changed, but Cesar was sure Walnut Hills hadn't turned him into a killer. It wasn't *that* different from regular high schools. Besides, he still talked like he used to.

What about the New Zealand commando? He seemed like a nice enough guy. But he was a commando. Commandos could kill, couldn't they? Squires was also in danger of losing his job. Well, actually, if Grace Golden had her way he *would* lose his job, only Squires hadn't known that yesterday. Do you kill someone over a job? Maybe. If you've got a retarded kid and big house payments and want a good life and like your gadgets and you're a nice guy who has to be nice for a living and a loudmouth with a lot of power dumps all over you, would you be tempted? Cesar hadn't thought that commandos bashed their opponents with statuettes, as a rule, but he wasn't too familiar with commando training. He knew even less about New Zealand commandos. Maybe they were taught to use whatever was handy.

What about Rosemary Meynell? She certainly didn't look or act like a boss bonker. Was it physically possible? He tried to picture Rosemary wielding a Tina. Very hard to imagine. What did high-class English ladies do for exercise? Christen ships, maybe? Could Rosemary swing a blunt instrument if it had a big silk ribbon tied to it? Possibly. Also, very unlikely. Irving treated her nicely.

Irving's family? How could they get into the office without a key? Oh, boy, he had spent all that time in Amberley without asking any of them where they were Thursday afternoon. Nice work, Cesar. Now you've got to find out where Irving's safety deposit box is and whether the key is still in it and whether anyone took the key Thursday. Don't forget. When he stopped for the light at McHenry he wrote down "bank—key" on the back of one of Donna Creech's phone messages.

Cesar devoted the last leg of his drive to worrying about the Top Hat. When he came into the house, Lillian was asleep in front of the TV. He pulled a Hudepohl from the fridge and went back to the living room to read the *Post*. Irving was the headline story. They ran the picture of Irving with Menachem Begin. He checked the story to see if the quotes he had fed Lt. Tieves made it intact. They did. Time for the nightly battle.

"Mom! Mom!"

"What? I'm not asleep."

"Mom, why don't you go to bed?"

"'Cause I'm not asleep."

"The hell you're not."

"Don't talk like that."

"It's stupid to sleep in here when you could be in bed."

"I'm going to watch 'Dallas.'"

"You'll be asleep."

"No, I won't."

She was right. She'd snore through the "Dukes of Hazzard," but when the "Dallas" theme came on she'd wake right up. What a talent.

"Well, I'm going to bed. I've got to go back out late."

"How come?"

"I've got to meet someone."

"In the middle of the night?"

"Yeah."

"That's crazy, Gus."

"I know. If you're up at eleven-thirty, make sure I get out of bed, okay?"

Cesar went to bed and slept hard. When the alarm went off he was completely befuddled. It took him five minutes to remember what time it was and what he was supposed to be doing. He dressed carefully. There was no disguising the fact that he was a white guy, but he didn't want to look too goofy to the Top Hat regulars. Cesar checked himself in the mirror: green knit pants, boots, flowered knit shirt, white policeman face. As a final touch he added a bullshit diamond ring he had kept from his vice squad days.

Lillian was still in the recliner.

"Mom, I'm leaving." She woke up.

"Are you coming back?"

"Yeah. I don't know when. Shouldn't be too long. How was 'Dallas'?"

"Okay. 'Falcon Crest' is getting to be better, you know."

"Goodnight."

"Be careful."

Cesar sat in his Camaro outside the Top Hat. He was frozen, but he couldn't face going in there without Henry, and Henry's Mark IV wasn't in the lot. Henry was going to have a problem parking. He preferred angling across three spaces, preferably under a light, in order that lesser cars and hubcap fanciers might not approach. Lt. Tieves hated Henry's car. It was too expensive for a cop and, since Henry was black, it smelled of corruption. The car wasn't to Cesar's taste, but then neither was Lt. Tieves' indulgence. Lt. Tieves spent his money on his basement.

Cesar watched the cars and motorcycles pulling in off Baltimore. The Top Hat looked crummy outside but it sure packed them in. The patrons who noticed him gave him tough looks and stepped up their badness. It wasn't necessary. He was plenty nervous.

Just as Cesar was ready to start the engine so he could run the heater, Henry pulled in. Cesar watched him case the parking lot, then pull the Mark right up to the front door. Cesar joined Henry and his gorgeous date.

"Calquetta, this is Cesar Franck. Cesar, this is Calquetta."

How did he do it? Calquetta was five inches taller than Henry and looked like a movie star, but she smiled down at Henry's bald dome as if he were a big dish of ice cream and she held on to his fat arm like a winning lottery ticket.

"Nice to meet you, Calquetta."

"Calquetta's a med student."

Wouldn't you know.

Henry took in Cesar's costume and smiled without comment. Cesar took in Henry's three-piece pinstripes and wondered who was right. "I sure hope your date's on time, Ceez. Calquetta and I have other plans." Calquetta plastered herself to Henry and beamed a smile at poor pale Cesar. He was supposed to imagine the plans.

"After you, Henry." He watched Calquetta's backside as she and Henry pushed into the Top Hat.

It must have been 90 degrees inside. The air was thick with smoke—marijuana and Kools. Cesar watched as all eyes turned on Calquetta. He was grateful for the distraction. Henry stood and looked for a table worthy of Calquetta. She apparently rated a booth all the way across the large room. Trailing behind them he heard all the groans of envy. Calquetta had no competition. He looked for Donna. There were only about six white Bad Dude groupies. None of them was Donna. Please, Donna, don't drag this out.

Henry had to stand on tiptoe to help Calquetta with her coat. When they were settled in to Henry's satisfaction, he waved for a waiter. A woman in tight pants, halter, and a top hat came for their order. She shot Calquetta a filthy look, ignored Cesar, and grinned at Henry. "Hi, Junebug, where you been?" Junebug?

"Working, Weeze, working."

"J&B?"

"Make it two. And my friend will have . . ."

"Beer."

"A Michelob," said Henry.

Why couldn't he have a Hudepohl?

"I'll be right back." The waitress pinched Henry's earlobe as she left. Another fan.

"Sorry to do this to you," Cesar said to Calquetta.

"Oh, that's all right. I think Henry's work is *so* interesting."

"You're in med school?"

She nodded.

"You like it?"

"I love it."

"Are you from Cincinnati?"

"Dayton."

What else could he ask? What he wanted to know was what she saw in a fat bald detective, but he couldn't see a way. She turned sideways so she could adore Henry a little better.

Henry favored Cesar with one of his cat smiles.

"How's your mother, Henry?" It was the only thing Cesar could think of to rattle his friend's composure. Henry had his own place but his mother was very involved in his life, a lot more than Lillian was in Cesar's.

"Am I going to meet your mother tonight, Henry?"

"No, baby. Not tonight." Henry kicked Cesar under the table. Cesar smiled and turned to watch the crowd at the Top Hat.

There was a lot of ostentatious weed-passing, but Cesar couldn't see anything worthy of the Top Hat's menacing reputation. Bad Dudes swaggered. There was lots of leather. The white girls and the black girls screamed insults at each other once in a while, but it was no worse than Thirteenth Street in July.

"So, Cesar, are you going to fill me in on this case sometime?" Henry asked.

Cesar looked at Calquetta.

"Her lips are sealed," said Henry. "Calquetta, don't listen. If you hear anything, forget it."

"Baby, are you going to talk business?"

"Got to."

"Okay." Calquetta settled into her corner and lit a Virginia Slim.

Cesar talked quietly. Henry was too cool to lean over the table but he concentrated like crazy. He really did want to know. Cesar told him everything, start to finish. Calquetta was invited to dance several times during the narration and Henry allowed her to go. When Cesar was through, Henry said, "Wow."

"I know," said Cesar. "It's a mess."

"White people," said Henry.

"What do you mean, white people?" Race. Always race.

"White people's crime."

"You mean white-collar crime."

"No."

"All right, Henry, what *do* you mean?"

"I mean that only white people could come up with something like this. No girls. No gambling. Just business."

"I didn't say there was no gambling or girls."

"You didn't say there *was* any."

"I just haven't heard anything more than what I told you." Cesar felt silly. He was going on the defensive about how and why white people went off the tracks. They weren't *his* white people, for crying out loud.

"You're not going to hear anything but business, Cesar. This is business crime."

"Black people don't have business crime?"

"You all don't let us have much business, Ceez."

"You've got businesses, Henry."

"Not big business."

"Oh, yeah?"

"What about politics? You've got politics."

"I said business."

"Okay. Business."

Cesar thought, but he couldn't come up with any black corporate capital offenses. Shit.

"I hate it. All you've got is talk," said Henry.

"It's more than talk, Henry. It's jobs and money. Irving Golden was a very big guy. Some of those people might just as well be slaves."

"Cesar, really."

"No kidding, Henry. Golden owned everybody at that meeting."

"Except the English guy."

"Right. And maybe his girlfriend."

"And your buddy."

"No. He owned him, too. I think. But he's okay."

"Because he's your buddy?"

"Why not?"

"Yeah, why not. What's the secretary like? Was she into the boss?"

"Henry, secretaries don't all fall for the boss. She's beautiful."

"Did you get a date?"

"Down, Henry. I told you, she goes with Osborne."

"Okay." Henry respected no arrangements. "So what are you going to do? What have you got to go on?"

"Nothing. Motives. That's it."

"That's worse than nothing," said Henry.

Cesar agreed. It meant picking minds. In this case he had to pick minds that he was afraid were stronger than his own. Advertising people. Production man. Rich brother. That was probably why he was at the Top Hat waiting for Donna Creech. She had a mind at his level.

Donna didn't arrive until the second round of drinks. She and a black woman were hanging on to a very large black guy. He had on a leather jacket with "Black Lugers" printed on the back. The Black Lugers and Millvale Fury seemed to be the two largest fraternal organizations represented tonight. Cesar started to get up to go talk to her, but she made a quick motion for him to sit down. Jealous boyfriend? Cesar didn't feel like a threat.

"She's here, Henry. Just came in."

"About time."

"I guess she wants to come over by herself."

"Which one is she?"

"White, black hair, sunglasses, blue dress."

"One of those, huh?"

"One of those."

"Calquetta, don't you have to go to the bathroom?" Calquetta looked at Henry. She looked at the bathroom. Cesar couldn't blame her for wanting to avoid it. She was going to get it from the regulars once she was detached from Henry.

"Sure, honey," she said.

"As a favor to you, Cesar, I'm going to pry your girlfriend loose."

"Thanks, Henry."

Cesar watched as Henry ambled over to Donna's booth and gave her boyfriend a moderately complex soul brother handshake. After a minute the boyfriend allowed Donna to leave while he and Henry and the remaining girlfriend dealt with today's thorny issues. Basketball, Cesar guessed.

Donna sure wasn't much to look at. She got only one half-hearted comment from the crowd as she headed for Cesar, but she played that for all it was worth. She giggled and flashed her false teeth in the direction of the comment. Then she sucked in her cheeks and tossed her hair like Charlie's Angels. What a mess she was. "Hi, Donna."

"Detective Franck, I'm so glad you got my message. Now, I can only talk for just a *second* because Alfred, he's my boyfriend, he gets real jealous, you know."

"Sure. What's the problem?"

"I'm scared, Detective Franck, I'm awful scared. Somebody is checkin' up on me."

"What do you mean?"

"Well, I've been gettin' calls. And I've got an unlisted number. You have to when you're datin' black men, don't you know. Well, them calls, it's like they're checkin' on me. I answer and they hang up."

"Maybe it's a wrong number."

"I don't think so. And here's why, because if it was a wrong number they'd say something or call back right away. But this one's different. He calls about every hour like he's seeing if I'm there. And I wouldn't have called you if it was only that but, Detective Franck, I'm pretty sure someone was following me last night."

"When?"

"After you let me go home. I'm pretty sure I heard something in the alley by the parking lot when I was getting in my car and then when I was driving home I was watching in the mirror and there *was* a car followed me all the way to Millvale. I swear."

"Are you sure, Donna?"

"I'm real sure and what I think is that whoever killed Mr. G. is after me now."

"Hey, Donna, that's pretty—"

"No. I figured it out. That person that's callin' me and followin' me thinks I saw him or knows who he is and that I'm tellin' you but honestly, I didn't see no one. No one. I told you everything I saw."

Cesar wanted to cry. Last night he had suspected that Donna Creech saw life as a TV show. Now he was certain. He could have been in bed, resting his brain for encounters with smart people. Instead he was watching a rerun of "Perry Mason."

"Donna, is that all you wanted to tell me?"

"Yes, sir."

"Does that guy live with you?"

"No, hon. He can't. My husband would find out from the kids. He'd *kill* me."

"Do you have a good lock on the door at home?"

"Yes. I put it on myself. It's a Kwikset."

"Okay. When you go home from here, you lock your door. Put some furniture in front of it if it'll make you feel better. Then unplug the phone and go to bed."

"What are you going to do?"

"About what?"

"About finding him."

"I'm going to go home and go to bed. I'll look for him in the morning."

"But I'm scared!"

"Well, you've had kind of a shock. I don't blame you."

"What if something happens to me or my kids? I don't want my kids to get hurt!"

"Your kids aren't going to get hurt, Donna. You do what I say and you're going to be all right. Look, if you have any more trouble, call the police emergency number. They'll get someone over fast—faster than I could get there."

"Oh, you don't know. I live in Millvale and they take their time when they get a call to go there. They don't like the projects."

"Donna, I'll put a word in at the district office. You just tell them who you are and they'll be right over. Quit worrying."

"Oh, thanks, Detective Franck. I know you think I'm bein' silly, but I can't help it. I've got this bad feelin' about those calls." She looked over her shoulder. "I'd better get back to Alfred. He doesn't like me to talk too long to other men, but thanks again."

"You're welcome, Donna. Any time."

Henry detached Calquetta from her dancing partner and brought her back to the booth. "Was it worth the trip?" he asked Cesar.

"Hell, no. She's decided she's being tailed."

"Maybe she is."

"I doubt it. I think she just wants to be a star."

"Crime lover?"

"Probably."

"I used to know her boyfriend."

"What's he do?"

"He's a garbageman."

"What do you suppose he sees in her?"

"White chick."

"He could have found someone better looking."

"Alfred isn't real smart. Are we through?"

"Yeah. Thanks, Henry."
"You going to need me tomorrow?"
"I might."
"Call my mother if you do."
"Right."

8

It was nearly two when Cesar got to bed. He got up at six, fixed bacon and eggs, did the dishes, and faced his first dilemma of the day—how to look collegiate.

What he came up with was a blue blazer, grey knit slacks, white shirt, red tie, and black wing tips, and when he checked in the mirror he looked like he worked for Delta Airlines. Well, shit. It was the best he could do. When it came to coats, he rebelled. It was too damned cold for his topcoat. He wore the foul weather coat. Lillian was still asleep when he left.

Cesar stopped at the office to look up addresses. There was a note from Sgt. Evans on his desk.

"Lieutenant Tieves asked me how you were coming with the budget forms. I told him you were nearly done."

Thanks a lot.

Phillip Bennett lived off of Madison on Wold Avenue in Walnut Hills. East Walnut Hills. White Walnut Hills. Cesar had been nearly blinded by the clear winter sun on Madison Road. When he turned onto Wold, he had to slow to a crawl to allow his eyes to adjust. Even without their leaves, the trees were sufficiently dense to create a cathedral twilight. Once his vision returned it was rewarded with a procession of mansions, all in perfect repair, all very large. Heating bills, heating bills, heating bills. Cesar resisted intimidation.

Phillip Bennett's house, the duplicate of a Portsmouth, New Hampshire masterpiece, was at the end of the block. Like the others, it was well back from the street. Its yellow clapboards shone through the oaks in the yard, welcoming all, even policemen.

A black woman answered his ring. Mr. Bennett was home, would he be seated while she saw if he was available? He would stand. While he stood in the large entry he noticed that the wallpaper, while handsome, was getting old. He noticed galoshes and coats under and on what appeared to be very delicate antique chairs. There was a stupendously flashy Big Wheel parked under a very tall chest of drawers. The place was clearly not under Lillian's management. Cesar heard a television set going someplace. An elderly collie wandered in from the

74

living room, looked up at him, barked once sharply, and wandered back to collapse under the piano. A grey-haired man emerged from a door at the rear of the hall, smiled, and offered his hand.

"I'm Phillip Bennett."

Cesar knew at once that Phillip Bennett was dying. When he had been in uniform, Cesar had patrolled Elm Street and Race Street and Vine Street, and he had seen too many old men on their way out not to recognize the symptoms. Phillip Bennett wore an Izod gold shirt instead of a cotton work shirt, but it hung away from him the same way Elm Street shirts did. He had lost weight fast; his skin hung on him. If there was a critical difference between him and the dying men downtown, it was that he was still fighting. Cesar's old men had spent lifetimes working for other people and when death came it was simply one more order to follow. Bennett still had a grip to his shake. He was forcing his body to keep moving. Cesar wanted to pardon himself and leave. Instead he let Bennett lead him into the living room where a big Sony was tuned to the Smurfs. When Bennett sat down, the collie heaved himself up and plodded over to recollapse at his owner's feet.

"I apologize for that," said Bennett, nodding at the television. "I have to keep an eye on the competition."

"No problem."

"Julia's bringing some coffee. She said your name was Franck?"

"Detective Franck, yes, sir."

"Are you here about Irving Golden?"

"Yes, sir."

"I'm not sure I know anything helpful, but I'll be glad to try. What would you like to know?"

I would like to know if you killed Irving Golden, because if you did I'm going to walk out of here and let you die in peace.

"Thanks, sir. What I'm interested in is anything you can tell me about your meeting with Mr. Golden Thursday and anything relevant that might have happened afterward. We're interested in that time period right now, but if you know anything else that might shed some light I'd appreciate that, too."

But Bennett was staring at the tube. He turned up the volume on the TV; Angela Dellaire, star of "Boston," had replaced Smurfette. A voice sang, "Boston Babes! We've got the cutest little Boston Babes!" and Angela smiled and chuckled and wriggled. The camera zoomed in to show, in the palm of her hand, a tiny doll dressed just like the star. The zoom continued until the doll's face filled the screen. Cesar didn't think it looked too much like Angela's except for the mole by her mouth.

"Is that . . ." He started to ask if this was a Bennett ad, but Phillip Bennett held up a hand to shush him.

"Flexy knees! The tiny Boston Babes just love to please!" Angela posed the doll so that she sat on her heels like Brigette Bardot used to do.

No minidoll you'll ever see
On TV
Has so many features,
They're such darling creatures.

The close-up shot now clearly showed that the doll was anatomically all there under the tight blouse. Then Kathy Madigan, Angela's "Boston" co-star, stepped in and hugged Angela, then held up a little Kathy Madigan doll.

Exercise!
The brand-new Boston Babes can exercise!
Squeeze her thighs
Boston Babes can kick out
She's the doll you'll pick out!

Bennett turned the sound off and slumped back in his chair. Cesar watched the screen as the Whizbang trademark monkey pushed the plunger on the Whizbang trademark detonator, making a big mushroom cloud that said Whizbang on it—same as when Cesar used to watch.

"Have you heard about the meeting?"

"Some."

Bennett's story was very nearly as complete as Tom Cleary's. Unlike Tom, however, Bennett went out of his way to put everybody, including Irving, in the best possible light. He wasn't flattering, Cesar knew that, but he seemed incapable of saying something unkind. Cesar could see why the Bennett staff didn't go in for any of the sniping he was used to hearing from your usual employees. Phillip Bennett wasn't your usual boss.

Bennett's account of the discussion in the parking lot after the meeting was no different from any of the others.

"Where did you go when you left Golden Time?" asked Cesar.

"I drove home."

"By yourself?"

"Yes."

"Did you come straight home?"

"Yes."

"Can you verify that, sir?"

Bennett thought a moment. "No. I guess I can't. My wife was out and the housekeeper was off. Is that going to be awkward?"

"I'm sure it's not, sir. I am trying to find out who went where, though. It helps if someone can back you up."

"It's known as an alibi, I believe," Bennett smiled gently.

"Yes, sir."

"Well, I'm sorry. I don't have one. It's a little embarrassing." Bennett bent over and fondled his collie.

"Maybe you got a phone call—or called someone when you got home?"

"No such luck. Would you like more coffee?" They had emptied the silver pot.

"No, thanks."

"Have I been any help at all?"

"Yes, sir."

"Good, I hope so."

"Sir, you've known Mr. Golden a long time, haven't you?"

"Years and years."

"And your companies worked together?"

"We are Golden Time's only advertising agency. Yes. It's a close relationship."

"Well, did you work close enough—did you have to know what was going on with his business?"

"Pretty much, yes."

"Did you know about any serious problems at Golden Time? Any staff problems? Labor problems?"

"Well, he's had something of a labor problem for years. Not serious, not really, but there were efforts to organize his work force. I'm sure you know about that."

"Yes."

"But staff problems? I don't think so."

"Is the company solid? Any financial problems?"

"It's very solid. Irving made it a strong business. Very attractive. And it's in a good position to get stronger. They've got good product lines and new lines in the works."

"Like the new dolls?"

"Yes. Have you seen them?"

"Not yet."

Cesar hesitated to ask more questions. He had watched Bennett's strength evaporate while he talked. The lines of pain around his eyes and mouth were deeper, too. But there had been no mention of the strain. Cesar would try to keep his questions short.

"Mr. Bennett, we don't think we're dealing with an ordinary break-in here."

"I don't either."

"It's possible that someone was hiding in the building, but the security guard keeps pretty good records and it doesn't seem likely."

"Leonard's thoroughness is legendary."

"So, what we're looking for is some reason besides money."

"I understand."

"Have you thought about that at all?"

"Yes."

"And?"

Bennett shrugged. "I can't help you."

"You don't know about any enemies he might have had?"

"Enemies?"

"Well, it seems to me he could be kind of a tough guy."

"Oh, he was tough all right, but not . . . not movie tough."

"He had a lot of power, though."

Bennett laughed. "I suppose so. Not as much as you might think, though. No one has much real power these days."

"Did he make all the decisions for Golden Time?"

"All the important ones."

"Were advertising decisions important?"

"To him? Yes."

"So he would pass on anything your company did?"

"Almost everything. We agreed that marketing was as vital as production. He had to be interested."

"Were there—" Cesar stopped. He was about to be less than candid with a dying man and he wasn't happy about it. Bennett was waiting.

"Were there any problems—did *he* have any problems with your agency?"

"From time to time. Of course, after thirty years the two businesses were almost a family. Families fight. But no, it was on the whole a good relationship and I'm sure it will continue to be."

Damn. Wrong answer. It wasn't just that Grace wanted to fire the agency. She said her father wanted to. Who should he believe, a pushy, ambitious girl or a dying gentleman? The pushy, ambitious girl was frank and direct. She didn't apologize for herself. The dying gentleman apologized for everybody.

"Do you know who will be running Golden Time now?"

"Mr. Golden's brother will."

"Frederick Golden?"

"Yes."

"There won't be any big changes?"

"I don't expect any. And by the way, if you're wondering about Frederick Golden gaining anything from this accident, he won't. Irving's family will have his share of the company. Have you met Frederick?"

"Not yet."

"You'll like him."

"Nice guy?"

"Very."

Cesar stood up. He had to help Bennett from the sofa.

"This is a nice house, Mr. Bennett."

"You like it? It's way too big. We never did fill it even when the children were here. But we like having it for the grandchildren. Would you like the tour?"

Cesar did want to see the rest of the house. Never pass up a chance to snoop around. But his host was tired.

"Thanks. I'd like to, but I've got a lot to do."

He followed Bennett to the front door. The man was nearly shuffling. Even the ancient collie was ahead of them. Cesar opened the door figuring one that big would weigh a ton, but it was beautifully balanced. A child would have no trouble. The things you can do with money.

"Thanks for your time, Mr. Bennett. I appreciate it."

"Any time."

The collie was picking its way down the stairs to the yard.

"Do you want the dog back in?" Cesar asked.

"No, that's all right. He's too old to go far." And, indeed, the dog only went a few yards beyond the house where he stopped and stared at the trees.

"Well, I'll be going. It was nice meeting you, sir."

"Nice meeting you, officer. Good luck."

9

CESAR FOLDED INTO the Camaro and headed back to Madison Road. He should have gone to the toilet while he was at Bennett's. Too much coffee. He found a gas station at DeSales Corner. When he got back in the car he pulled out his sheet map. Frederick Golden lived on Medoc Circle in Mt. Lookout and Cesar knew he would get lost. Mt. Lookout was worse than ever to navigate since the city tore down the old Grandin Road viaduct. He made an X on Medoc Circle, put the map on the passenger seat, and turned back out on Madison Road.

He couldn't stop thinking about Bennett. Up until Bennett lied to him, Cesar thought he was one of the best men he'd ever met, someone who deserved everything he had. Big house, good income, antique furniture, collie. It took a lot of guts to live with great pain and not mention it. Bennett's staff only knew that he was sick.

Why did he have to lie? Lying is for jerks, not gentlemen.

How did he stand Irving Golden for thirty-five years? Maybe Irving wasn't all bad—he was Grace's father—but he was a loudmouth and a steamroller. He called people names, dumped on them. Did he finally push Phillip Bennett over the brink? Pain could drive you crazy. Pain combined with an irritation like Irving would make Cesar go nuts.

He turned onto Observatory.

Suppose that's what happened. Suppose Bennett snapped. Wouldn't you think he would yell back? Tell Golden what a jerk he was being? Tell him to apologize for being a pig to Marianne Kelly? That's how people snapped in the movies. But maybe a lifetime of biting his tongue kept Bennett from doing that. Or maybe he had slow reactions. Was he physically capable of swinging that statue? Weak as he was?

In Bennett's state he'd have to swing it in a pretty big circle to get the momentum going. Hard to do a hammer blow and cave in a skull the way Golden's was caved in.

He turned onto Linwood.

Maybe it wasn't rage. Maybe he didn't snap.

Back to the lie. Everything's just fine. The Bennett Agency and Golden Time Toys will always be together. Everyone will have a job and Bennett will get top price when he sells out. You'll like Frederick Golden. Good guys are in charge. Grace isn't a good guy. Grace is a girl. But if you don't know about Grace, everything's fine now that Irving's out of the way. Is that it?

Cesar believed in hell. He didn't know what it looked like, but he believed there was hell even more than he believed there was heaven. Hell was where you went when you did something wrong and you were smart enough to know better. He didn't really see dumb people in hell. Phillip Bennett shouldn't go to hell, Cesar liked him, but, dammit, if he killed Irving Golden that was where he was going. Cesar had no opinion about Golden's destination.

He turned right on Tweed.

For crying out loud, Cesar, you're not being objective. Bennett only said that he was sure the Golden Time connection would continue. Maybe that wasn't a lie, maybe it was just business talk. Maybe if he was incapable of saying bad things about business like he was about people and . . .

Shit. Cesar was lost.

He stopped to consult his map and found that he was probably at the intersection of Stanley Lane and a substantial erosion due to much folding and refolding of the paper. He backed his car into a driveway and retraced his path at a crawl, seeking his error. He was passed twice by joggers, both of whom made a point of memorizing his license number. Cesar was embarrassed. He was in a Camaro in BMW country and, creeping as he was, he did look like an intruder. He stopped the third jogger and asked for directions. The jogger did not want to help. Cesar became irritated and nearly said that he was a cop, but thought better of it. The public does not need to know that policemen can lose their way. He explained that he was looking for the Frederick Golden residence, using his idea of an insurance salesman voice. He got the directions and drove away. That guy memorized his plates, too. Bunch of paranoids. He had yet to see a burglar in wing tips.

It was no wonder that he had missed Medoc Circle. The entrance to that exclusive ring was unmarked and looked like a driveway. It was a private street. The houses were all 1920s' Tudor. Driveways seemed to be important here. They were wide, most of them semicircular, and all were freshly sealed asphalt. There were fewer trees than in Walnut Hills, and as Cesar jerked over the speed bumps he decided he liked Walnut Hills better. This street was too much like a convention of clubhouses. He belonged to no clubs.

Cesar found #14 and swept up to the door. No doubt about it, though, clubhouse driveways were certainly preferable to his own concrete chute. The sounds of domestic debate reached him as he reached for the doorbell, so he tried a little professional eavesdropping. Couldn't hurt. But the great oak door made the argument unintelligible. What he did notice was a vicious ring to both voices. Sounded pretty much like downtown. He rang. A lady with whales all over her pants yanked the door open and glared at him.

"Mrs. Golden?"

"Yes."

"I'm Detective Franck, Cincinnati Police. Is Mr. Golden in?"

"He's in the living room." She pointed, snatched her purse off a table and stomped out, slamming the front door behind her.

Cesar stepped in with caution. The Goldens' entry hall was as big as the Bennetts', but there was no peeling wallpaper. Here it was oak paneling and an oak staircase built for giants. The floor was stone, partially covered by oriental rugs. There were no overcoats or Big Wheels adrift. He looked around the edge of an arch where Mrs. Golden had pointed and saw Frederick Golden.

"I'm Detective Franck, sir," said Cesar.

"I know. Phil Bennett called me. Come in here."

Cesar stepped down into the living room and followed Golden to a door in the corner. Like all the doors, it was paneled oak. Golden waved him in.

They were in another world. The only trace of Old England was a diamond-paned window looking onto the backyard. There was a solid wall of books to the right and to the left a wall with one bright painting hung slightly off center. A large rosewood desk stood with its business side facing the books; a leather sofa sat across from the desk. The walls were white and the carpet grey. "Want a drink?"

"No, thanks, sir."

"Well, I'm having one."

While Frederick Golden poured a drink, Cesar crossed to the window. The backyards on Medoc Circle flowed together, unfenced, increasing the golf course effect. There wasn't a Weber kettle in sight. Cesar walked over to the painting.

"You like that?" asked Golden.

"It looks kind of familiar."

"It's a Gauguin. You'll find Duveneck and Farney and School of Duveneck and crap like that in the rest of the house. They belong to Mrs. Golden. That," he waved his drink at the Gauguin, "is mine."

"It's a nice painting."

"Yes, it is. Sit down. Give me a minute to cool off."

Cesar sat on the sofa while Golden walked behind the desk, sat down, and stared out the window. Cesar watched Golden cool off. His face, which had been scarlet, regained a normal color. His neck muscles loosened. After a moment he ran a hand through his thick silver hair, turned away from the view, and smiled at Cesar.

"You've come about my brother," he said.

What a change. Everybody Cesar had talked to about this man had painted him the opposite of his brother—polished, poised, and cool—

but Cesar's first impression had been that he was seeing Irving come to life. It must have been a real stinker of a fight to make him lose his cool like that. Now he fit his public image.

He answered Cesar's questions politely. Frederick Golden was windier than Bennett but nearly as careful about being nice. His way of being not so nice when he had to, which was any time he talked about Irving, was to say less than usual. Cesar noticed, too, that when he had to talk about his brother, a vein in his forehead bulged. They were on the topic of Thursday's meeting when Frederick's telephone rang.

Cesar stood up to leave the room as Golden answered the phone, but he was waved back into his seat. He turned to look out the window and eavesdropped like a maniac.

'Hi, Bob . . . no . . . no, I'm just talking to one of our local detectives . . . unarmed . . . as far as I know . . . could be worse . . . what? . . . no . . . you know I don't watch those cartoons, Bob . . . and you know why . . . Oh? . . . they did? . . . isn't that kind of fast? . . . Oh . . . well . . . no, Bob . . . I don't . . . not a bit . . . " Cesar stood up and walked over to the window.

"Bob . . . Bob, I'm keeping this detective waiting . . . yes . . . I'll call you . . . later." He hung up.

"Sorry, I don't like business on Saturday."

"It's OK, sir."

"That was Bob Atwood—from Bennett. Have you met him?"

"Not yet, sir."

"Very bright. Good—a good finance man. Maybe a little too MBA for the long run, but very good. He's had to step in for Phil Bennett a lot lately. Did you know Phil's terribly sick?"

"I didn't know for sure."

"Well, he is." Golden stared out the window for a moment, then swung himself back to face Cesar.

"Anyway, we're all agog about the competition . . . not to mention my brother's unfortunate . . ." He cleared his throat. "It seems the Whizbang Toy Company has beaten us out of the starting gate with their rival tasteless doll."

"The Boston dolls?"

"You know them?"

"I saw an ad this morning." said Cesar. Then, in case Golden thought he watched the Smurfs. "At Mr. Bennett's. He was watching."

"Bob seems to think they're going to blow us out of the water. He's probably right." Golden didn't seem too upset. "Do you have any children, Detective Franck?"

Children?

"No, sir."

"Perhaps you will. If you do, you will, no doubt, see why it is no shame to be beaten by a firm like Whizbang. You'll hate every toy they make. Well, you saw their new doll."

"It's like yours?"

"Worse. Or better. Depends on your viewpoint, but it's typical of Whizbang to *copy* our most tasteless products. Have you seen the Denver Doll?"

Cesar had not. Frederick opened a drawer, pulled out a tiny woman in blue jeans, and handed her to Cesar.

"Take a look and tell me what you think. I'm interested."

Cesar was plunged into embarrassment. It reminded him of his sister's Barbie doll, which had provided some of his earliest anatomy lessons. This doll, however, had something Barbie never had, which was sex appeal. She really looked like Banner Strathmore. He moved the arms and legs gingerly while discreetly peeking down the cleavage. They had the details down right. Little girls wouldn't be the only fans. He tried to stand her on the desk, but she couldn't manage it so he sat her with her legs in front. She fell off the edge and he picked her up.

"What do you think?" asked Golden.

"I don't know much about dolls, sir. She . . . I guess she looks a lot like Banner Strathmore."

"I saw you blush."

Cesar blushed again.

"Don't feel bad," said Golden. "That's my reaction, too. I don't know how much you know about the toy industry."

"Not much, sir."

"Our name is only slightly better regarded than the Whizbang Toy Company. This isn't going to help much."

"Why's that?" asked Cesar.

And Frederick filled him in on the toy industry. He talked about the good companies which made durable toys that increased a child's aesthetic awareness and sharpened cognitive skills and the bad companies which made garish and tasteless toys and how the garish and tasteless toys had changed the market, driving out some of the fine old companies, and also how the end of the baby boom had begun to change the picture again. Cesar drifted off to a recollection of his stamped metal gas station. It was probably garish and tasteless, but he hadn't thrown it out. He tuned back in as Frederick was explaining how professional couples were demanding higher quality toys and would probably refuse to allow things "like that" into their homes. He pointed to the toy in Cesar's hand. Cesar had been idly twisting the inflexible arms and legs. No matter how he arranged them, she could not look relaxed.

"And I think what distresses me most is that *all* the girls we test, regardless of income, love the doll."

That's bad?

"It's going to sell millions. It's so cheap that every girl can have one. I'm afraid it will become part of the national consciousness."

84

Frederick spoke of his fears. Fear of talk-show jokes. Fear of feminist retribution. Fear of PTA and NEA. Fear of Jerry Falwell. Fear of the pope. Above all, fear of the permanent association of the lewd little figure with the Golden family, meaning, Cesar understood, Frederick Golden. "That is why," he said, "I am seriously considering withdrawing this toy from production."

Have you talked this over with your niece?

"I realize that's a drastic move," Golden continued, "one that will cost money, but it is my firm intention to make the Golden Time brand stand for quality if it stands for anything. If that means a temporary reduction in profits, I find the sacrifice worthwhile."

Frederick Golden turned to gaze out his window, giving Cesar the benefit of his chiseled profile. He paused, and Cesar wondered if the pause was to allow his audience time to appreciate the nobility of Frederick's management.

"But you didn't come here to talk my plans. We were discussing my brother." Golden turned full face to Cesar.

Actually, the glimpse into Frederick's plans interested Cesar a great deal. He was interested in the imminent war between uncle and niece as well as the confirmation of Irene Golden's tale. But he returned to the topic—Thursday night.

Frederick cast no new insight into the meeting. He did remember who had talked to whom after the meeting and he recalled the order of departure up until his own. He was, however, unable to account for what was to Cesar an unusually long commute to Mt. Lookout. He did not arrive at home until eight o'clock that night.

"I drove, Detective Franck. I was angry and distraught, and I drove."

No one had seen him. He had bought no gas. He agreed to search his memory and call Cesar if he could recall a witness. He understood Cesar's need to know very well. Cesar didn't push. He would be in touch.

As he was standing to leave, Cesar remembered the Cadillac in the parking lot and the order from Sgt. Evans to report in. Do it here or from a phone booth? Golden was getting restless, but Cesar didn't want to hunt a phone. Besides, it would be nice to try out the desk. Golden granted his request and left the room, but he left the door open. Cesar stood and called.

Sgt. Evans was not thrilled with his report. He even got a little sarcastic about the Top Hat. Cesar felt injured. True, he had not sprung a confession from anyone. True, he had not come up with a witness. It was not true that he was wasting the city's time and money visiting the hotter night spots. Sgt. Evans wanted to know if he was getting anywhere this morning. Cesar didn't know if Golden was eavesdropping or not.

"I'm making progress, Sergeant."

"Making progress? Are you *learning* anything? Are you getting *information,* Detective Franck?"

"Affirmative, Sergeant."

"What's the matter? You got an audience?"

"Yes."

"Franck, don't do that. When you call me again, call me without an audience. Will you do that?"

"I will, Sergeant."

"Thank you, Cesar. Where are you going next?"

"Terrace Park."

"Are you dressed correctly?"

"I think so. I don't know."

"What color are your pants?"

"Grey."

"Good." And Sgt. Evans hung up.

The next call was even trickier. Cesar didn't want Frederick Golden to hear him begging for help with Irving's marooned Cadillac. He checked around the door to see if he could be overheard. He could not. The huge living room was empty. Even so, he closed the door.

Ten minutes later, he had negotiated a deal with Henry. It cost Cesar another night shift, but Henry agreed to break into the Cadillac, hotwire the ignition, and ferry the car to Amberley. The devoted Calquetta would follow in Henry's Mark to bring him home. Henry was so nasty and charged such a stiff fee that Cesar was tempted to report him to the Amberley cops. Better not. No need. Two luxury liners with two black people at the helms would cause plenty of consternation without Cesar's contribution.

He hung up and went in search of Golden. They met in the hall. Cesar thanked him for his time and the use of the phone and started to leave, but Golden stopped him.

"That's one of the Duvenecks," he said and pointed to a small oil painting.

"Nice picture," said Cesar.

"It's Mrs. Golden's. She wanted something Cincinnati there. Better that than a tiger, I suppose."

Cesar got the impression Golden wanted to tell him something but didn't have the nerve.

"She's something of a Cincinnati chauvinist. She's a Neff."

What is a neff? Should Cesar know? He almost asked when Golden finally said what was on his mind.

"You talked to my sister-in-law."

"Mrs. Golden? Irene?"

Frederick nodded.

"Yes, sir."

"I hope you'll . . . consider . . . she's quite upset. She's not always . . . completely logical in the best of circumstances. And now . . . " He trailed off.

"It's a bad time for her. Yes, sir."

"Yes," said Frederick.

"Thank you, sir," said Cesar. "I've got to be going."

10

CESAR'S GUESS THAT a downward progression would get him out of Mt. Lookout and onto Columbia Parkway proved, eventually, to be correct. He headed for the Frisch's Mainliner outside Mariemont.

Half an hour later, tartar sauce level restored, he was back on U.S. 50 headed for Terrace Park and Bob Atwood. His brain wasn't working too well. It never did after lunch. Keeping the Hornet well under the limit, he spent his time wondering what was a neff. Was Lt. Tieves a neff? Was he himself a neff? Nice thing to call someone if you know what it means. Mrs. Frederick Golden was a neff because she liked Cincinnati pictures. Or maybe she was a neff because she yelled at her husband. As he reached Terrace Park he remembered. Neff Valves. Big money and old Cincinnati. Jesus. Cesar had almost worked the word into his vocabulary. What if he'd tried to drop it around someone he knew? He broke into a light sweat and then forgot the whole thing as he concentrated on navigation.

Five minutes later he put himself in the hands of a kindly gas station attendant who drew him a little map, and four minutes later he was parking at the Atwoods.

Why did he feel he had been here before when he knew he hadn't? Ahhh! This was where "My Three Sons" lived, and before them the Cleavers, and before them "Ozzie and Harriet." He rang the bell expecting a squared-away lady in high heels and a dress. What he got as a five-year-old girl in pink pants and Nikes.

"Hi. Is your dad home?"

"No, but my mother is. MOM! MOM! Do you want to come in? It's okay."

"Thanks." Cesar stepped into the vestibule. The little girl leaned against a wall and bounced her bottom.

"What's that you've got?"

"It's my new doll. Want to see it?" She stuck out her hand and Cesar saw his second Denver Doll.

"Neat. What's her name?"

"Well, it's supposed to be Banner because she looks just like Banner Strathmore on television, but I named her Mrs. Wilhelm like for my teacher. She looks like my teacher, too. I don't watch 'Denver' because it's on so late, you know."

"Nice doll. That's a good name, too."

"I know. She's neat because she's tiny. I keep her in my secrets box my friend gave me." She folded the doll into a fetal position and stuffed her into a cough drop box. "My friend, her name is Laura, she wants her secrets box back because she doesn't have a tiny doll but she's going to get one."

"Are you going to give her the box back?"

"No." The girl put the box in her pocket.

"I wouldn't either."

"Here comes my mom." Cesar heard someone coming up basement steps and the thump of a laundry basket in the kitchen.

"Julie, who are you talking to?"

"I don't know, Mom. A man. He wants to talk to Daddy."

Mrs. Atwood came through a swinging door into the dining room. Cesar was a little disappointed to see a pink warm-up suit and running shoes instead of pumps and pearls. June Cleaver's nice hairdo had been replaced by a frizz.

"I'm Detective Franck, ma'am. Cincinnati Police."

She blinked at him. She wore great big glasses with a blob of rhinestone on one lens.

"Is something wrong? Where's Daddy, Julie?"

"He went to get some beer and his raincoat from the dry cleaner. He said he'll be right back."

"There's nothing wrong, ma'am. I just need to talk to your husband if he's going to be available."

"Oh. Well. Sure. Come in. Sit down."

She crossed the vestibule and led him into the living room.

"Julie, go watch television, okay?"

"Are you a detective?" Julie asked.

"Julie, I said go watch television. Go! He doesn't want to talk to you." The little girl left the room, but Cesar didn't hear the kitchen door swing. She would listen.

"I guess Bob's coming right back. Do you want to wait?"

"If you don't mind."

"Sure. Listen, I've got . . . I'm doing things. Will you excuse me?"

She left the living room and Cesar heard her grab the little girl and drag her into the kitchen, muttering all the way.

He leaned back into the couch and stared at the large picture of a tiger's head. Go, Bengals.

The Atwoods' living room was big, but not nearly as big as the Goldens' or the Bennetts', and it was a lot more like the living rooms Cesar was used to. They had spent money—the furniture was big and new— but it was from Shillito's or Pogue's, he guessed, not from a museum. He stretched his legs and stared at his wing tips. He would give Atwood fifteen minutes to show up. As he started to doze off he heard a car in the drive so he got up and walked to the window. Atwood got out of a maroon 98, loaded with groceries and dry cleaning.

Jeez. It wasn't fair. Atwood was wearing a blue warm-up suit. What was the point of dressing like a Delta agent if you're going to talk to people in warm-ups, he'd like to know. In fact, his was the only tie he'd seen all day.

Atwood burst into the house and slammed the door. He stuck a dry cleaning bag in the coat closet, turned, saw Cesar, and did a double take.

"Mr. Atwood?"

"Right."

"Detective Franck, Cincinnati Police."

"Whoa. Wait." He held up his six-pack. "It's legal. I'm twenty-one. Hahahaha."

"Can I talk to you for a few minutes?"

"Sure! Sure! I'll sing. Just let me get warm before you take me in. Hahahaha."

Very funny. You wouldn't freeze if you wore an overcoat, dummy.

"It's about Irving Golden," said Cesar.

"Don't tell me! He's alive. I knew he was too mean to die. What a toughie! Hahahaha."

"No, he's dead. He's . . . "

"I confess. I did it. I couldn't take it anymore. I wanted his secretary. I'd do anything to get her. Hahahaha."

Cesar became discouraged.

"Mr. Atwood, I'm with the Cincinnati Homicide Squad. I'm interviewing everyone who was at the meeting with Irving Golden on Thursday. According to my information, you were in attendance. I'd like to ask you some questions, please."

"Sure, sure. You're Tom Cleary's buddy, right? You were at Arnold's Friday?"

"That's right. Now, if it—"

"Hold it. Hold it. Let me get rid of this. You want one?" Atwood held the beer up.

"No thanks."

"Linda! LINDA! Will you put this beer away?"

Why don't you put it away yourself?

They waited until Linda Atwood came for the beer.

Atwood's interview required different tactics from those used with Mr. Golden and Mr. Bennett. With them he had been the good listener, the polite young policeman. To be the polite listener around Atwood would be to ask for ninety minutes of smartass baloney. For Atwood, Cesar would have to be all cop, Mr. Bureaucrat. The interview became a contest, a duel. The Procedures Manual questions vs. the snappy response. Atwood was outgunned.

As he wore Atwood down, Cesar watched the man's attitude change from bouncy arrogance to sullen cooperation. Atwood was used to giving orders and receiving flattery. He was used to a brown nose's laughing when he laughed. Cesar began to sympathize with the Bennett employees.

Cesar's victory notwithstanding, there was no new information to be had. Atwood was not a good narrator. He couldn't remember what people said, too busy listening to himself. He was short on details.

With some probing, Cesar learned that Atwood had been the last to leave the parking lot after the meeting. No, he hadn't seen anybody hanging around. Frederick Golden and Joe Enneking were pulling out of the parking lot when he left. Atwood's car was parked on Ninth Street near the agency. He had cut through the alley to get there. No, he hadn't seen anyone. Cesar asked whether he went straight home. He had. What time did he get home?

"Linda! LINDA!" Atwood yelled. "What time did I get home Thursday?"

"What?" she yelled from the kitchen.

"Come in here!" he ordered, and she obeyed. He repeated the question.

"I don't know, Bob. Whatever time you usually get home. Seven o'clock?"

"Come on, babe. This is important. The detective needs to know if I had time to commit murder."

"Bob! No!"

"Just kidding, hahahaha. No, just try to remember. You were here."

She racked her brain, but she wasn't a clockwatcher. She thought "Entertainment Tonight" was on, but she wasn't paying attention. She was on the phone when he came in.

"That's my wife. Always wide awake." Cesar thought Atwood was a really lousy husband.

"Did you see 'Entertainment Tonight' last night?" Atwood asked him.

"No, sir."

"Oh. Too bad. They showed the party in L.A. for the Boston Babes."

"Please?"

"New dolls from Whizbang? Like the Dallas Dolls. Only," and he shook his head, "I've gotta say they're cuter. Sexier." He smacked his wife's seat and she sidled away. "Should have seen it. They got Burt Reynolds to come."

Big deal. Cesar would leave Atwood with a little thrill.

"Thank you for your time, Mr. Atwood, Mrs. Atwood. Mr. Atwood, will you be in town this week? Are you planning any trips?"

"Not now."

"I may have more questions. I'd appreciate your letting me know if you do contemplate leaving the area." Cesar gave Atwood his card. Take that, hotshot.

"Sure, sure," said Atwood. "Listen, good luck, all right? I really hope you get the jerk who did this. I liked Irv. I really did. Great guy. Sharp manager."

"Goodbye, Mr. Atwood. Ma'am."

11

THREE DOWN, ONE to go. Joe Enneking was last on today's list. Was there time to look up Tom Cleary and talk to him again? Cesar needed to process what he'd learned and what he hadn't learned. Tom could help. He found a phone and called. Tom would be glad to see him, but he had to go out. Could they get together tomorrow? Tom would be at the office. Cesar agreed.

What the hell was Enneking doing living in Winton Place? Enneking was pretty high up at Golden Time. Surely he could afford someplace nicer than that. There were some charismatic Catholics down there. Maybe he was one of those.

Cesar drove and thought what a jerk Atwood was. Any man who couldn't put his own beer in the fridge had to be a creep. And he sure as hell didn't work up a sweat in that sweatsuit. He looked soft and overweight.

Cesar sucked in his own stomach as far as he could. So maybe he was a little overweight, too, but he didn't go around in a sweatsuit trying to convince everybody that he was a jock. Mrs. Atwood wore sweats, too. Is that collegiate attire? Should Cesar have jogged out to Terrace Park? Would that meet with Sgt. Tieves' approval? Had he dressed right for any of his interviews? A nice guy like Bennett wouldn't care what he wore. What about Golden? Golden probably didn't even notice. As a matter of fact, his mind seemed to be on other things the whole time Cesar was at his house. What was Golden thinking about? What was the fight with his wife about? Mrs. Golden was steaming when she left. Irene Golden didn't like Mrs. Fred. Maybe the fight was about art. People went crazy about art.

Grace Golden was going to have a fight on her hands. She was a tough girl, that was obvious, but Cesar didn't think her uncle was going to roll over and play dead. So maybe Frederick had been ashamed of his brother and the toy business; he had plans for it now. There was no way to tell if they were spur-of-the-moment plans or if he'd been hatching them for a while. Was it possible to get so upset about a business that you would kill your own brother? In Cincinnati? Cesar tried to imagine pissing off his sister to the point that she would smash his head in. He could get her mad all right, but her preferred and effective method was to appeal to Supreme Court Justice Lillian Franck. Of course, the Goldens were different. They were rich. They had something substantial to go to war over. Cesar and Kathy didn't.

Phillip Bennett must have cancer. That had to be it. That was what he looked like. Cancer. Jesus. He shouldn't lie, though, even if he had cancer. But then, what was a lie if you had already killed somebody? Bennett didn't have much to lose even if he got caught. A life sentence wouldn't be more than six months. He seemed to be pretty friendly with Frederick Golden. Suppose they were in this together? Not a bad deal. Remove Irving and you solve both their problems. The Bennett Agency keeps the Golden Time account and Frederick gets the company—as long as Grace loses the fight. Bennett sells his agency, staff stays on. He's a hero—dies rich.

But Irving Golden's death didn't seem planned. At least it didn't seem like long-range planning at work. Whoever killed Irving worked fast and took a lot of risks. He-she could have been seen going in or coming out of Irving's private door. Donna Creech could have . . .

Donna Creech. No wonder he was so sleepy. Stupid woman. Okay, not stupid, silly. What did she do with her kids when she was out partying in the middle of the night? She was a mess. No doubt about it. And it was too bad. You couldn't help liking her at least a little. And even if she did dumb things like making Cesar miss his sleep, she wasn't dumb. But she was a mess. She must have black kids if she lived in Millvale. White kids wouldn't survive out there any better than black kids would in the white projects. Was she really getting strange phone calls? Could they really have anything to do with Golden's murder?

Golden's murder. Irving Golden's murder. How do you murder Irving Golden? You palm his keys as you pass his desk. You wait around out of sight until the parking lot's empty. You go quietly up to his office, pick up the Tina, and smash his head in. And then you leave. That's how you do it. But you have to know that he's not going to hear you because he's a strong man and a fighter. Why would he sit at a conference table and let someone walk up behind him?

Maybe Tom would know. How long would all that take? Couple of minutes. Who could do it? Anyone. Bennett couldn't account for his time—Golden couldn't either. But you don't expect people to account for two minutes at the end of a workday. Maybe it was longer, but not much. What about bloodstains? Donna cleaned up the statuette, but there was blood on the conference table. If you swung a blunt object hard enough to cave in a skull like Irving's, there had to be some splashing. He'd have to talk to the lab guys.

Cesar's thoughts had carried him nearly to Winton Place, and it was time to prep for Enneking. Louis Golden said he lived in a grim place, called Schloss Enneking. Look up Schloss before you use it. Don't call anyone a neff. Joe Enneking's family used to own Golden Time Toys.

Louie's theory: Joseph thinks he's been robbed. Grace's caution: Louie slings the bull.

Cesar understood a little better why Enneking stayed in Winton Place when he saw the house. It was big. The house stood smack in the center of an acre of lawn and it looked like a castle. A German castle. Blue spruces and thick hedge separated the Enneking lot from the neighbors on either side. Every other house on the street was run-down ordinary. Most of them were pretty dreary looking. Cesar knew that Winton Place was going through the same problems as a lot of other neighborhoods. The old people, people who had spent lifetimes here, were dying off and the hillbillies were moving in. Appalachian persons and older citizens. Cesar appreciated the intent of the human relations nomenclature training the City Manager had ordered, but it was a pain in the neck. He never once heard a hillbilly call a fellow hillbilly an Appalachian person. They called each other Gene or Bobby. But Joseph Enneking was well isolated from the culture clash. The castle walls were thick enough to withstand full-scale war.

Cesar, prepare yourself for dogs . . .

He pulled an old-fashioned bell knob and heard a low gong. Dogs there were. Please, God, don't make them Dobermans. Dobermans are crazy. Whatever they were, they were right behind the door and they wanted his liver.

"Who is it?" Someone was at the door.

"Detective Franck, Cincinnati Police. I'm looking for Joseph Enneking."

"Just a minute."

Please. Chain the dogs. Muzzle them. A man slipped out of the door.

"I'm Joseph Enneking."

At last. Someone else in a tie.

Enneking was a big man; he looked down on Cesar. His thin blond hair was plastered straight back from his forehead. His suit and tie were black. His appearance, the baying dogs, and the menacing bulk of the castle combined to convey a less than cordial welcome for Cesar. Maybe he should listen more carefully to Louis Golden.

"Mr. Enneking, I'd like to talk to you about Irving Golden."

Enneking stared down at him for a moment before he answered.

"Of course, come in." He opened the door. There was a moment of stark terror when Cesar saw that the dogs were loose and headed for the door. Before he could bolt he saw that the dogs were going to run past him. They were interested only in the shrubbery.

"My Weimaraners. Do you know Weimaraners?"

"No, sir."

"Beautiful dogs. They are a little excited. I had to lock them up while I was away. I have been to see Mrs. Golden. Please come in."

They weren't going to believe this in Westwood. It really was a castle. Schloss Enneking featured a two-story hall as big as the sanctuary at Harrison Avenue Reformed. Enneking's ikons were animal heads, moose, deer, deer, possible boar, more deer, what must be an elk, a mountain goat, and over the walk-in fireplace, three bears. The staircase made Frederick Golden's look spindly. It led to a gallery from which the second-story rooms opened. Two enormous iron chandeliers provided feeble illumination.

Cesar fought and lost the battle to keep his chin from dropping.

"You have not been here before," said Enneking. "I don't have many visitors."

"How old is it?"

"Not as old as it looks. My grandfather designed the house in 1886, but my father did not complete it until 1928. I was born here. It is unusual. Will you come with me?" He opened a door into a corridor and marched ahead. Cesar followed.

After the stupendous space of the hall, the corridor felt cramped. Where the hell were they going? Torture room? Armory?

"This way." Enneking opened a door and waved Cesar in. "This is my office." Not a torture room—a toy room. It was full of toys, all displayed in open cases. The display very nearly distracted Cesar from his mission, for the toys were not the Denver Dolls, Patty Raccoons, or exploding crayons he had seen in Irving Golden's office. These were toys from years past. Toys that did things. Rich kids' toys, poor kids' toys. Toy jugglers, toy cars, toy dragons, tumbling Chinamen, clawing tigers. A toy Chrysler Airflow called to Cesar and he came. He touched it—couldn't help himself. The doors worked.

"Do you like that?"

"It's an Airflow, isn't it? I've seen pictures of them, but I never saw a real one."

"That's correct. Do you like cars?"

"Sure."

Cesar moved to look at the fire wagon when his eye fell on the toy of his dreams. It was a service station. Not the one he had had as a boy. This was a twenties version of the gas station of the future. For a moment Cesar understood murder. He wanted that gas station very badly. It sat on its own table, surrounded by cars from the same era in the same scale. Pipes led from the tank on the roof to gas pumps with real hoses. Had it been real it would have covered half a city block. There was an up ramp and a down ramp, an elevator, a bizarre automobile washer, a pit, thousands of tools, a body shop, a showroom, an office with desks, and, for some reason, a small radio station. Cesar stepped back to admire the front. Printed across the upper half in bright blue letters a full story high were the words "Joseph's Mammoth Garage."

"I like that," said Cesar.

"It is nice, isn't it?"

"I've never seen one like it."

"As far as I know it is the only one. My father had it built for me."

"Did you collect all these?" asked Cesar.

"No. My grandfather started the collection. My father added to it. It is not the largest collection, but there are several things that make it unusual. Would you like to know about it?"

"Sure."

"Every toy in this room was made here in Cincinnati," Enneking began. Cesar followed him from case to case. Some of the toys were one of a kind, some had been mass-produced. Many were products of the Queen City Toy Company, the business started by the Ennekings which was now Golden Time Toys. A few of the toys besides the garage had been commissioned by the family. The majority of them were for boys. There were no dolls, but there were stoves that worked, washing machines and a spectacularly real bungalow with central heating and a roof that lifted off. There was one other theme besides local origin that unified the collection. The toys were meant for children. These weren't political toys. There was no Early Learning, no effort to ape the Indians or the Africans. There were lots of sharp edges and plenty of places to catch tiny fingers. Enough to give Ralph Nader heart failure.

"I've never seen anything like this," said Cesar when the tour was over.

"There *is* no other collection like it." Enneking's answer was without arrogance. It was a statement of fact. "And now that I have shown you all of this, I must ask you not to speak of it," said Enneking.

"All right," said Cesar.

"You're puzzled?"

"It's your business."

"Security. I have no alarm system, no Israeli locks." There was a touch of contempt. "I have only my Weimaraners. They serve to discourage the hoodlums who live in Winton Place, but the dogs are not killers. You are a policeman. You know that dogs can be handled by anyone with a little intelligence. And my dogs are gentle at heart."

Cesar wouldn't have put the Weimaraners to the test. The three of them outweighed even a slightly overweight policeman.

"Now, would you care for something to drink? I am going to have some whiskey."

"No, thanks."

"Please carry on with your questions. I am quite ready."

Cesar put Enneking through the obligatory questions about the meeting, but he found himself distracted by Enneking's speech, which sounded foreign, even though he was born in Winton Place. It wasn't so much his accent, although that didn't sound like a Cincinnatian's, but there was something formal about the way he put things. He made no effort to be a regular guy, the way most businessmen seemed to. Maybe that's the way you talk if you live in a castle, Cesar concluded.

"And now I imagine you wish to ask me about the order of departure after the meeting. *I* would ask that since it obviously has significant bearing on Irving Golden's murder."

"Well, yes," said Cesar.

And Enneking listed the order. It fit with the other versions, but Enneking had noticed more and was able to say which way each person had gone and to estimate the approximate time of each departure. He had even listened for automobiles to start and could therefore verify, at least to his satisfaction, that some people had left.

"Now that I have told you these things I must say that it tells you nothing. I have thought a great deal about this event and I have reached certain conclusions. Certainly you have, too. You must agree with me that it will do you no good to determine who left the parking lot and when they left unless they can prove that they went someplace immediately and were seen there from that time until the murder was reported. I assume, by the way, that Mrs. Creech reported the murder. Am I correct?"

Cesar nodded. Enneking went on.

"Those of us who cannot prove that we went straight to a cafe or church or some such thing, we have a problem. We are aware that Mr. Golden was bludgeoned to death. We also are aware that he was probably bludgeoned very soon after the last of us left and that such an act would not take long—no more than two or three minutes. Even those of us who drove straight home will have a difficult time proving that we did so. Who notices a car on the road? Have you also reached this conclusion?"

"I've looked at that angle, yes, sir."

"I cannot prove that I was not two or three minutes late coming home. I came home to my dogs. They don't remember these things."

Cesar understood that Enneking had made what was, for him, a joke.

"I have nothing to tell you that could eliminate me as a possible candidate. If I could, I would."

"What do you know about Donna Creech?"

Enneking turned red immediately, but Cesar couldn't tell if he was angry or embarrassed.

"I know that she is a slut. That she lives with Negroes. That she is indiscreet and nosy. That she had filthy habits and that she is a lazy and ineffective worker. She is also a liar."

So this is not your favorite cleaning lady.

"I will strongly recommend to Frederick Golden that he fire Mrs. Creech at once. That is what I would do if the company were mine."

Cesar thought the man was going to start banging tables in a minute.

"Why do you suppose Irving Golden kept her on?" he asked.

Enneking barked a laugh.

"There is no point in asking me why Irving Golden did anything. If I were completely demented I could not make my brain work like his. He had one concern and that was profit. After profit he thought life was a joke to be played on honorable people. I can only guess that Mrs. Creech was one of his jokes. Will you excuse me, Detective Franck? I must recall my dogs. Please wait here."

Enneking left Cesar with the toys. They were distracting. This was the time to look for the keys to Joseph Enneking, but when would Cesar see the Mammoth Garage again? He carefully placed a red Maxwell on the elevator and took it to the roof and was about to send it down the ramp when he heard a loud flurry of toenails in the corridor. The pack of Weimaraners burst into the room and Enneking followed to find Cesar holding the Maxwell high in the air as the hunting dogs kissed his neck.

"Rudi! Max! Toni! Down!" The pack obeyed. Nice doggies.

"I was playing with the garage," Cesar confessed.

"That's all right. Please sit down."

When they had sat and the dogs had settled down, Cesar started to speak but Enneking beat him to it.

"It occurred to me that I should explain my feelings about Irving Golden. There is no reason you should not know. I detested Irving Golden as my father detested Irving's father. Do you have children, Detective Franck?"

"No, sir."

"Neither do I, but that does not mean I do not understand paternity and paternal feelings. My grandfather and my father considered the Queen City Toy Company to be their child. They loved the company and they loved their toys. Like fathers. Had it not been for the financial ruin caused by this house, I should have been the father of Queen City Toys. But we Ennekings are not smart about money. The Goldens— Irving and his father—were very smart. More important, they were cold-blooded in a way we could never be. Irving's father watched my father like a hawk all the time that he was an employee. It did not matter that my father had given him a job and his trust. When he saw my father's financial weakness he took advantage of it without a qualm. Without mercy. And my father was very weak. And sentimental. He had to choose between the family company and the family home. I do not blame him. I would have chosen the home, but perhaps I would have fought more thoroughly for the business. The Goldens thought he was stupid, but they had no sense of the finer things. They do not understand what a house can mean. Have you ever seen their house?"

Cesar nodded.

"It is so vulgar. I was just there. I called on his widow. Have you met her?"

"Yes."

"I do not know when I have felt so uncomfortable. The family made me feel like an intruder when I was in fact behaving properly. They made it abundantly clear that they consider me responsible for the death of Irving Golden. Can you imagine such rudeness? I am glad I went, though. It was the correct thing to do whether they know it or not."

Enneking snapped his fingers and one of the Weimaraners trotted over and placed its head on Enneking's knee. Enneking stroked its ears.

"They're probably pretty upset, sir," said Cesar.

"That was obvious. I have seen such wailing and moaning only among Negroes and Italians. Even the son was keening. Such a false young man."

"Mr. Enneking, could we talk about the toy company for a minute? I just have a few more questions and I'll get out of your way." Cesar did not like hearing about the Goldens from Enneking. So what if Louis was a phoney? His father was dead.

Cesar asked if there were any major problems within the business, anything besides the Denver Doll commercial. He didn't expect a full answer from Enneking, but he might hear something reflecting poorly on the Goldens.

"Security" was the prompt answer. Enneking thought Golden had been penny-wise and pound foolish about security measures. He had trusted in a slow learner, Loyal Leonard, rather than a Doberman service recommended by Enneking, and he had cut labor costs through the use of seasonal and part-time help rather than permanent employees such as the Ennekings had. It was Enneking's opinion that the recent and fairly steady leak of developmental secrets could be traced to one of those economies. There was no loyalty to be had from seasonal employees. And the mention of seasonal employees led to a diatribe about the failure to develop true industrial craftsmen dedicated to the art of fine toys. To Cesar it sounded as if he were in agreement with Frederick Golden. So he asked.

"Did Frederick Golden go along with his brother?"

"I consider Frederick Golden to be much more reasonable than his brother. He was, however, unable to influence Irving in any matter of taste. He is not a strong man."

Cesar looked at his watch. He wasn't getting anywhere that he could see. He stood up and began to take his leave.

"I will see you to the door," said Enneking.

In the afternoon gloom the corridor seemed like a tunnel, and when they reached the great hall it was so dark that Cesar could not see the ceiling. After the cheer of the toy room the rest of the house was cold. Cesar did not envy Enneking his castle, only his toys.

The dogs had followed them to the door, and as Enneking opened it they burst out for another run. Two of the dogs dampened Cesar's radials and all three ran out toward the street to bark at a group of boys. When the three dogs sang together the noise was unbearable. Suddenly there was a screech and a hound came racing back to the house with its tail between its legs. One of the boys must have thrown something. Enneking raced to the street but the boys had scattered. When he returned his face was twisted with rage.

"Is your dog all right?" Cesar asked. He sincerely hoped Enneking wasn't going to have a stroke; he didn't care about the dog. Enneking examined the animal which was still whining and licking its side. Enneking's hands shook as he stroked the point of impact. There was no blood.

"Kids," said Cesar. What could he say? He had zinged a few dogs in his youth.

"They are filth. Those boys are filth," said Enneking. He continued to stroke, crooning softly, "Rudi, poor Rudi." It was Enneking who needed the calming. Rudi had forgotten his wound and was basking in the attention.

Cesar left Enneking with his dogs. He drove slowly through Winton Place, switching on his headlights in the twilight. The little houses looked less depressing. There were lights on inside, and he could no longer see the peeling paint outside. The abundance of aged Oldsmobiles and Chevrolets parked in the street gave the only visible sign that Winton Place was ailing. It would be nice to go straight home to healthy Westwood, but Cesar dutifully headed for Central Station.

His route skirted Spring Grove Cemetery. He wondered if that was Irving Golden's destination. Must be. That was the final club membership for all the big industrial families. He was willing to bet the Ennekings were buried there in a small castle. It wouldn't be the only castle either. There were plenty of efforts to take it with you when you went to Spring Grove.

Since it was Saturday evening, Spring Grove Avenue was nearly empty. Cesar decided to follow it on into town. The same twilight which had softened the edges of Winton Place worked its charm on Spring Grove Avenue. Normally the six lanes were full of trucks, but tonight Cesar and a few other motorists found themselves on a spacious, almost grand thoroughfare. The towers of the grand Clifton mansions were still barely visible, high on their hill to the east. The factories to the west were darkened for the weekend. They bore the names of the mansion builders to the east, and those same builders rested in Spring Grove Cemetery, just over Cesar's shoulder. A tidy triangle.

12

By the time Cesar reached Central Station it was dark. Detective Griesel was on duty, eating yogurt and reading a law volume.

"You've got messages." She waved her spoon at Cesar's desk.

"Surprise," said Cesar.

"And Lieutenant Tieves wants to see you. He'll be here in a few minutes."

"Terrific."

"You getting anywhere on the Golden case?"

"Carole, I'm trying to read my messages. Wait a minute."

"Got your budget narrative done?"

Cesar ignored her.

Ms. Creech called. Will call back.

Ms. Franck called. Message: Pick up some ammonia.

Ms. Grace Golden called. Message: Thank you for the car. (You never gave *me* a car. C.G.)

Leon Wilson (*Enquirer*) called. Please call.

Ms. Creech called. Will call back.

Sgt. Evans called. Message: I told you to call twice.

Cesar took a deep breath and called Sgt. Evans. The Sergeant's habits were well known. Abstemious through the week, Saturday evenings he plowed his way through a six-pack of Hudepohl. Mrs. Evans, when their children were young, had found it prudent to take the children out for a Saturday night supper and movie, leaving her husband to kick the cat and the television. The children were grown now, but she still sought refuge elsewhere. Occasionally she dropped in on Lillian Franck.

The call was all that Cesar had feared. Sgt. Evans was into his fourth can. He was blistering in his contempt of Cesar's efforts. Cesar was an idiot, an overeducated bum, a tea drinker, a pussy footer. Did he think he was working for some suburban police force? Did he hope Golden's murderer would be polite and turn himself in because Cesar was such a nice guy? Did Cesar really think he was going to solve anything by going out and kissing a lot of asses in Walnut Hills,

Mt. Lookout, and Terrace Park? Did he anticipate at any time taking off the kid gloves? Kicking ass? Taking names? Was Griesel on duty? Was she eating yogurt? Would Cesar mind slipping over and sprinkling rat poison on her wheat germ? Did Cesar know that Lt. Tieves was coming in? Was he going to have some evidence of work for the lieutenant? Were there any real cops left in Cincinnati? Cesar heard a snarl from the cat and a clatter of beer cans. It was hard to believe that this same maniac would be sitting in the Westwood Methodist Church tomorrow morning, clean shaven and asleep. But he would.

Cesar heard Lt. Tieves arriving.

"Hang on a second, Sergeant," said Cesar, and he put his superior on hold.

"I'll be right with you, sir. It's Sergeant Evans."

The lieutenant nodded and walked over to talk to Detective Griesel, who had trashed her yogurt carton just in time. She favored the lieutenant with her exhausted-but-still-at-work-smile, and the lieutenant favored her with his I'm-a-cop-but-I'm-a human-being-too grin. Politics. Always politics. Cesar punched back in on Sgt. Evans.

"N'T EVER DO THAT, YOU HEAR ME? NEVER DO THAT! FRANCK! FRANCK!"

"I'm back, Sergeant. Sorry."

"IF YOU EVER PUT ME ON HOLD AGAIN, DETECTIVE FRANCK, I WILL PERSONALLY KILL YOU MYSELF. DO YOU HEAR ME?"

"Right, Sergeant."

"Where was I? Oh, yeah. Tieves. Who's on duty, Griesel?"

"Right, sir."

"Did she get her yogurt under the desk in time? Is she kissing ass?"

"Right on both counts, Sergeant."

"I've changed my mind. If you ever put me on hold again I will find some way to team you permanently with Detective Griesel. How do you like that, Cesar?"

"I'll try to avoid that."

"You do that. And listen, sonny, I know how you're going to handle Lieutenant Tieves and I know he's going to buy that crap about how many miles you've traveled and how you're starting to get a picture and a feel for things, but you remember that I *don't* buy that crap and I'm going to want to hear that you've got your hands on something besides smoke tomorrow, understand?"

"Right, Sergeant."

"And you're going to check in with me at least twice tomorrow, understand?"

"Right."

"Only not in the morning because I'll be at church, understand?"

"I've got it, Sergeant."

"And Cesar, don't forget the budget."

"Right, Sergeant. I won't forget."

Sgt. Evans dropped the phone on the hook.

"Sorry, Lieutenant. The Sergeant wanted to go over some things."

"No problem, Franck. Come on into my office."

Cesar followed him into the operating theater, studiously ignoring whatever wise-ass grin Detective Griesel might have pasted on.

"Saturday night. Sergeant Evans' party must be well under way," said Lt. Tieves. Cesar grunted respectfully.

"Well, Cesar, what do you know?" asked the Lieutenant.

Cesar filled him in on his day. The Lieutenant was particularly interested in Enneking and his castle.

"So that's who lives there. I've been by it plenty of times but I never knew. It's a screwy place. What's it doing there?" Cesar told him what he had picked up about the house and described it, but he didn't mention the toys. He did tell the Lieutenant about Enneking's relationship to the company and his disagreement with Golden's way of doing things.

"Did you piss off any of these guys, Cesar?" asked the Lieutenant out of the blue.

"No, sir. I don't think so. Maybe Atwood a little, but not much."

"Good. That's good, Cesar. Okay, go on."

And Cesar launched into a listing of the problems and angles associated with each of the interviews. Lt. Tieves got up and paced while Cesar talked. Cesar figured the Lieutenant stood up when he wanted to look even more impressive, so he expected to hear a little disagreement.

"Cesar, it sounds like you're doing okay, but I can't help thinking . . ."

Cesar waited.

"Do you *know* what you're doing?"

"Sir?"

"It looks to me like you're following up on a lot of business angles, and I see what you're doing, but . . ."

Cesar waited.

"You've got a violent murder here. Violent. But you're dealing with executives. And I know we don't limit murder to blacks and Appalachian persons, but it is rare—and I mean really rare—that you see someone as far up in management as the men you're dealing with go off the tracks like that."

"I know that, sir, I—"

"I'm not stopping you, Cesar. I've got confidence in you. Just like anyone in the squad, but I'm not sure you know enough about business. What I'm saying is that business is tough. It's dog-eat-dog. But businessmen are used to it. Some of the angles, some of the motives you're looking at may sound a lot worse to you than they really are. Do you follow me?"

"Yes, sir."

"But?"

"But that's the group I've got to work with. That's who was with him. They're the only ones who could have gotten back in that building." Cesar explained the security system and Irving's Israeli lock again.

"What about other keys? Have you checked that out?" asked Lt. Tieves. Cesar told him about the duplicate in the safe-deposit box, but as he did he felt his stomach drop. He hadn't checked to see if anyone had gotten it out.

"All right, Cesar. You know what you're doing. But be careful. Keep checking back with me about these business angles. I'll handle them, you understand? If you don't . . . understand them."

"Right, sir."

"What did you say to Atwood? That you think pissed him off?"

"Nothing, Lieutenant. What happened was he's kind of a wise guy. I didn't think he was very funny."

"And you let him know it?"

"I didn't get tough, sir. If that's what you mean."

"Good. Don't." The Lieutenant seemed to be satisfied. "What are you doing tonight?"

"I was going home, sir. Try to work a little on the budget. I'll be out again tomorrow."

"Good. Good. Keep it up. You're doing fine. You'll still be pretty much on your own, you know. I told the Chief we didn't have the manpower to pull to help you. You can have Chapman if you absolutely have to or if things get too hot, but I want you by yourself if possible. Understand?"

I understand. Budget move. Manpower politics. The Homicide Squad has been crippled by recent budget cutbacks and is doing the best it can with extremely limited resources. Panic to the Council.

"Yes, sir," said Cesar.

"Take off. See you Monday."

"Right, sir."

Cesar beat it back to his desk where he found the budget forms. There had been no miraculous completion by elves while he was out.

"Your Mrs. Creech called again," said Detective Griesel.

"She did? Why didn't you get me out?"

"I didn't want to interrupt the Lieutenant."

"Thanks a lot, Carole. Jeez. Did she leave a number?"

"She said she'd call back."

"Well, listen. If she calls back, give her my home number. Okay? Can you remember that, Carole?"

"I can remember that, Cesar. Can you remember to finish your budget narrative?"

Cesar didn't have an answer. If he said what he wanted to say, he'd have the Human Relations Commission on him like a ton of bricks. He got his coat and papers and turned to give her a shitty look, but she and Lt. Tieves were back to their professional discussion. Wishful thinking on both their parts. Cesar had met Mrs. Tieves. She might dress like Donna Reed, but she would run her sewing scissors through Detective Griesel's neck if she thought there was a threat from that quarter. Lt. Tieves could kiss his promotion goodbye if he was known to monkey around with the lady detectives. Let them dream.

Cesar headed for the parking lot.

13

CESAR'S HOUSE FELT small. He had spent the day in grand houses, houses with entry halls bigger than the Franck's living room, dining room, kitchen, and vestibule. Heating bills, he reminded himself. Heating bills.

Lillian was washing up.

"Did you remember the ammonia?" she asked.

"Oh, Mom, I'm sorry. I'll go get some."

"No, that's okay. Get it tomorrow. I was thinking I'd do a few windows before we go to Kathy's. There won't be time to strip the floor."

They both looked at the gleaming linoleum. To most eyes the floor would have appeared spotless and superbly waxed. But Lillian had been a Fletemeyer, and the Fletemeyers had set for themselves the highest standards of household cleanliness. In a city of tidy kitchens, the Fletemeyers had no equals. And since Lillian had trained her son, he was able to distinguish the palest beginning of a yellow cast in the wax. She was right. Time to strip.

"I'll get it next week, Mom."

"There's tuna casserole in the fridge."

Cesar warmed the tuna in the microwave, poured a glass of milk, and sat down with the Saturday papers. He ate and read. A slug of carbon tetrachloride making its way down the Ohio from Charleston had pushed Irving Golden from the front page. Cincinnatians were not to worry immediately. The city would close its intake until the slug was downriver and on its way to Louisville. There was supposed to be plenty of water in the reservoirs to handle the washing and drinking until the crisis was over. Cesar would pick up some bottled water when he got the ammonia. Why take a chance?

The third page had a feature on Irving and Golden Time Toy Company. There was no information new to Cesar, but he was interested in the highly flattering tone and stress on the Golden management skills. According to the article, the Queen City Toy Company was a bankrupt, two-bit firm which had been run into the ground by the previous (unnamed) owners. Irving and his dad had turned the company around and made it a real powerhouse, using hot new marketing concepts and twentieth-century management. If Cesar hadn't seen the beautiful toys from the pre-Golden years he wouldn't have given the article a second thought. Maybe Queen City Toys wasn't a powerhouse, but it had been a high-quality outfit. Enneking wasn't going to enjoy reading this.

Cesar looked up the obituary. Funeral Sunday, tomorrow. Interment, Spring Grove.

He went back to the third page to see if Lt. Tieves had gotten his licks in. He had. The Homicide Squad was doing the best it could with the highly limited resources and manpower available. He regretted that recent budget actions had made it impossible to bring the squad to a level of readiness appropriate to a city of this size. Cesar expected an editorial supporting a budget hike for the Homicide Squad in the next couple of days. Big deal. Budget hikes equal bigger staff, not bigger salaries.

Budget. Do the Budget Narrative Forms.

Cesar washed his dishes, wiped the counters, and damp mopped the floor. When he couldn't think of any other delays, he spread his budget forms on the dinette, sharpened two pencils, fixed a cup of Maxim, and sat down to work.

When, after half an hour, inspiration would not come, he began to use the large budget form as a scratch sheet. He wrote:

Phillip Bennett—Saves agency contract. Nothing to lose (dying).
Frederick Golden—Thinks he will run company. Wants money and new products.
Bob Atwood—Saves agency contract (but probably didn't know). General jerk.
Jos. Enneking—Revenge. Wants different products. Hates Irving.
Jack Squires—Saves job. Needs money. Commando.
Tom Cleary—My buddy, not a tough guy.
*Marianne Kelly—Hothead, insulted by Golden.
Rosemary Meynell—No known grievance.
*Evelyn Osborne—No known grievance.

And for the asterisks he put *needs interview*.

He read and reread the list until it became as baffling to him as the Budget Narrative Form. Every last person on the list was intelligent, successful (or about to be so), and fairly normal. Even if Golden Time and The Bennett Agency closed their doors forever, these people would do all right. Some of the motives were strong. He could see that. But none of them seemed the kind to make you run in and club somebody to death on the spur of the moment. This was stuff for lawyers, accountants, or politicians. He hadn't heard a single mention of gambling, woman troubles, or drugs. Maybe Lt. Tieves had a point. Maybe Cesar couldn't understand business problems. Maybe business problems had it all over gambling, women, and drugs. But if that was the case, why weren't there daily businessmen's shootouts on Fourth Street? Out of this whole group of people, only one seemed to be anywhere close to unhinged and that was Enneking.

Cesar remembered Enneking's fury when his dog got hurt. Was that normal? It was hard to say. Cesar had been kind of edgy himself just from being in the Enneking castle. What did Louis Golden call the place? Schloss Enneking.

"Mom!"

"I'm in the bathroom." Time for her weekend soak. He went to the door.

"What does 'schloss' mean?"

"Castle."

He went back to the kitchen, sat down, and stared at his forms and his notes. Maybe he shouldn't think it was all business. Just because people had filled him full of business talk for the past two days didn't necessarily mean that Irving Golden died for profit or loss. Who started the business talk anyway? Donna Creech. She came to the station and told him that the toy people and the advertising people had been up in arms over business. Everybody else had followed her lead. *Everybody* assumed this was a corporate offense. Drugs? Women? Gambling? Why not? Who's to say Irving didn't run a profitable coke operation? Maybe someone is in love with Irene Golden. Maybe Irving took bets. Maybe Irving had the hots for somebody's wife. All right, maybe those don't sound like your winning theories, but that doesn't mean there's not an angle besides business.

Cesar blushed to think how polite he'd been all day today and yesterday. He was so respectful of people with money and slick jobs that he hadn't even considered leaning on them about drugs or women or horses. Could he go back in and get tough since he'd been such a polite policeman? Did he need to? What would it get him? Lies. Lies for sure if there were drugs. Drugs made the best people into liars. Everybody who did drugs thought it was okay to lie about them. Not so bad when it's poor people, they don't have much time for truth and truth doesn't pay. But Cesar's people. Middle-class people. People who went to school and had plenty of clothes and both parents. People who weren't going to get the goofy kinds of cancer and blood problems poor people got. They were lying now. Habitually. Because of drugs.

Cesar wondered if Tom did drugs. Had Walnut Hills High School taught him how to lie and not be bothered by it? When they were kids they didn't lie. Cesar knew that for a fact. He would ask Tom tomorrow. Give him a test. Tomorrow. What about tonight? What about these Budget Forms and was Donna Creech ever going to call?

Lillian came in. She was bright red from her soaker. She asked Cesar what he was doing and why he had to do it at home and why did he have to do budgets when he was a detective and when did he think he was going to bed and whether he had some plan for getting out of Sunday dinner with Kathy.

Cesar told her he didn't have a plan he really had to work and guess who he was going to see—Tom Cleary—and he didn't know why he had to do the stupid budget and yes he would drop her off at church and he was really sorry he couldn't eat at Kathy's and don't give him the fisheye he really had work to do. He also asked if Donna Creech had called while he was driving over.

No.

Lillian went to bed with *The Thornbirds*.

Cooey bono. He didn't know how to spell it, but he loved to say it. His brother-in-law, the lawyer, tossed it off one day and Cesar like the sound so much he swallowed his pride and asked Fred what it meant. Cooey Bono. Sonny's brother. Cooey and Cher. Who gets the bono from Irving? Everybody except Irene and Grace and maybe Rosemary They're going to miss him. Maybe Menachem Begin will, too.

Cooey bono? Joesph Enneking, Frederick Golden, and all of The Bennett Agency. Please, God, let it be drugs. Too much bono. Maybe Tom knew how to spell it. He would ask.

Cesar stacked his papers neatly and put them on the stereo in the living room. He gave up. He was tired and confused.

He checked the locks and turned out lights and had started up to bed when he remembered something.

Cesar went down to the basement and searched through the boxes marked *Cesar*. The bottom two were toys and in the first one he found what he was looking for. His stamped metal garage. He set it on the laundry table and fiddled with it. It was still in good shape. Ed the mechanic still stood smiling, printed on a wall beside a stack of tires. It was not Joseph's Mammoth Garage, but it was worth hanging on to. He put it back carefully and started restacking the boxes. The telephone rang upstairs. Would Lillian get it? No. She would know it was for him. He hustled the rest of the boxes back into place and ran up the stairs, but when he picked up the receiver he was too late.

Donna Creech. Had to be Donna. He called Communications. It was Donna. No, she didn't leave a number.

Damn it.

Cesar went to bed.

14

AT 1:00 P.M. SUNDAY afternoon Cesar sat in his Camaro, which was parked on Ninth Street in front of The Bennett Agency Offices. He was still enjoying a state of Sunday well-being and hoped that Tom Cleary would not destroy it by arriving late.

Cesar had slept until eight-thirty, taken a long shower, fixed a big breakfast for himself and Lillian, and read the paper. Mrs. Franck had been prepared to wear him down with her powerful fisheye. She still wanted him to come to dinner at his sister's. But Cesar was in a good humor and his breakfast of sausage, eggs, and biscuits deflected his mother from her planned attack. By the time Cesar had done two or three imitations of his brother-in-law reacting to the newspaper, Lillian fell in with his good mood. She even did the dishes while he drove to the Kroger for ammonia and allowed him to drive her to the Harrison Avenue Reformed Church. He had watched her climb the long front steps to the church door and concluded that, of all the grey-haired ladies in purple church coats, she had the most class.

Cesar's mood was improved even more when, stopping at the station to drop off his budget forms and pick up news, he discovered Henry on duty and in a grossly hungover funk. The black detective was hiding behind mirrored sunglasses, but Cesar knew that his eyes would look like maps of West Virginia. Henry's fringe of hair was spikey, and he was slumped behind his desk in a position of surrender. Cesar switched on Sgt. Evans' desk radio to country music. He sat on his own desk and watched Henry deteriorate even more. After a few minutes Henry began to groan. When he had decided that Henry was sufficiently weakened, Cesar went to the sandwich machine and got a tuna sandwich, which he proceeded to eat in front of his associate. Halfway through the sandwich Henry snapped. He jumped from his chair, knocking it over in the process, staggered to Sgt. Evans' desk, and smashed his fist down on the radio, silencing it forever. Cesar smiled, finished his tuna, and began to whistle.

Cesar's sister had once told him that when her dog would prick up his ears, whine, and crawl under the sofa for no apparent reason, she knew that somewhere in Greater Cincinnati her brother was whistling. She had further informed him that she would bet on his whistle against an industrial laser any day. For Henry's benefit Cesar launched into a highly ornamented version of "Hey, Jude." Henry began to cry and staggered off to the toilet, leaving Cesar very gratified. It was not right that Henry should be so dumpy and obnoxious, yet blessed with a string of sensational girlfriends. It pleased Cesar to punish him whenever possible.

Cesar sat in the car and smiled at the memory.

Ninth Street was empty. Even during the week when the streets to the south were hopping, Ninth Street, untouched by urban development and lacking any draw for shopper or diner, was quiet. On Sunday it was downright sepulchral. Flanked by empty dark red brick buildings, Cesar's Camaro was the only car on the street. Cesar, sitting inside the Camaro, began to feel not only chilly but slightly spooked. When a battered green Volvo pulled up behind him and parked, Cesar checked in the rearview mirror to make sure it was Tom before he got out.

"Been waiting long?" asked Tom.

"Nope," said Cesar.

Tom let him into the Bennett offices. The agency shared a six-story building with a printing firm. On his first visit Cesar's attention had been absorbed by the astonishing Haitian receptionist. Now he noticed how small and almost shabby the lobby was.

"It's a dump, isn't it?" said Tom. "Mr. Bennett won't fix it up. He keeps saying we'll move. Come on back. Hit those lights, will you?" He pointed to a row of switches by the receptionist's window and Cesar complied.

"Is there an alarm?" asked Cesar.

"What's to steal?" asked Tom. Cesar shrugged and followed him through the door leading to the offices.

"Welcome to the glamorous world of advertising," said Tom. "Did you ever see such a mess?" They were in a narrow passageway possessed of the glamour of a wino hotel. Cesar recognized the paint as navy surplus pea green. Glancing up he saw that the walls stopped at seven feet. The ceiling was well beyond that. The Bennett Agency filled what was once open industrial work space. High overhead, the great long banks of fluorescent bulbs washed the cubicles in a cold green light, revealing dust that could have been laid down before Bennett moved in, as well as black fingerprints on every door frame. The place was grimy. And messy. Dusty boxes, piles of paper, rolled up posters, and dead coffee makers made the passageway an obstacle course. Cesar's good manners fought a round with his housekeeping instincts and lost.

"Who does your cleaning?" he asked.

"Nice of you to call it that," said Tom. "There actually is somebody paid to tidy up. It's a guy named Ted Harris. He owns a bar on Burnet and comes down here to rest from the rigors of management. Taught Donna Creech everything she knows about maintenance."

"Why do you keep him?"

"I don't. Mr. Bennett does."

"Why does he?"

"Apparently thirty years ago he decided Ted was oppressed. It's a gesture."

"He ought to be sued," said Cesar.

"What's funny is when we have clients in for a meeting, Mr. Bennett calls a real cleaning firm himself to do the meeting rooms. He *is* aware of the problem. This is my office."

All the talk about cleaning reminded Cesar that Donna Creech, girl office cleaner, was trying to reach him. "Can I use your phone?" he asked Tom.

"Sure. Dial nine."

Cesar called his office and raised Henry from the dead. He told Henry where he was and gave him the number of Tom's phone in case Donna wanted to reach him. Henry's only response was a directive to Cesar to commit an offense upon himself, but Cesar felt certain that Henry had recorded the information. He whistled through the telephone to remind Henry who had seniority as well as a clear head and then hung up. He looked around Tom's office.

Like the rest of the offices, it was a topless cubicle decorated in dust and paper. There were a lot of memos taped to the walls. There were also a couple of ads and what looked like comic strips drawn by children. Two things caught his attention more than the others. One was a little black and white school picture of a girl about ten or eleven. The other was a Denver Doll. The girl in the picture looked vaguely familiar. The Denver Doll was tethered to Tom's in-tray with tiny handcuffs. She had been stripped and someone had drawn net stockings and a garter belt directly on her skin. Cesar tackled the picture first. "Who is that? Someone we went to school with?"

"It's Grace Golden," said Tom.

Cesar looked again. There was no hint of the tough executive to come. She had an open grin and her curly hair was completely out of control. Cesar recognized a Girl Scout scarf. He couldn't help smiling at her.

"How did you get this?" he asked Tom.

"I stole it from her. She hates it. Reminds her she was a human being once."

"She's not now?"

"Not if she can help it." Tom was flushed. He stared at his shoes so Cesar wouldn't see, but he had forgotten his hair loss. Cesar noticed.

"You said you used to go together. What happened?"

"What happened was we stopped going together," said Tom. He was real talkative today.

"But she's pretty nice, isn't she? I mean, she seemed like a really nice girl when I talked to her. I even thought about hitting her up for a date until she said she was going to take over the business." Oops. He hadn't meant to give that out yet.

Tom looked at him. "She told you that? What do you know. Well, you're right. She's a really nice girl, only don't call her that. She's a person now. And she's not going to have time for either of us in her new starring role, but don't feel bad. She probably won't have time for anybody."

"She didn't seem stuck-up to me—or not yet, anyway," said Cesar.

"She's not stuck-up. For Christ's sake, that's the last thing she is. She's the least stuck-up person I ever met."

"Sorry, Tom."

"No, I'm sorry. Jesus. I'm not rational on the subject."

"Did she break it off?"

"No, I did."

"You mean you could still be going with her? Why'd you stop?" Cesar was worried. Maybe Tom was losing his marbles.

"Because I thought she was being stupid about her career. She got it in her head to be a leading businesswoman, and I told her she was a fool. She could afford to stay out of a job, and here she was going after it as if it were something desirable. And for some people I suppose it is."

Cesar didn't say anything. It didn't seem strange to him. Lots of women went into business now. Lillian went into business years ago.

"She thinks she's tough, you know. Real tough. But that's something she's taught herself. She's not a natural bastard. Not like Irving," said Tom.

"Does she have to be a bastard?" asked Cesar.

"No. I don't know. I'm in advertising. I don't *know* anything. Shit. Forget it. Let's talk about something else. You like my Denver Doll?"

Cesar would have been happy to keep talking about Grace, but he looked at the Denver Doll.

"Cute," he said.

"Not cute enough. I only got an honorable mention in our Dollsarama '83 event. But I like it. Should have won."

"Who did win?"

"Come on, I'll show you. All the prize winners are still up."

"Just a second," said Cesar. "How do you spell 'cooey bono'?"

"Hunh?"

"Cooey bono. It's Latin. You should know. It means 'who benefits?'"

114

"Cooey bono? Oh. Wait." Tom muttered to himself a minute and then said "*cui bono*" and spelled it.

"Why?" asked Tom.

"I wanted to use it. It comes in handy, but I wasn't sure about it. My jerk of a brother-in-law told me about it."

"Why didn't you ask him?"

"I didn't want to give him the pleasure."

"Who is he?" asked Tom.

"Fred Kuhne. Remember him?"

"Fred the weasel? Kathy married Fred the weasel?"

"Yeah. He's a lawyer now."

"Gee. I'm sorry."

"Yeah. Let's see the dolls."

"Cui bono," said Tom. "When you're talking about Irving it's easier to say *cui non bono*."

"How much Latin did you have to take?" asked Cesar.

"Years. I don't remember any of it."

"You remembered that."

Tom led Cesar through the maze of cubicles and explained the Dollsarama '83 event. It was an office contest for the best use of a Denver Doll. There were no rules other than the use of the new product in a tableau that would fit on a desk. Most of the tableaux embarrassed Cesar. The grand prize winner had been moved to a table by the coffee maker. Evelyn Osborne had worn for "Chain Saw Mama." He had posed his naked doll with a tiny and bloody chain saw. At her foot lay pieces of what used to be a Soldier Bob doll. Jack Squires took second place with "Reach Out and Touch Someone," which involved the Denver Doll, a toy telephone, and the cheery visitor from outer space who was applying his curative finger to one of the more sensitive spots on the Denver Doll's body.

"They just won because they had movie themes and everyone likes movies," grumped Tom.

Cesar thought there was a lot of goofing off on company time. They continued to tour the building. They poked into Marianne Kelly's office. She hadn't participated in the Dollsarama '83 for political reasons. Her cubicle was a lot neater than Tom's but just as dusty. She had St. Francis' prayer on a poster and pictures of Jane Fonda and Alan Alda.

Jack Squires rated a double-sized cubicle. He had decorated in stuffed kiwis and pictures of the Royal Family. Underneath the Queen Mother was a hand-lettered sign that said "What a gal." He, too, had a dust problem.

"Come on. I'll show you what you get when you're a top dog," said Tom. They worked their way to the back of the building and entered the grandmother of all freight elevators. "How's your insurance?" asked Tom as he pushed the button for the second floor. Cesar's answer was drowned in the creaking and rattling and whining of the lift. He looked at his friend, who was wearing a sadistic grin. "It almost always works," Tom yelled over the noise and indeed it did stop at the second floor, but the thump of the brakes was heart stopping. Cesar followed Tom through an alley of boxes and file cabinets and a plain door into a much more pleasant set of rooms.

"This is where we bring the clients," said Tom. "They never see the crud below. Mr. Bennett's office and Bob Atwood's are up here— and their secretaries." He showed Cesar a large conference room and a "media center" and they poked their heads into Bennett's and Atwood's offices. Bennett's was paneled and carpeted and pleasant. There were pictures of his family on the desk and there were bookcases on the walls. While not completely tidy, it was definitely a cut above the hell-holes on the floor below.

Atwood's office had been done more recently and at greater expense. The paneling was top of the line and the carpet was knee deep. No Atwood family portraits graced the rosewood desk. There were, instead, trophies from the local advertising council awarded to the agency for various efforts. Tom stretched out full-length on the leather Chesterfield sofa.

"I'm pretty sure this cost close to my annual salary. I've been trying to figure out how to booby-trap it."

"How does he rate all this?" asked Cesar.

"I told you. He's the golden boy. The heir apparent. Phillip's great hope for the future."

"Must be nice."

"Nice isn't the word. Go push that button under that picture."

Cesar did as he was told and a section of the wall slid away to reveal a wet bar. Tom stood up, jumped up and down on the sofa a couple of times to scuff it up, and bounced over to the bar. "Name your drink."

Cesar almost declined, but settled on Wild Turkey. Tom poured two. "Marianne spends hours up here. We assume she finds the sofa more comfortable than her modest chair," Tom said. Cesar tried the couch himself. It was indeed comfortable. They sipped their drinks and Cesar popped his question.

"Are you doing drugs?"

Tom stared at him. He didn't answer.

"I'm not going to lock you up. I promise."

"Why?" asked Tom.

"I was thinking last night. About Golden. It's unusual, you know," said Cesar. "This case. You get a big-time murder these days and there's usually drugs somewhere, but I haven't hit any yet."

"What would you say if I said yes?"

"I don't know. Don't do it. You're not supposed to."

"You're such a cop."

"I know."

"I'm glad."

"Why?"

"It means we've got a good police force."

Cesar laughed.

"You remember my dad?" asked Tom. Cesar nodded. "You remember how he was so professionally Irish? He always used to bitch about all the Germans on the police force. He said it wasn't natural. Every other city has Irish cops. He said any place else in the country he could talk or pay his way out of a ticket, but in Cincinnati? No way. Pissed him off. I used to tell him to be grateful—we had the only completely honest police force in the country. But he said it was embarrassing. He still thinks Boston is the highest form of urban life."

"We're not completely honest," said Cesar. "I mean, we've got a couple of funny guys."

"That's what I mean. If all you've got is a couple of 'funny guys,' we're in good hands. Like I said. I'm glad you're one of them."

Cesar wasn't sure he understood.

"No, Cesar. I don't do coke. I don't even do marijuana anymore. I'm getting too old. Some people here do coke and most do marijuana, but not a lot and certainly none of the people at the meeting with Irving. Except maybe Marianne. But she doesn't deal. Nobody deals. We're all basically chicken. We buy."

"Just thought I'd check," said Cesar.

"I take that back. Not about buying, but I'll bet Atwood takes advantage of other people's coke at parties. He'd never buy it himself, but I'll bet he doesn't want to be thought uptight. What a jerk."

Tom walked back over to the bar and looked behind the bottles. "It figures," he said.

"What does?"

"He had a really dirty Dollsarama '83 entry, but it's gone. Banner was down on her knees in front of Cowboy Jack, and when you squeezed her she pushed him on his back. Looked like he'd OD'd on pleasure. But they're gone. I'll bet he cleared it out when he heard Bennett coming back. What a hypocrite."

"Who's Cowboy Jack?"

"Shh . . . " Tom shushed him. "The phone's ringing downstairs." He picked up Atwood's phone, punched two numbers and said, "Bennett Agency." It was for Cesar and it was Henry. Cesar listened, wrote something down, and hung up.

"How do I get out of here?" he asked Tom.

"What's the matter?"

"Donna Creech. Somebody's killed Donna Creech. They just found her. Now how do I get out of here?"

15

"DAMMIT," SNAPPED CESAR. "Dammit. Dammit. Dammit." He hit the steering wheel in his frustration. He was doing eighty on the Mill Creek Expressway and heading for Millvale. What a jerk! What a bum! He had laughed at her. Ignored her. He didn't take her seriously because she was goofy and hung out with Bad Dudes and now she was dead and it was his fault. What a jerk.

He nearly sideswiped an innocent hippy in a Li'l Hustler as he aimed for the Hopple Street ramp. Slow down, Cesar, you dumbass. Jerk. Bum. Jesus. She'd been calling all day yesterday and he never talked to her. He could have gone out to see what she wanted or stayed at the office to catch her call, but he thought he'd done a hard day's work and she would just want to run her mouth. He ought to be fired. Well, not fired. Yelled at. *Something.*

Cesar slammed on his brakes to avoid rear-ending a Buick. He cursed the driver for observing the speed limit. When he reached the housing project where Donna Creech had lived, the speed bumps forced him to a crawl. He wound his way through Millvale searching for the address Henry had given him.

The Millvale project consisted of what seemed to be an endless series of two-story buildings the size and shape of army barracks. Physically it differed only slightly from the other public housing projects in Cincinnati, but it had a well-deserved reputation as the toughest. Cesar had unpleasant memories from his uniform days.

He didn't need to see the house number to know he had found Donna's unit. There was a crowd of residents surrounding the last unit in the last building on Deerpath. Kids were climbing all over the two patrol cars. Two news units had arrived. Cesar parked as close as he could and worked his way through the crowd, bracing himself for the customary verbal abuse. Normally, when there was violent death in the project, the residents could be counted on to punish the visiting cops for failing to prevent the crime. But this crowd was quiet—almost friendly. By the time Cesar reached the door he had heard enough to understand. Donna Creech was white and, in the crowd's estimation, trash. She had gotten no more than she deserved. That made Cesar feel worse. He didn't blame the black residents. Most of the white people he knew were going to take the same stand. But death was a pretty heavy punishment for flouting the rules of race. He flashed his badge to a young cop who didn't know him and went in through Donna's front door.

Henry was inside in the living room talking to a big black policeman. Cesar recognized him as Calvin McFarland. Donna knew McFarland. She had asked Cesar about him Thursday night.

He looked around. The place was a mess. His police eye and his housekeeper's eye separated the recent disorder from the permanent disorder and located underneath both disorders Donna's attempts at black decoration. She had hung pictures of Martin Luther King, Jr., and Malcolm X as well as the Kennedys. Two velvet paintings hung over the sofa, one African warrior and one African princess. Two huge pink ashtrays full of Kool butts sat on a gold coffee table. The twenty-five-inch color set facing the sofa was a Magnavox. There were wires leading to a video game control box which seemed to have been knocked off the top of the television. Still on the television was a family portrait. The family was Donna and a surprisingly middle-class-looking black man with a small boy and a smaller girl.

A white plastic bookshelf lay smashed on the rug; its contents were scattered underfoot. Cesar saw a wooden warrior head, a broken plaster falcon, several *People* magazines, and a smashed pair of gold "Praying Hands." Most of the pieces of a very ornate chess set had rolled under the television. The fake onyx chess board had cracked in two.

He stepped carefully over to Henry's side and asked where Donna was. Henry pointed to the short hall which led to the kitchen. Cesar went to look and wished he hadn't.

There is, occasionally, dignity in death, even when it is violent, but Donna's bad luck had stuck with her. She lay on her side on what was once off-white linoleum. Her legs were drawn up slightly, her hands almost grasped in prayer in front of her. Cesar thought how pathetically skinny she was. Her long thin feet were bare and boney. Blood trickled from a wound in the back of her head, but that was not the detail that nearly wiped Cesar out. It was her teeth. She had fallen so that one ear was pressed to the floor and in her fall her false teeth had dislodged slightly. They were too far forward and she looked horribly like a rodent on the highway.

Cesar went back to Henry.

"What happened?" he asked.

"You know Calvin?" Henry asked.

"Sure. Hi, Calvin."

Calvin nodded.

"Calvin knows Donna's cousin. She called him when she couldn't get Donna on the phone this morning. Donna's kids were staying with her last night. She saw Donna's car outside and got worried. Thought she might have been beat up—OD'd.''

"Does she live here, too?" asked Cesar.

"Couple of buildings over."

Calvin's glare dared Cesar to say something about white women in a black project or white women calling black cops in an emergency, but he didn't know Cesar.

"Calvin came over this afternoon and picked the lock. He called me when he found Donna."

"How long has she been dead?" asked Cesar.

"Looks like last night some time."

"What do you know?"

"Not much," said Henry. "The lady next door said she heard fighting last night, but she didn't think anything about it. She said it happened a lot. We're looking for Alfred—the guy she was with at the Top Hat."

"Why?"

"Why not?" asked Henry. "I told you he's dumb. Linda says—"

"Who's Linda?" asked Cesar.

"Cousin. She says Alfred beat her up pretty often."

"Yeah, but he didn't kill her real often."

"So what? Looks like he did this time."

"Henry, what about the guy who was calling her? The guy who followed her?"

"The one she was talking about at the Top Hat?"

Cesar nodded.

"You didn't believe her, did you, man?"

"Not then, but I do now," said Cesar.

"Come on, man, she was seeing things. You know what she was like. She was crazy."

"No, she wasn't, Henry. She was goofy, all right, but she wasn't crazy. Take a look. She's dead."

"Cesar, her boyfriend beat her up every weekend. I'm telling you."

Cesar glared at his friend. It seemed ricidulous for Henry to back the boyfriend as the most likely suspect.

"What did he use?" he asked Henry.

"On her head? Don't know. Hammer maybe. Or wrench. Haven't found it yet."

"That doesn't sound like what happened to Irving Golden?" asked Cesar.

"Maybe. Maybe it sounds like boyfriend, too."

"Let me check something," said Cesar. He went back into the kitchen and looked, not at Donna but at the kitchen. There was the same pattern of new disorder on top of old that he had seen in the living room. At one level there was bologna and bread on the table and unwashed dishes and cruddy dish towels, but at the other level there were drawers pulled out and, in a couple of cases, the contents of drawers dumped over the floor. He went back to the living room.

"Have you been upstairs?" he asked George.

"Not yet."

Cesar climbed the skinny staircase. It was a wreck upstairs, too, and in all the rooms there was the same pattern of old and new mess. Even the kids' rooms hadn't escaped. Cesar went into both of them and came out sadder. The rooms weren't clean, but he could tell the kids had made some effort to put order into their lives even if they couldn't have cleanliness. They weren't going to like what had happened to their toys. Donna's room was a total wreck. Her fuzzy blue headboard had been ripped from the bed and was now lying halfway under it. Pillow cases were ripped off pillows. The contents of the closet were spilled out in the space between the closet and the foot of the bed. There were Polaroid pictures scattered over the clothes. Cesar picked up a couple of the pictures and blushed (Alfred aroused by passion). He went back downstairs and cornered Henry. "You see what a mess this place is?" he asked.

"Yeah, I see. I saw. I'm not blind. I told you they had a fight."

"Sure. They probably did, but this place is really torn apart, even upstairs. It looks more like a burglary than a punchout. Don't you see? Somebody's been looking for something."

"No, I don't see. And I have looked." Henry lowered his voice so Calvin wouldn't hear. "Look, man. I hate to say it, but your lady friend was a pig. This house is filthy and messy from *her*. It's disgusting. I'll buy those shelves getting knocked over in a fight, but that's it. And I'll tell you something else, it's tough for the lady, but it might be a good thing for the kids. No kids ought to have to live in this kind of mess. Or with that kind of trash either."

"Well. Judge Henry Chapman."

"Would you want a kid to grow up here?"

"No."

"Was she your idea of a mother?"

"No," said Cesar. "But she was theirs." He pointed to the portrait on the television. "They didn't know any better. And I'll tell you who else didn't know any better is poor dumb Alfred who's going to go to prison for this. Jesus Christ, Henry. You're assuming he did it. Aren't you even going to look for anyone else?"

"Yes. I know what I'm doing, all right? I'm a detective, too. You remember that." Henry was going cold on Cesar. That made problems.

Cesar got along with Henry better than anyone else in homicide did. They worked well together and Henry had learned to open up with Cesar. It was a matter of trust. But, from time to time, Cesar would do or say something wrong and Henry, or the Henry Cesar thought he knew, would disappear, leaving a stoney black cop in his place. It always made Cesar feel white, stupid, and slightly angry. He could not, for Christ's sake, keep up with Henry's list of possible offenses. It was too long and too complicated. Cesar thought fast to figure out how he had offended (he had suggested incompetence?) and answered accordingly.

"Henry, you're probably right. I'm crazy. All right? You know the guy and you know your job and I'm not stepping in. If it looked like it, I'm sorry. I've got Golden on the brain, all right? I don't know what I'm doing. I can't get my hands on anything and I kind of hoped I'd get some more out of Donna and I kind of blew up when you called. Understand?"

He watched Henry's eyes and thought he saw a slight thaw. Christ, he hoped so. Cesar *knew* this wasn't a domestic spat. This was Golden Toy business. It had to be. But Henry was Henry and he was going to need his help when it turned out that Donna's lover was in Dayton at the time of death.

"I'll call you when we bring Alfred in. You can talk to him." If that was Henry's peace offering, Cesar would take it.

"Thanks, Henry. Where are the kids? Still with the cousin?"

"Yeah."

"Do they know yet?"

"I don't know. Calvin!" he called the vice squad detective over. Calvin gave Cesar another mean guy glare. "Do the kids know what happened?" Henry asked.

"Yeah, they know. Linda sorta fell apart."

"Would it be okay if I talked to them a minute?" asked Cesar.

"Whatever you want, man," said Calvin. He was very cool.

"How do I get there?"

"Out the door and turn left. It's 33E."

"Thanks."

Cesar had to work through the crowd again to get to Linda's apartment. He listened to the crowd noise and picked up a change. He heard Alfred's name a couple of times and put that together with the new and surly sound. Somehow the people on the sidewalk had learned that Donna's boyfriend was the number one suspect and they didn't like it. How did they learn? Who leaked the news? Maybe no one. It didn't take much to connect him with the crime. You didn't need police help. Cesar felt an urge to yell, "He didn't do it. Go home and forget it." He got a couple of elbows in the ribs from the crowd. Even though they hurt, he didn't acknowledge the challenges or insults or whatever. No point.

The name on the mailbox at 33E was Fitzgerald. Cesar's knock was answered by a boy in brand new Nikes. Donna's kid or Linda's? He was light brown.

"I'm looking for Linda. Is she here?"

"Yeah."

"Is she your mom?"

"Yeah."

"What's your name?"

"Dante Maurice Fitzgerald."

"Okay, Dante, can I come in? I'm a policeman."

"You know Calvin?"

"Yep."

"Okay. Come in."

The unit was identical to Donna's as far as layout, but it was a world away in housekeeping. Even though the kids were watching television with the curtains pulled and the lights off, Cesar could sense the cleanliness and order. There were three other kids besides Dante, two boys and a girl. They were all sitting on a long sofa, all neatly dressed, sharing a big bowl of popcorn. They only gave Cesar a brief look. "Mission Impossible" was on.

"Where's your mom, Dante?"

"In the kitchen." Dante reclaimed his spot on the sofa as Cesar left the room. The lights were on in the kitchen. Linda Fitzgerald was sitting at a small dinette. Cesar saw the family resemblance right away. She had that mountain-boney look and the same rounded shoulders. Her hair was lighter than her cousin's. It was cleaner, too. She was cleaner. Everything was cleaner here than at Donna's. She looked up at Cesar. Her eyes were red from crying.

"Mrs. Fitzgerald?" She nodded. "I'm Cesar Franck. I knew your cousin."

"Detective Franck? The one she's been calling?"

"Yes, ma'am."

She blew her nose.

"You want some coffee?"

"Is it made?"

She stood up and got a mug from the cabinet over the sink. She was shorter than her cousin. She had to stretch to get the mug.

"What do you take in it?"

"Black's fine."

She brought the carafe to the table, filled his mug, and refilled hers. Her movements were precise. No splashes. Before she put the carafe back on the Mr. Coffee she wiped the hot plate with a dish cloth. Cesar approved. They drank silently for a couple of minutes. She kept her eyes on the table. He watched her.

Cesar couldn't tell if she was younger than Donna or simply less battleworn. Her clothes were K-Mart, he could tell that, but she was one of those lucky women who make their clothes look more expensive. Her blouse was perfectly ironed and there were no pills on her polyester pull-ons. She took care of her nails.

"I'm sorry about your cousin, ma'am," Cesar broke into the silence. Linda Fitzgerald gasped involuntarily and then tightened herself. She was, apparently, not going to cry in front of strangers.

"I didn't know her all that well. We met only a couple of times, but I liked her."

"She liked you, too, Detective Franck. She said you were real nice and smart. She liked smart people."

"I don't know how she could tell. I've been pretty dumb for the past couple of days."

"She knew you were smart." Linda looked at her coffee a minute. "Did you know she was trying to call you?"

"Yes."

"Why didn't you call back?"

"I'm sorry. I should have. But her messages said not to. I should have."

"Don't worry about it."

"I wish I had."

Linda sighed. "It wouldn't have done you any good if you did. Her phone's unlisted and she unplugged it after she started getting those calls she told you about."

"Did she get any more of them yesterday?"

"I don't know. I didn't see her. She sent the kids over by themselves in the afternoon."

"How are the kids taking it?"

"They're all right, I guess. Their daddy's coming down from Chicago, so that's got them excited."

"I guess it'll hit them later," said Cesar.

"Maybe. Maybe not." Linda straightened up in her chair and grasped her arms. "You saw her, Detective Franck. I guess you saw what she was like."

"I don't think—"

"You don't have to be nice. I know her. I grew up with her. She acted like trash. She always did. The kids don't like her and I guess I don't blame them. She didn't know anything about kids and she'd whip them too hard. And then she'd spoil them. I guess they were over here more than they were there. She didn't cook much so I fed them a lot. And their daddy was nasty about her whenever they went to stay with him, so it's no wonder they didn't think much of her."

"Maybe they'll forget. I hear kids do." Cesar hoped that was right. He had to say something.

"Maybe," said Linda. She stood up and straightened some dish towels on a rack and then circled the room. "But I loved her," she finally said. "We were raised like sisters. There's just a couple of months between us. We'd fight sometimes. We fought this week. But she was always sorry. And listen, if anybody else did anything to me she'd go crazy. She'd fight ten boys at once when she was little. I never did 'cause I was always scared, but she wasn't scared of anything. I guess she didn't have good sense."

Linda had stopped in front of a window and was staring out. Cesar finally realized she was weeping without a sound when he saw tears on the floor by her feet.

After a few minutes she wiped her face hard with her hands and sat down. "We're from Rat Trap, Kentucky," she said. "It's near Harlan. She tried taking her kids down there once. I never did 'cause I was afraid to, their being black and all. But she did it. She drove down there to Mamaw's and Mamaw wouldn't let her in, so she sat on the front porch with the kids all day. Right there by the highway. And she waved at everybody that passed and she didn't leave until it was dark." Linda smiled and said, "She was a fool."

Linda was pretty when she smiled even though, like Donna, she had false teeth. Cesar thought how lucky Donna and the kids were to have her around. And maybe Linda had needed Donna, too. He wondered how Linda would make out with the neighbors now. Maybe she wouldn't stay. Linda offered more coffee. He accepted half a cup and then began to ask her about the calls Donna got. Did she ever hear them? Did Donna ever recognize a voice or a background noise? Had she been followed anymore? Linda didn't know anything new, but she asked if Cesar thought this had something to do with Donna's murder. Cesar explained that he wasn't the investigating officer on this case, but that he was interested.

"Don't you think Alfred did it?" she asked.

"Maybe. Like I said, it's not my case."

"I don't think he did it either. Alfred's dumb, but he's no killer. I think whoever killed Mr. Golden killed Donna. I saw her face when she got those calls and she was scared. She really was. And I told you she didn't get scared easy."

"Do you suppose I could ask the kids about it?" asked Cesar.

"I don't think they knew what was going on."

"Maybe they heard something . . . maybe they answered one of the calls. Could I talk to them?"

She went into the living room and brought back a boy and a girl. They didn't look too happy to leave the television.

"Stacey and Mitch, this is Mr. Franck. He's a detective and he wants to ask you some questions, all right? Now you cooperate with him. You tell him whatever he wants to know. You hear me?"

125

"Nice to meet you, Stacey and Mitch." He offered his hand, but they weren't buying.

"Shake hands, Mitch," said Linda.

"It's okay, ma'am."

Linda started to say it wasn't, thought better of it, and excused herself, leaving the two black children to stare at the white cop. Cesar recognized the look on Mitch's face as the one he had just seen on Henry's. This wasn't going to be easy.

"I'm sorry to get you away from your show. Is it good?"

No answer.

"Well, I won't keep you long. It'll still be on."

"It's almost over," said Stacey.

Good. They can talk.

"I'm sorry about your mother, kids."

No reaction.

"Did your mom ever take you to the toy factory?"

No reaction.

"That's a neat place to work, don't you think?"

No reaction.

"Your mom said she used to bring home toys for you."

No reaction.

"Didn't she?" he asked. Come on, kids, take me off the hook.

Stacey spoke. "When she bring home toys, she take them to K-Mart."

"What for?" asked Cesar.

"She wanted money, so she told them she got them at the store."

Mitch glared at his sister and then hit her hard on the arm. She punched him back.

"Hey! Stop that!" said Cesar.

They glared at him. None of his business.

"Look, you shouldn't punch each other. No kidding."

Stacey opened up again. Probably wanted to piss off her brother some more.

"She tried to take my new doll back, but she forgot they don't sell them there, so I still have it."

"Is it a Denver Doll?"

She nodded, dug in her pocket, and pulled out Banner Strathmore.

"You know who this is?" asked Cesar.

"Sure. I watch 'Denver' all the time."

"It's stupid." Mitch's first contribution.

"The doll or the show?" asked Cesar.

"Both," said Mitch.

"It's a good show," said Stacey. "And you wish you had a doll, too."

"I ain't."

"Yes, you do. You said it was sexy."

"I ain't. That's a stupid doll."

"Look," said Stacey to Cesar and she collapsed the doll into a ball and rolled it on the table. "She do gymnastics."

"Do you do gymnastics?" asked Cesar.

"I'm gonna. We gonna live with my daddy and he say we can do anything we want to."

"Do you do gymnastics, Mitch?"

"Naw."

"Karate?"

"Yeah."

"Are you good?"

"Pretty good."

"I had to learn some at police school. Want to try?" He stood up and poised for an attack. Mitch countered and they did a lot of weaving and chopping. They were both terrible, but it loosened Mitch up a little. Cesar sat down.

"You're already way past me, Mitch."

"Yeah, well, I be practicing *all* the time."

"That's what you got to do," said Cesar. "Now, listen, you know what my job is?"

"Yeah. You a detective," said Mitch.

"Right. So you probably know what I'm here about."

"You looking for Alfred?" asked Stacey.

"No. I'm not. I mean we want to talk to him, but that's not who I'm looking for."

They stared at him.

"I'm looking for someone else."

"Don't you think Alfred kill Mamma?" asked Stacey.

"No. I don't think so. But I'm not sure."

"See, Mitch! I told you. You said Alfred kill Mamma, but I said no 'cause she'd kill him first."

Mitch hit her arm in the same spot.

"Hey! Quit that! You're not supposed to hit people when you know karate." Cesar invented a new rule.

"Who killed her?" asked Mitch.

Well, so you're interested.

"I don't know," said Cesar. "But she said someone was calling her and maybe following her. Did she tell you that?"

They nodded.

"What did she say about it? Did she ever see anybody? Did she ever tell you who she thought it was?"

"She say a man follow her. She say he the one calling her," said Stacey.

"Did he follow her here?"

"Yeah."

"Did you see him?"

"Unh-unh." She shook her head.

"Did you?" Cesar asked the boy.

"Unh-unh."

"Did she know him, Mitch? Did she say who it was?"

"She say she think she know and she say she gonna make sure and then she gonna call the police."

"Did she say . . . did she say what kind of car it was, maybe?"

"No."

"But she was scared. She say he scare her to death," said Stacey.

Cesar looked at the children. He saw no signs of nerves or fear on their part. If they weren't totally detached from their mother's murder, they were certainly not grieving. And they seemed to enjoy being interrogated. Probably, like their mother, they were deeply into television.

"Kids," said Cesar, "I need help."

They didn't answer, but they were paying close attention.

"You know what happened to your momma, right?"

They nodded.

"You know the police think that Alfred hit your momma."

"Don't you think so? You're the police," asked Stacey.

"He a *detective*," said Mitch and hit her.

"Quit hitting her. I'm a police detective. You're both right." Stacey rubbed her upper arm and made a move toward Mitch, but Cesar grabbed her.

"Quit it. Knock it off. No. I don't think Alfred killed your momma. I think someone else did. I think maybe it was the guy your momma was scared of. The one that called her up. And followed her. And I think the reason is that he wanted something your momma had."

"Her money? He want her money?" asked Stacey.

"Stacey, you are so *stupid*. Momma don't keep money."

"I don't think it was money," said Cesar.

"Well, what he *want*?" asked Stacey.

"I don't know. That's why I need your help. I want you to think if your momma ever brought anything home that she thought was important, something she had to hide."

The children stared at him, then Stacey asked, "What you mean?"

"I mean papers, maybe, or something in an envelope. Something small. Did you see anything like that?"

"No, sir," said Mitch. Sir?

"Why? You think she steal something?" asked Stacey.

"No. I think she *had* something. Maybe she found something. Whoever was in your house was looking for it. That's what I think. He sort of messed up your house—even your rooms—looking for it."

128

"My Atari! Did he take my Atari?!" Mitch panicked.

"No, that's still there. I saw it. But he was really looking hard. He pulled everything out of the drawers and closets."

"He got my Nikes, I kill *him*," said Stacey.

"I don't think he was looking for those." Cesar thought a minute and then asked. "Does your momma have any hiding place?" Kids almost always knew if they did. Cesar knew where Lillian hid stuff.

"Yeah, she got a hiding place. We know all about it." Stacey started to giggle. Cesar wondered what was funny. More than that, he wondered where the hiding place was and if Donna's murderer had found it. Whatever it was. If it was there. If there was anything.

"She got pictures of Alfred in there and he—" Stacey didn't have a chance to finish. Mitched grabbed her and covered her mouth which made her laugh again. Her brother was painfully embarrassed.

"It's okay, Mitch. I saw them. They were in the closet, weren't they?"

"Yeah. That's where they were and that's where this nosey little bitch always be sticking her head and—" Mitch stopped talking and started slamming his little sister against the wall. She kept laughing until her head took a knock and then she started screaming. That brought Linda into the kitchen. Cesar pulled Mitch off his sister and let Linda take the little girl back into the living room.

Cesar looked at Mitch. The boy was miserable, but he wasn't going to cry in front of a cop. Maybe he didn't miss his mother, but his life was a mess just then and there wasn't anybody around but Cousin Linda to smooth things out. Cesar hoped the boy's father would get here fast.

Cesar sat down at the table and asked Mitch to join him. Mitch sat down, but he wouldn't look at Cesar. He glared at the stove instead, and as he looked at the boy's sullen profile, Cesar for the first time saw the resemblance to Donna under the black skin. He had the same sharp chin, hollow temples, and Lyndon Johnson ears. And he was sitting not as a black man but as a mountain man, with his shoulders curled in. For a moment Cesar was helpless. He could not imagine a rougher existence than that of half-hillbilly, half-black boy in the projects. Furthermore, he knew that Mitch was smart. Smart enough to know just what lousy cards he had been dealt. Cesar drew in his breath and tried to reconnect with this boy.

"Mitch, my dad died when I was about your age."

"So?"

"So, I sort of know what you're going through about your mother."

If Cesar had hoped Mitch would pick up on the television dialogue, he was out of luck. "Aw, she was *stupid*."

"Come on, you don't mean that."

"She was stupid, man. A stupid white woman. She thought she was cool, but she was stupid. And mean."

"Come on, Mitch. She's dead."

"So what?"

"What are you mad at her for? She didn't *try* to get killed." Cesar stopped trying to help.

"I'm mad 'cause she was stupid. Keeping stupid pictures like that. She a ho!"

"Dammit, Mitch. Stop talking like that! She was your mother."

"I don't care."

"Well, I do. I liked your mother."

"Yeah, well."

"Well, what?"

"You like her 'cause she white."

"Oh, *brother!*"

"Well, my dad's *black*. And I like him. He thinks Mamma's stupid, too."

"Well, that's his mistake," said Cesar and then bit his tongue. He had forgotten he was fighting with a boy. He stood up and went over to the window to stare at the grim backyards of Millvale. After a minute he went back to the chair.

"Look, Mitch. I'm sorry. Let's just leave it at that, all right?"

Mitch didn't answer.

"I've just got a couple more questions, okay?"

Still no answer.

"Mitch, I'm trying to keep Alfred out of jail. You understand? You want him to go to jail for something he didn't do?" Cesar waited and Mitch finally said no. "All right. Now. Did you ever look in your mother's closet? Where she hid those pictures?"

"Maybe."

"I don't care about the pictures. You shouldn't either. People just do that when they get Polaroids. I want to know if there was anything else in there?"

Mitch shook his head without looking at Cesar.

"Are you sure?" asked Cesar.

"Yeah."

"When was the last time you looked?"

"Yesterday."

"No papers? No envelopes? No packages?"

"No."

"Okay, Mitch. That's all I want to know. Thanks." The boy slipped out of the room and Cesar called, "Wait a second!" but he didn't come back. Cesar took the coffee cups back to the sink, rinsed them, and went back to the living room. Linda was watching television with her boys and Stacey. Mitch wasn't in sight.

Linda stood up and joined Cesar by the front door. Cesar apologized for upsetting Mitch. He really did feel bad. He didn't like not being liked. Linda told him not to worry. She'd keep an eye on him.

She wanted to know when she could go over to straighten up and get some things for the kids. Cesar told her it might be hours before the guys from the lab were through, but he would see that she was allowed to get some clothes. Straightening up would have to wait.

He said goodbye to Stacey and walked out onto the stoop. The afternoon had begun to fade. He turned around to say goodbye to Linda. Standing behind the storm door in the darkened living room as she was, Cesar could see no difference between her and Donna. He walked back to Donna's house.

The crowd was gone, and in his depressed mood Cesar concluded that their interest lasted only until the departure of the news crews. He went back into the house and looked for Henry. Henry was on the telephone in the kitchen. Donna's body was gone.

Cesar listened to Henry long enough to tell that there was a woman on the other end of the phone and that she was not talking homicide business. He stepped around and over the technicians and wandered upstairs. Two uniforms were having a laugh over the Polaroids. Cesar stared at them until they got embarrassed. He went back downstairs. Henry was off the phone. He asked if Cesar had seen the kids.

Cesar told Henry the kids were okay and asked what was new. Henry told him they had a good lead on Alfred and expected to pick him up pretty soon. His expression dared Cesar to bring up the business about Donna's mystery guest. Cesar let it ride. He asked Henry if there was anything he needed. There wasn't. He left.

Instead of going straight to the station, Cesar headed downtown. There was a chance of finding Tom still at work.

16

TOM'S CAR WAS still there.

Cesar parked in the same spot he had had earlier in the day. There was no night bell on the door and the place looked dark. He beat on the door anyway and, in a couple of seconds, he saw a light come on somewhere inside. Tom came to the door, peered out, and then let him in.

Once he was back in the offices Cesar wondered what he wanted here. Tom looked tired. Cesar realized he had returned only because he had rushed out. He had planned to spend more time with Tom than Donna had allowed. He started to figure out how to get out gracefully when Tom asked what he was going to do about supper.

"Go home, I guess," he answered.

"You want to eat out?" asked Tom.

"No. There's nothing open but Frisch's."

"Arnold's?"

"No, thanks."

Tom looked disappointed.

"Come on with me," said Cesar.

"To your house?"

"Yeah. Why not. Mom'll get a kick out of seeing you."

"Nah. She's not expecting company."

Cesar picked up the phone, told Lillian he was bringing company and they would want supper. He hung up on her reply. She would be pissed until she saw Tom. Tom closed up the building. He was headed for his Volvo when Cesar offered to drive. Cesar said it was a waste of gas to take two cars up when he was coming back anyway. Besides, he wanted to talk. Tom checked the locks on his car, then got in with Cesar. As they drove to Westwood, Cesar told him about Donna and her house and kids. Tom listened without comment. Cesar looked over at him and saw that he had paled. They drove without talking for a couple of miles. Finally Tom spoke.

"This stinks, you know?"

"You mean Donna?" asked Cesar.

"Both of them. Donna and Irving. I mean it's the same person, isn't it?"

Cesar didn't answer.

"Isn't it?" asked Tom again.

"I don't know," said Cesar finally.

"Don't know? Okay, what do you *think?* Don't you think it's the same guy? Look. Two people who know each other, work together, get killed the same way in three days. You don't think that's the same person at work?"

"Yeah. Yes, I do."

"But what?" asked Tom.

And Cesar explained about Alfred and Henry's assumption. Tom screwed himself around in the bucket seat until his back was nearly to the window. He listened closely. When Cesar finished, Tom asked, "Why don't they check out both theories?"

"Because I goofed up and because the boyfriend is the natural in this case. You always go for the obvious."

"You don't think it's obvious that she and Irving are connected?" asked Tom.

"Sure. I do. But I'm on the Golden case. And I have to admit that if I weren't, I'd be out looking for the boyfriend, too."

"How did you goof up?"

Cesar told him about his run-in with Henry.

"How is that a screw-up?" asked Tom.

"Competition. I put myself in competition with Henry. At least as far as he's concerned. Now he's going to hang onto his own angle for dear life. And because Donna was a white hillbilly going with a black guy and living in a black project, everybody's going to assume it's just one more black-on-black mugging and they'll agree with Henry."

"But she's white."

"Sure, but she was living with blacks. So she's one of them, only worse. That's how it works," said Cesar.

"Judgmental bastards, you cops."

"Yeah," said Cesar. "We are."

"So what are you going to do?"

"What I'm going to do is assume that I've got a crazy man on the loose who doesn't discriminate. Hits the high and the low."

"Middle class next?"

"Maybe," said Cesar. "Only I want to find out who he is before he decides to go after the middle class."

Tom shivered.

"Crummy business, isn't it?" asked Cesar.

"No kidding," said Tom.

They were home.

Cesar was right. Lillian was glad to see Tom. She grilled Tom about his family and what he was doing and why he wasn't married and why

133

Cesar wasn't married and what was the matter with kids now that they didn't want to have families. Cesar let her go on for about five minutes then asked about something to eat. She told him to fix it himself. She wanted to talk to Tom.

Cesar went into the kitchen and found rib eyes laid out and a salad tossed. Lillian had put a cloth on the dinette and set out her good dishes. Cesar laughed. She was expecting a girl.

Lillian left Tom and Cesar to eat alone, and they talked about Donna while they ate. Tom told Cesar all of the standing jokes about Donna. When he came to a joke about blackmail, Cesar slowed down on his chewing and said, "You know, I thought about that."

"Blackmail?" asked Tom.

"Yeah. I had to wonder. She could have seen a lot of things cleaning up those offices."

Tom pulled a piece of gristle from his mouth and thought for a minute. "It's possible," he said. "But I don't know what she could see to blackmail anybody with."

"I don't either," said Cesar. "But I don't know what all was going on there either. I just wondered. I was trying to figure how she could get herself into so much trouble."

"Maybe she saw more than she told you?" Cesar thought about that.

"I don't think so," he said. "You didn't see her when she came over to the station. I'm pretty sure that if she had a chance to be a witness she would have told me. She would have liked to go to court."

"But papers, Cesar? I don't think Rosemary Meynell would leave anything sensitive lying around. She's too thorough for that. Now at our place . . . Christ, it's leak city. Anybody who wants to know what we're up to can walk straight in during business hours and read it all. We've got no security and no Rosemary."

"What about Golden? He could have left things out. Bosses do."

"Not him. He was careful."

"Except about his keys," said Cesar.

"Except about his keys," said Tom. "Anyway, Rosemary cleaned up after him."

They went back to their food. When they finished the salad, Cesar got out some ice cream, dished that out, and turned on Mr. Coffee.

"Was she listening at the meeting?" asked Cesar.

"Probably. But there wasn't anything to hear."

"What do you mean? You told me it was a circus," said Cesar.

"It was. But there wasn't anything blackmailable. Not at that one."

"You sure?"

"Yeah. It was just nasty."

"But maybe she heard something she shouldn't have," said Cesar.

"Cesar, there wasn't anything to hear. There wasn't anything secret. You can't have a secret in a meeting like that."

134

"Maybe not. I wish I could ask her about it, though. I bet she'd give me better information than I got out of you guys."

"What do you mean?" Tom got huffy.

"I mean everybody who told me about that meeting cleaned up some or all of the story. I know that. I just wish I could have talked to her about it some more. She'd remember the worst for sure. What are you staring at?"

"I feel like Alexander Butterfield," said Tom.

"Who?"

"Alexander Butterfield. Remember? The guy at Watergate who revealed the tapes?"

"Yeah."

"We've got tapes," said Tom.

"Tapes of the meeting?"

"Yeah. Or we don't. Irving does. Rosemary does. She always tapes meetings for Irving and for her notes. She taped the last one. I saw her doing it."

"No kidding."

"No kidding," said Tom.

Cesar poured coffee. Why hadn't Rosemary mentioned the tapes? Why hadn't anybody mentioned the tapes? Why hadn't Richard Nixon mentioned the tapes? "I'd really like to hear those," he said finally.

"Shouldn't be too hard," said Tom.

"You don't think so?" asked Cesar. He had a fast vision of a trip to the Supreme Court to plead for them.

"Just ask Rosemary."

"Sure. That's the most loyal secretary I've ever seen. I don't think she's going to hand them over to the cops without some sort of warrant."

"Hm. Might be right," said Tom. He drank his coffee and thought for a minute. Cesar waited.

"Maybe I can help you. What's it worth to you?"

"What's it worth to me? Cripes, you just got a free supper. Come on!"

"Right," said Tom and then yelled into the living room. "Mrs. Franck? Is it okay if I use your phone?"

"What are you asking her for? It's my phone, too. I pay half the bill," said Cesar.

"It's your mom's house, Cesar. I'm supposed to ask *her*. Is it okay, Mrs. Franck?"

Lillian came into the kitchen. "See how polite he is, Gus? I'll bet he never gives *his* mom any back talk. Sure you can use the phone, Tom. Help yourself." She checked the sink and the garbage. "Did you finish your supper?" she asked.

"Yes, thanks. It was delicious," said Tom.

"I fixed it," said Cesar. He was put out.

"It was delicious," Tom said again to Mrs. Franck, who chucked him under the chin.

"I'm going to be sick," said Cesar.

Lillian frowned at him and took Tom to the phone, clutching his arm fondly.

Cesar listened to the call.

"Grace? . . . it's me . . . yes . . . I know . . . yes, I'm sorry . . . no, something else . . . I'm at Cesar Franck's . . . right . . . no, I had supper here . . . no, we go way back . . . right . . . listen, it's about some tapes he needs . . . from the meeting, the ones Rosemary made. He needs them and I wondered if you could get them for him without a lot of fuss . . . oh, you do? . . . can—could he borrow them? . . . tonight, I guess. Cesar? You want those tapes tonight?"

"Sure!"

"Okay . . . he'll be out tonight. You sure it's okay? . . . I could. You want me to? . . . are you sure? . . . all right. I'll see you." Tom hung up.

So they were speaking. Or speaking again. Cesar cleared the table. Tom came back into the kitchen. "You want to go now?" he asked.

"I've got to clean up first."

"I'll do the dishes, Cesar. You boys run on," Lillian called from the living room. Cesar looked at Tom. Tom smiled sweetly at Cesar. They both knew whom Lillian was rewarding.

For half the drive to Amberley they fought about the fairness of mothers and the duplicity of friends and then Cesar asked, "How come she had the tapes?"

"She asked for them," answered Tom. "I guess she's making her move."

"And Miss Meynell just handed them over? What about Frederick?"

"Rosemary worked for Irving. Grace is Irving's daughter. Besides, they're friends."

"Rosemary and Grace?"

"Yep. Grace used to go to Rosemary with her problems when she was in college. Irene's not much help in a crisis."

"That'll be helpful, won't it? Having Rosemary on her side?"

"Very," said Tom.

A few miles later Cesar asked, "Are you two going together again?"

"I don't know."

They drove on silently to the Goldens' house.

136

17

GRACE OPENED THE door. There was a brief and awkward moment when no one spoke. And then somehow she was in Tom's arms and Cesar gave up altogether his small hope of dating a corporate president. When they separated Cesar saw Grace flustered for the first time. It made her even more attractive, of course. Tom was sheepish.

"Can we come in?" Cesar asked.

Grace took them to the den. Mrs. Golden was in bed. Louis was out and the funeral guests had left. Cesar saw for the first time just how big the house was. Grace offered drinks. Cesar declined but he made Tom have one. Cesar and Tom sat on a huge leather sofa and watched Grace at the bar. When she kept dropping ice cubes, Tom went over to help her.

A micro-cassette recorder and two cassettes sat on an end table next to Cesar's sofa. "Are these the tapes?" asked Cesar. Grace nodded. Cesar picked up the cassettes. Someone, Rosemary probably, had stuck on typed labels with the date of conference and the order of sequence. All very neat. He wanted nothing more than to lock himself up somewhere and listen. Someplace where he wouldn't see Tom and Grace having such a good time. He rattled the cassettes discreetly in his hand. Tom and Grace brought their drinks over and sat on the other huge sofa.

"Tell me more," said Grace. "I want to know how you two know each other." So they told her. They told her about Westwood and their school. They told her about each other. Grace was vitally interested to hear about Tom as a schoolboy. Cesar was surprised to hear that he was the smartest kid Tom ever knew.

Grace kept smiling at Cesar. It made her more attractive than ever. She hadn't smiled much on Friday. But Cesar knew that he was getting those smiles because he was Tom's friend. Tom knew it, too, from the look of him.

Tom had started to tell Grace about Lillian when Cesar finally rattled the micro-cassettes once too often and lost one in the crack of the sofa. He blushed and fiddled his hand around trying to get it to come out. It stopped the conversation. When he finally extracted the damned thing, Grace had recalled the reason for his visit. She straightened her back and put on a more businesslike expression. Tom sobered up, too.

"Why don't you play these now?" she suggested. Cesar didn't want to. He wanted to play them by himself, where there were no distractions. He started to put that politely but she interrupted.

"You're going to need to know who's talking." She had a point. Cesar had talked to everyone in attendance at the meeting, but he was going to need help matching all the voices to all the faces.

Grace took the micro-cassettes from him and stooped over the player, searching for and inserting side one. The first voice was unfamiliar to Cesar and he looked at Grace.

"My father." He should have guessed. Grace had tensed herself, gripping her glass until her knuckles were white. Had she listened before? She hadn't said.

One by one she identified the speakers. Cesar realized that he would have no trouble with the voices. The recorder at the meeting must have been a good one, and Rosemary had set the audio levels correctly, of course. He interrupted. "I think I know who's who now."

"I want to hear it again," said Grace. She didn't look as if she would accept any discussion.

The three of them sat together on the sofas in the den in Amberley and listened without comment. From time to time Cesar looked at the other two, wondering at their reactions. Neither one looked back at him. Grace concentrated on one spot on the carpet. She didn't move, she just stared. An occasional shiver was the only sign of her feelings. Tom leaned back into the sofa and let his eyes wander. From time to time he blushed, usually when he heard himself. Once when Irving became particularly abusive Tom started to put his hand on Grace's shoulder. A tiny twitch warned him off as effectively as a slap.

Cesar listened first for deviations from the stories he had been given. He would have to listen again and again for details, for background noises, anything new. He was surprised to see that he had picked up a lot of the jargon already. He followed the conversation. Harangue, usually. So far he had heard nothing to surprise him. He heard plenty to shock him, though. Irving's treatment of Marianne Kelly, for example. Cesar could not recall anything like it on the police force. Man to man, maybe, but never man to woman. Too bad Irving never had a chance to work Carole Griesel over at a meeting. There was no doubt about it, Irving Golden was a real mean son of a bitch. The tape moved on and they heard Tom fighting for his copy. For the first time Grace looked away from her spot on the carpet and turned to Tom. Cesar was surprised to see no pity or embarrassment as her father lit into her friend. To Cesar it appeared that she was assessing Tom's response. Tom's expression was almost frightened. Did he know he was being judged by the daughter as the father found him wanting? No one interrupted the tape.

And then Donna came in and Cesar forgot the other two listeners. He listened and listened hard. What could the poor screwy hillbilly snoop say or hear to get herself killed? Nothing was revealed. She was herself, the only funny thing on the tape.

There was no missing the key business.

As the first cassette popped out, Grace sighed. "Daddy thought Donna was so funny. He really didn't care about her cleaning. He just thought she was terribly funny."

The last side was short and confusing. Grace punched the off button.

"What was that last bit about?" Cesar asked. He referred to Irving's exchange with Evelyn Osborne.

"You mean about pushing the start button?" asked Tom.

"Right."

Tom looked at Grace. She wanted to know, too.

"Evelyn made up a tape from the outtakes. Bad shots, unused shots, goofups at the taping session. There were quite a few. Banner Strathmore couldn't remember her lines and, according to Evelyn, she can barely read."

"So that was set up to go? After the meeting?" asked Cesar.

"Evelyn set it up himself. Mr. Golden wasn't very . . . wasn't comfortable with the video controls."

"My father was all thumbs with things like that," said Grace. "What I want to know is did everybody know about it—about the tape?"

"Yes. We all saw it before the meeting."

"Should I see it?" asked Cesar. "Who has it?"

"It's silly," said Tom. "It won't tell you anything unless you're into Banner Strathmore's . . . " Tom interrupted himself.

"Unless you're into Banner Strathmore's breasts, Cesar." Grace glared at Tom.

"I said it was silly, Grace."

"But you watched?"

"We all did. It was *funny*. You know Evelyn, Grace."

"I do know Evelyn, Tom. And I do know what Evelyn's time costs. And I can imagine how much that little joke cost Golden Time Toys."

"Grace, your father *expected* that sort of thing. You heard him."

"That didn't mean Evelyn had to do it. Or that you all had to watch it." Grace was angry. "I'll bet you all watched it and laughed about my father watching it, didn't you? *Didn't* you?"

"Grace, we—"

"So you all had a good time laughing at that poor stupid woman with the big tits and my poor stupid father watching her, right?"

"Was there a sound track?" asked Cesar.

Grace and Tom both stared at him, Grace angrily and Tom in confusion.

"Did these outtakes have a sound track?" he asked again.

"What does . . . " Grace started to snap but Tom interrupted.

"Yes. Evelyn spent a lot of time on it. He liked to match the scenes to classical music."

"Noisy stuff?" asked Cesar.

"Partly. Well, mostly noisy. He used a lot of 'Zarathustra.' It *was* funny."

"What does it have to do with anything?" asked Grace. "Why are we talking about it?"

"I guess," said Cesar, "I guess it explains why your father didn't hear anyone come back into the office after the meeting."

Grace considered that for a moment and then, looking at Tom she said, "And it also explains how someone felt free to come back. If you all knew what the tape was like."

Tom said nothing. Cesar thought for a minute.

"Except for the two from Golden Time. Enneking and Mr. Golden's brother. They didn't watch the show beforehand, did they?"

"No," said Tom. "But they didn't need to. They've seen Evelyn's private productions before. They're all pretty much the same."

Cesar looked at Grace. She was starting to wilt. Cesar wasn't surprised. On top of her father's funeral she was now seeing in some detail her father's death scene. He felt sorry for her. He wished he had taken Tom and the tapes and left right away.

"Tom, I've got to get back to town. Would you mind leaving now?" There was a good chance Tom would mind. The good feeling between him and Grace had evaporated as the tapes played. Repairs were needed. Tom opened his mouth to plead for time, but Grace shook her head.

"Can I take the tapes with me?" asked Cesar.

Grace nodded and asked, "Do you need the recorder? You can borrow it."

Cesar thanked her, stood up, and retrieved his coat from one of the bar stools. The recorder fit into a pocket. Tom hadn't gotten up so Cesar stood and waited.

"Cesar wants to leave," said Grace.

"Grace, I want . . . "

"Tom, we'll talk tomorrow. I'm tired. Cesar needs to go."

Tom looked miserable. He finally stood up and put his coat on. Cesar led the way out through the great icy foyer. Grace followed him closely and automatically. Tom trudged along at the rear. Cesar stopped at the front door to wait for Tom. He and Grace turned to watch Cleary until he caught up. When they were all at the door Cesar offered his hand to Grace and said, "Thank you for the tapes, Miss Golden. It's really going to be a help to have them." She started to laugh as she shook his hand.

"Do I have to keep calling you Detective Franck? My name is Grace."

"Oh. My name is Cesar."

"I know, Cesar. You're welcome. Thank you for sending the car home."

Cesar let Tom pout and sulk for five minutes as they drove. Five minutes was long enough for a grown-up. Then he charged in.

"That's some girl, Tom. You let her get away this time and I will personally sign you into Longview myself."

No answer.

"And you know what? She's right—I do have very good manners." No answer.

Finally Cesar said, "Look, Tom. I can't slap you around the car, I'm driving. It would be dangerous. So quit pouting, all right?"

Tom almost smiled, but managed to recall his misery in time. "You see what I mean?" he said.

"No. What are you talking about?"

"Ms. Executive. Ms. Business. How am I supposed to deal with that?"

"Are you serious?" asked Cesar.

"Yeah, I'm serious. She chewed me out. *Me.* Because Evelyn made a goofy tape on company time."

"Give her a break, for Christ's sake. Her dad got murdered while he was watching that."

"No, you don't understand. That was business," said Tom.

"Bullshit. She's upset. She's got a right to be. And anyway, what's wrong with being serious? You haven't noticed that's what women are doing now?" Surely it wasn't going to turn out that Cesar the policeman's consciousness had been raised higher than Tom the adman's.

"I do know that, Cesar. I've even gotten a ticket from a lady cop. And that's fine. That's the way it's supposed to be. I'm all for it."

"Except for Grace."

"Except for Grace."

The car hurtled down I-75 as Tom wondered why he couldn't stand Grace in pinstripes. "I suppose it's like abortion," he said. Cesar looked at him for a second. It was a confusing remark.

"I'm for abortion," said Tom. "I really mean that."

"You're not Catholic anymore?" asked Cesar.

"I'm Catholic, I suppose. I'm not anything else yet. But I don't like abortion. I don't think I could handle it if someone aborted my kid. But I'm for abortion."

"What does that have to do with Grace?" asked Cesar.

"It has . . . Nothing. What I mean is I'm completely for women in the corporate jungle. I mean it. I'm just not for *Grace* in the corporate jungle. It screws her up."

"Tom, my mother has been working for twenty years. I don't think it's screwed her up."

"Of course not. I don't mean that. Your mother's not into the eye-gouging business. She has a job and she goes home, right?"

"Yeah."

"Well, Grace wants to be an eye-gouger. That's what Irving was. That's where the money is. That's what I mean by business."

"Oh. Are you afraid she'll get killed?" asked Cesar.

"No."

"Well, she really likes you, Tom." Cesar gave up on Tom's dilemma.

"You think so? I don't know. She likes *you*. That's for sure."

"Not the same way."

"She *loves* your good manners."

"Don't be an asshole."

"I don't know what to do," said Tom. And Cesar shut up so Tom could think about it. Cesar's thoughts shifted to the tape recorder and the micro-cassettes nesting in his pocket. The desire to lock himself in a room and steep himself in the meeting returned. It made him want to get rid of Tom. He was ready to work.

Tom's car was where he left it and still in one piece. Cesar waited to make sure the car would start. It did, and Cesar started to pull away from the curb when Tom got out again, flagged him down, and came to Cesar's window.

"Thanks for supper," he said.

"My pleasure."

"Don't go away thinking I'm a jerk, all right? I'm afraid of another twenty-year freeze."

"What are you talking about?" asked Cesar.

"Like when you rode off on your bike and wrote me out of your books."

"Oh."

"Okay?" asked Tom.

"Sure," said Cesar.

"Grace is right, of course. You do have excellent manners."

"I'll see you tomorrow."

"You coming back here?"

"I still have to talk to Marianne Kelly."

"Goodnight. Thanks. Thank your mom."

"Right." Cesar sped off.

18

CEASAR HEARD THE television set before he reached the squad office. What the hell? Lt. Tieves doesn't allow that. He walked in and saw Detective Griesel sitting in Sgt. Evans' chair watching a small black and white portable.

"What's up?" asked Cesar. Detective Griesel put a finger to her lips to shut him up. He walked around behind her to see the screen. It was a live instant-porto-cam news broadcast. Cesar stooped over Carole's shoulder to see better. The screen was tiny and the hand-held camera was jiggling. Cesar was able to make out the front of a small white house. The house was washed with floodlights.

"What's going—" he started.

"Shut up. I'm listening," Carole snapped. One day, Carole. One day.

Cesar listened.

The Channel Three newsperson was unfamiliar. The big stars were off duty for the weekend leaving the lamer, blinder, junior news aces to cover the normally uneventful period. The screen identified the reporter as Don Beasle. Don Beasle recapped.

The SWAT team had surrounded the little house on Florence Avenue in Walnut Hills which contained someone believed to be Alfred Brown, who was being sought for questioning by the Cincinnati Homicide Squad. Cesar groaned out load. Carole slapped his knee.

Alfred had apparently gotten word that he was under suspicion and had barricaded himself in the house with his mother. When Detective Henry Chapman showed up at the house, Alfred fired off a couple of rounds from the front window. The SWAT team was summoned and the area sealed off.

"We've been talking to Mrs. Ozella Johnson, a neighbor of Brown's mother here on Florence Avenue," announced Don Beasle from behind his John Chancellor glasses. Cesar didn't think the kid was more than twenty-two years old, but he had certainly mastered the newsperson's voice of catastrophe. "Mrs. Johnson, can you tell us what you know about Alfred and his mother? Is there anything in his past to mark him as a potential killer?"

Mrs. Johnson was an old black lady wearing the goggle glasses issued after cataracts come out.

143

"Well, I don't know Alfred too good, but Mrs. Lewis, that's his mother who's in there with him, she's a real nice lady and I don't think she'd raise no killer. She's in my church and she's blind and she's got a bad heart and I don't think they ought to be scarin' her like this 'cause she's likely to have a heart attack."

"Did you see what happened here?" asked the reporter.

"I didn't *see* what happened. I *heard* shootin' and I looked out the window and I saw some man running away and I called the police."

"And this is your daughter with you?"

"Yes, she's my daughter."

"And your name is?" Beasle stuck the microphone under the nose of a very tall and very pretty woman.

"Jackie Johnson."

"Ms. Johnson, how much have you seen of these events?"

"I've seen enough to know they probably got poor Mrs. Lewis scared half to death. And I *do* know Alfred and if he's a killer I'm Nancy Reagan."

"You think they've got the wrong man?"

"Oh, they've probably got Alfred in there, but that man is not the killer."

"Well, why do you think he's barricaded himself in there?"

"He scared! What do you think? He hears they looking for him about a murder and a detective shows up at the door. What's he going to do? And now they got all these SWAT troops up here. I don't blame him."

"God!" said Detective Griesel. "They *have* to stick up for each other."

"You mean black people, Carole?" asked Cesar. He sniffed a chance to stick the knife in.

"Well, Cesar. You *know* how they are."

"I do?"

"Of course you do. I mean, when did you ever walk in and get straight information from black people when a black guy commits a crime? You know what I'm talking about."

"Did this guy commit a crime?"

"Ask his girlfriend. She's dead. Got her head smashed in. Henry was trying to bring him in for questioning."

"I know, Carole. I was out there today. I know the girlfriend even."

"Well?"

"Well, I don't think that guy had anything to do with it."

"Oh, you don't? Well, what the hell is he doing shooting at detectives, then? Hunh? If he's innocent, why didn't he answer the door for Henry instead of trying to blow him away."

"He's probably scared shitless, Carole. I think the lady's right. I realize nothing scares you, Carole. But us ordinary citizens get spooked when we hear we're murder suspects."

"Cesar, you're full of shit. If he's not guilty he wouldn't be going nuts."

"I didn't say he wasn't guilty. Everybody's guilty of something. I just don't think he's guilty of murder. Not this one."

"What do you mean everybody's guilty? What a stupid thing to say."

"Do you want your income tax audited?" asked Cesar.

"Shut up, Cesar. I want to hear this."

The scene had shifted back to the Channel Three News Alive Nerve Center where superstar anchorperson Hugh Semur had taken command. There is no rest for the weary in the battle of ratings. Semur apologized for his casual attire but he had rushed from his daughter's birthday dinner to the studio. There had apparently been enough time to have his hair done, and had the television been a color set, Cesar and Carole would have seen that he had on a fresh coat of Max Factor. Semur gave another recap and then announced that Don Beasle, "who, incidentally, has done a terrific job on this story," was ready to interview Henry Chapman, the detective shot at by Alfred Brown.

"Can you hear me, Don?"

"I hear you, Hugh. I've got Detective Henry Chapman with me. Detective Chapman, can you tell us why Mr. Brown would barricade himself here?"

The Instant-Porta-Mini-Cam swung from Don Beasle to Henry who was, like all non-newspersons, struggling to keep his earphone inserted. The cameraman was too dumb to open up his shutter for black people so Henry was not much more than a blotch on the screen.

Henry gave a careful account of his actions. Cesar relaxed. Henry was a good cop. He was definitely a better interview than Cesar, who tended to look guiltier than the worst sex offender on camera. If only Henry weren't completely wrong. He was after the wrong guy.

Sgt. Evans came in and joined them silently, slipping off his overcoat and fur gloves and piling them on the desk—his desk—beside the television. Detective Griesel got the point and got out of his chair. Sgt. Evans settled himself in and watched Henry.

Hugh Semur tried to pry out some information about Donna Creech, but Henry shifted automatically to his stonewall mode and Semur gave up. The crack news team broke for a commercial.

Sgt. Evans switched channels, but the other stations didn't seem to consider poor Alfred's plight to be worth disrupting their schedules for. Cesar agreed. It was sad rather than earthshaking.

"Detective Franck, I trust I know what you are doing here. You are completing your Budget Narrative Form and solving the murder of Mr. Irving Golden, right? However, I would like to know what you are doing here, Detective Griesel, since you had the duty last night. Not that I mind, of course. It's always a pleasure to see you," said Sgt. Evans, switching off the television set.

"I picked up the story on the radio, Sergeant. I thought they might need some help."

"That was very nice of you, Detective Griesel."

"What are you doing here, Sergeant?" asked Cesar. He knew that Sgt. Evans enjoyed a full night's sleep.

"I am here, Detective Franck, because Lieutenant Tieves called me at my house and informed me that he was on his way to the besieged residence in Walnut Hills. I suggested that it would be appropriate for me to cover the fort down here. Not that it is any of your business."

"Gee, I didn't see him on TV," said Cesar.

"Rest assured. He will be on."

Cesar reached past the Sergeant and rekindled the screen. Sure enough, right after the commercial the handsome lieutenant was sharing the scene with the much less handsome Don Beasle. Sgt. Evans turned the sound off and said, "Tell me what's going on, Cesar."

Cesar told him. He told what he knew as briefly as possible without omitting anything and, knowing Sgt. Evans' moods, he didn't editorialize. Sgt. Evans continued to watch the soundless television set. When Cesar was through, the Sergeant chewed on the story for a minute. Then he turned around in his chair and asked Cesar, "Does Henry know what he's doing?"

Oh, boy. That's not fair.

"Sure. He's good. You know him."

"But you don't think he's got the right guy."

"I didn't say that, Sergeant."

"Come on, Cesar. If you didn't have a problem with it you wouldn't be talking like you've got a poker up your ass."

"He already told me he thought Henry had the wrong guy," said Detective Griesel.

What a snitch. Cesar was torn between his conviction and a desire to say that Carole was lying and he never said anything like that. Sgt. Evans was waiting.

"I think Henry did what I would have done if I were in his shoes. But I also think in this case I would have been wrong. I think whoever killed Irving Golden killed Donna Creech, and Henry is chasing a panicked boyfriend for the wrong reason."

"I agree," said Sgt. Evans.

Detective Griesel gaped. Gotcha!

"You're surprised, Griesel?" asked the Sergeant.

"Well . . . I mean, that guy's gone crazy, Sergeant. He's shooting. He shot at Henry."

"So what?"

"So he doesn't want to go to jail for killing his girlfriend. He's trying to shoot his way out."

"That's an interesting theory, Detective Griesel. Cesar, would you mind discussing Detective Griesel's theory with me while I go to the toilet?"

"Sure, Sergeant," said Cesar. And he led the way out of the office.

"All right, Franck, what's this crap about the wrong man?" asked Sgt. Evans when they reached the men's room.

"What do you mean crap, Sergeant? I thought you agreed with me?" Cesar was hurt.

"I just wanted to piss her off. Now what's up?"

So Cesar told him why he thought Henry had made a mistake. He told him about Donna's mystery calls and about the ransacked house. He pointed out the similar uses of a blunt instrument, and he told about Donna's reputation as a snoop. He also told the Sergeant that he didn't have anything to back him up.

Sgt. Evans, who had long since emptied his bladder, made a sour face.

"What do you think, Sergeant?" asked Cesar.

"I dunno, Cesar. You're asking me to believe that this boyfriend who is black and who beats her up regular, who is this very minute taking potshots at my only black detective, who is mean enough to make his blind mother stay inside with him so she can get a face full of tear gas in a few minutes, you're asking me to say this guy is not capable of hitting his stupid girlfriend once too often and too hard, thereby causing her to become a deceased citizen?"

"I didn't say he wasn't capable of it. I just said I didn't think in this case he did it," said Cesar.

"Well," Sgt. Evans shook his head and started to leave the men's room, "I think you might be right." He stopped just outside the door. "Not because you've made a good case. You haven't. You haven't got anything yet. But it's a coincidence—Creech and Golden. I don't think much of coincidences. Find me something solid, Franck. Okay?"

"Okay, Sergeant. I'm really trying."

"Hubba hubba, Franck. If I wanted trying I'd rely on Mzzz. Griesel. Get busy. Also, get those damned budgets done."

Right.

Cesar took his tape recorder and Budget Narrative Form into a small conference room. He laid the form out carefully in sequence—last year's above this year's. He plugged in the recorder, shut the door, sharpened a pencil, and sat down to work. As he worked he played the cassettes. Over and over. Sometimes he paid attention to the tapes. Sometimes he wrote and ignored them. At times he wrote and paid attention. Occasionally he neither wrote nor listened. At 1:00 A.M. he allowed himself a break. Each of the sheets had at least one entry. Some of them were filled with his small naive script. It seemed to him that he was more than halfway done and that he had therefore earned a package of cheese crackers and a Dr. Pepper. He headed for the machines.

Cesar stopped in the homicide office after he hit the vending machines. Henry was at his desk, wearing his coat and hat and writing something.

"Henry! What's happening?" Try the cheery approach. "Close call?"

Henry glared at Cesar. His eyes were bloodshot and yellow. Not a good sign. He went back to his writing.

"I've been locked in, Henry. What happened? Did you take him? Everything okay?"

"Yeah." Henry didn't look up.

"You okay?"

Henry grunted.

"Is his mom okay?"

"Yeah."

"Well?"

"Well what?" Henry snarled.

"Well, did he give up? Was it a shoot-out? What happened?"

"He gave up. His mother fainted and he wanted a doctor."

"Watcha doing? Waiting for his lawyer?"

"No."

"Through talking to him already?"

"Not going to talk to him."

"Why not? Jeez! After all that?"

Henry lay down his pencil and rubbed his eyes. "He's not a suspect anymore."

"Oh. How come?"

"Because he's got two cops that say they were with him when Donna Creech was killed. They were on Burnet Avenue. And if you want to know what he was doing with two cops, he was letting himself be talked into selling them coke. Okay? So he's not a suspect."

"Oh."

"I don't have a suspect," said Henry.

"Oh," said Cesar.

"Are you happy? You were right."

Cesar let Henry go back to his writing. He was sorry that Henry was unhappy, but he wasn't sorry to be right. Henry wanted it the other way around.

Cesar flicked on the television. No cable. Nothing to watch. He considered putting some more time in on Henry on the off chance that he might turn reasonable after a while, but thought better of it. Time for that tomorrow.

"Goodnight, Henry."

Henry didn't answer.

Cesar went back to the conference room, started the tapes, and hit the budget forms. At 1:55 he gave up and went home.

19

CESAR WAS FIGHTING for his career, fighting hard. And the only weapons at hand were his teeth and his fingernails. He squeezed through his trouser fabric and reached the flesh below. He caused pain, but was it enough? No. He called his teeth into play and began to sink his molars into the sensitive flesh, bringing his jaws slowly together in a crescendo of agony. The enemy was sleep. The battleground was Lt. Tieves's *Police Management by Objective Seminar*, number eight in a series of thirteen. The time was 8:30. The day was Monday. Even though his inner cheek felt like the moon's surface and his doubleknits were beginning to ravel where he was clawing himself, Cesar was losing the fight. He felt the fatal shudder of involuntary sleep, which so frightened him that he became briefly alert. He looked around at his fellow soldiers. Except for Detective Carole Griesel, his fellow members of the Cincinnati Homocide Squad were engaged in similar battles at various levels. Henry had been vanquished early, but was safe from criticism behind his mirrored shades. Cesar prayed that Henry would snore or fall out of his chair. Either would be fair punishment for making Cesar feel like a heel simply for being right.

There was near disaster as Tom Schmidtmeier's head dropped closer and closer to the table, thereby placing his eye within an inch of the top of his Pentel which he held upright in a death grip. He had not taken a note since these interesting series of lectures began.

Carole Griesel hung on every word falling from Lt. Tieves' lips. Each time the lieutenant paused, Detective Griesel searched the faces around the conference table hoping to find someone as thrilled as she was and each time she was alone.

Sgt. Evans was alone in his exemption from attendance being, presumably, too old and too close to retirement to benefit from the lectures.

Lt. Tieves was no fool. He knew that his audience had dwindled to one even though there were at least ten open pairs of eyes pointed in his general direction. He knew that if he shifted his subject from *Police Management by Objective* to *The Ramifications of Supreme Court Decisions, 1965–1980*, no one but Carole would notice. Somewhere in the back of his handsome mind lurked the suspicion that even she might not really notice the transition.

Lt. Tieves did not indulge in theatrics such as slammed doors or boxed ears to revive his troops. He was subtler. Continuing his lecture, he arose from his seat at the end of the table and walked silently around one side passing behind Carole Griesel (who nearly broke her neck maintaining eye contact). He stopped behind Henry who was seated next to Carole.

Lt. Tieves was a strong man. Without any outward sign of strain and without missing a beat in his speech, he began to tilt Henry's seat slowly toward Detective Griesel. So discreet were his movements that the mesmerized Ms. Griesel had no hint of his intent.

At the edge of Lt. Tieves's excellent vision he noted with satisfaction that Henry had begun to tilt in the direction of Detective Griesel.

Cesar, who had begun once again to nod off, felt danger in the room and woke up. He saw the fleeting shadow of a smile in the corners of Lt. Tieves' mouth. Cesar, adrenalin flooding in, looked for the trap. When he saw Henry he knew that he himself had been spared and leaned back to watch the show.

Having set the works in motion, Lt. Tieves returned to his end of the table. He continued to lecture, never taking his eyes from Detectives Griesel and Chapman.

Henry, feeling falsely secure behind his Foster Grants, was in the deepest stages of sleep. He teetered closer and closer to Detective Carole Griesel, gradually picking up speed. Lt. Tieves pitched his voice deeper and made his eyes bluer—the tricks of a handsome man, assuring Carole's complete attention. At last, Henry's center of gravity, artificially low due to his plumpness, slipped beyond the point of no return, and with a FLOOP he slumped face down into the lap of his close female associate.

"*Jesus!*" yelled Carole. Her well-honed police reflexes came into play and she slapped Henry across the back of his head.

THONK. Fighting to regain his position, Henry slammed his head into the edge of the conference table. The uproar recalled the remainder of the detective squad from its collective trance. For Tom Schmidtmeier it was none too soon. His eye focused on the tip of the Pentel as it was about to enter his iris. Like the others he tried to identify the noises which had awakened him, but, also like the others, he was too late. Cesar and the lieutenant alone knew why Detective Griesel's nostrils were flared to her earlobes and why Henry's sunglasses were 13 degrees off the horizontal. There was no comment and no discussion. Lt. Tieves resumed his lecture.

Cesar's mind was racing as he trailed Henry out of the conference room. He had only a few minutes available for patching things up with Henry. Detective Griesel had detained Lt. Tieves after class for her usual post-seminar brown nosing, but as soon as she had run out of baloney questions the lieutenant would be out and looking for Cesar.

Cesar was sure that Henry would beat it out of the office ASAP. Even from behind, Cesar could feel the waves of cranky rage Henry was sending out. You couldn't blame him. He'd gone after the wrong man, been shot at by the same wrong man, and he had somehow awakened in Detective Griesel's lap. He had also bonked his noggin on the conference table.

Do Not Tease the Bears.

But what if you need the bear's help? What if you and the bear should be working together to rid the city of a vicious murderer? What then? You lie.

"Henry!"

"Nrnrnr." A bear noise.

"Henry. Mom wants you to come for supper."

"Nrnrnr."

"I was supposed to ask you last week and I forgot. She's pissed off at me. You're supposed to come this week."

Well, it wasn't a very big lie. Lillian did, after all, like Henry. She particularly liked his car. It made her feel safe and Henry made a point of driving very smoothly when she was a passenger. Henry also talked very smoothly whenever she or for that matter any grey-haired lady was around. He was so Catholic about mothers.

"So why don't you come, Henry?"

"Nrnrnr. When?"

"Thursday? Friday?"

"Nrnrnr."

"Thursday? Does that mean Thursday?"

"Yeah. Thursday."

"Good. Now. Listen, are you going to help me with this Golden stuff?"

By this time they had reached their desks. Rather than answering, Henry picked up the message slips and read the petitions from his harem.

"Henry! Where have you *been*?"

"Henry! *Please* call me."

"Henry! I *have* to talk to you."

"Henry! Are you coming over?"

"Henry! Why don't you call me?"

Henry opened a drawer and threw the messages in. His phone rang. While he was on that call, Cesar made five of his own. By the time he was through, having talked to seventeen different levels of management at the Fifth Third Bank where someone named Bunny had been most helpful, Cesar was certain that Irving's extra Israeli key was still in his safe-deposit box where it had been undisturbed for two weeks. Henry finally hung up.

"Are you, Henry?"

"What? Going to work with you, Cesar?"

"Yes."

Henry pulled a toothpick out of the air and put it in his mouth. He stood and stared out of the dusty window at the open expanse of brown grass and blacktop that separated the building from the rest of the West End to the north. He rolled the toothpick from one corner of his mouth to the other and jiggled the change in his pants pocket. Cesar waited. Finally, Henry sat down at his desk and said, "All right."

Attaboy.

"Good," said Cesar. "You know, you didn't fall, Henry. Back there. You were pushed."

"Tieves?"

"Tieves."

Henry's toothpick got another workout. Cesar was happy. Now Lt. Tieves was the bad guy and Cesar could be the good guy. He had just time to begin filling Henry in on all he had done to learn about Irving Golden when Sgt. Evans came to request their presence in Lt. Tieves' office. Sgt. Evans' smile was unpleasant.

Half an hour later Henry and Cesar emerged from Lt. Tieves' office. They were now strongly bonded by their anger toward Lt. Tieves, the police bureaucracy, the Chief, the Manager, and Council, all of whom, if Lt. Tieves was to be believed, were gravely disappointed over the labors of the two detectives. The lieutenant had left the impression that only Henry's blackness had prevented a race war over the treatment of poor Alfred Brown. In Cesar's case nothing stood between him and a riot of businessmen fearing blunt objects. The lieutenant was gravely disappointed. He actually said *"Gravely Disappointed."*

Henry and Cesar grumbled and whined their way back to their desks in approved police fashion. Cesar borrowed a toothpick from Henry. It did not give noticeable comfort, just a little distraction. They grumbled and whined for a few more minutes and then buckled down to their work.

Cesar resumed his narration and Henry listened. He listened well, grunting occasionally to show he was awake and concentrating. He even took off his sunglasses—a peace offering recognized and silently accepted by Cesar, and Cesar saw that his eyes were not veiled. Henry was helping.

When Cesar's story came to the point where Henry was involved, which was Sunday afternoon, the atmosphere thickened a little, but the sunglasses stayed off. The breach was well and truly healed.

Henry put his sunglasses back on as soon as Cesar was through, but this time Cesar knew there was no insult. Henry opened his message drawer and began to rummage. There was no filing system, but he quickly emerged with the slip he was looking for. He folded it once and put it in his shirt pocket without explaining. He opened another drawer and fished out a mentholyptus drop and handed one to Cesar. The two of them inhaled the fumes in silence.

Then Henry began to talk. And immediately Cesar was surprised. Henry had not ignored his pleas to consider Donna's murder as a spinoff from the Irving Golden Show. He had also thought it funny that the house was so thoroughly ransacked, although his first reaction was to think drugs.

Cesar asked if that weren't still a possibility. After all, Alfred's alibi was his involvement in a drug sale. But Henry didn't think so. Alfred was dumb, but not dumb enough to stash drugs at Donna's house. She was too crazy and she had kids.

But, Cesar wondered aloud, what about someone else's drugs? Wasn't it possible that Donna had hidden someone else's property? Cesar explained his sketchy blackmail hypothesis. Henry chewed his toothpick over that for a while. Cesar tried to keep his rolling, too, but he dropped it.

They agreed to think about that for a while.

Then Henry surprised Cesar again. After he had told Cesar that he wasn't going to talk to Alfred, he did just that. And Alfred confirmed the phone calls. He said they were real. But he also said that if Donna ever recognized a voice she didn't tell him. Henry also said that Alfred really did feel bad about Donna. Cesar was glad to hear that. That made three when you counted Cesar and Linda.

Cesar told Henry about Donna's kids and how far he hadn't gotten with them. Would Henry try to talk to them and see if he could get anywhere? Henry would. Was Henry planning to chat up the neighbors to see if they had noticed anyone unusual visiting Donna? Henry was. Cesar was going to interview Marianne Kelly, and then he was going to go another round with Lady Rosemary Meynell. Would Henry like to join him? Henry would not like to expose himself to Marianne Kelly, but he would try to join Cesar at Golden Time Toys. He had never met a Lady Anyone and he was intrigued. His arrival would depend on his progress in Millvale.

Cesar and Henry parted in the parking lot. To Cesar's great relief Henry favored him with his very rare, very small relaxed smile. For-giveness is pleasant even when no sin has been committed.

20

MARIANNE KELLY KEPT Cesar waiting for fifteen minutes. Cesar sat in the dreary little lobby of The Bennett Agency and watched and listened to Renée, the lovely Haitian receptionist. Her fingers, dazzling in at least eight rings, flew over the PBX as she connected the outside world with the people she thought they ought to talk to. Eventually she allowed each to speak to the person of his choice, but those connections seemed somehow accidental. During lulls she connected herself with what must have been a Haitian chum as she would launch into very rapid French. Every once in a while she acknowledged Cesar's presence with a very flashy and very sexy smile. At last she decided that Cesar had waited long enough. With an old-fashioned lewd wink, she stabbed a button on her console and broke into Marianne Kelly's conversation.

"Marianne! Marianne!" She pronounced the name in the French fashion. Loud squawks escaped from the earphone. "Marianne! Do not forget your person! Your person is here! Do you forget? Come and see, okay?" Cesar heard more squawks, which Renée the Receptionist cut off with a click of a button and a wild laugh. She could work the PBX just fine when she wanted to.

"She talks to her *maman*. It is not important," she told Cesar.

"Oh. Thank you."

"Marianne is a leetle beetch." Wild laugh.

"Oh."

The leetle beetch banged into the lobby. If she was going to yell at Renée she swallowed it. Renée had picked up a twelve-inch letter opener, which she ran thoughtfully over her fingertips.

"You can come back now," said Marianne to Cesar. She was truculent.

Cesar looked over his shoulder as he went through the door. Renée was again laughing wildly. He nearly had to run to catch up with Ms. Kelly.

"Now. What's this about? What are you here for?" Marianne's tough line of questioning lost some effect when she tipped her chair back too far and started to topple backwards. She threw her short legs out and saved herself. Neither she nor Cesar acknowledged the near fall.

"Am I a suspect? I don't have to say anything, you know."

"Ma'am, you're not a suspect."

"Why not? You're here about Irving Golden, aren't you? I was there, you know."

"Yes, I'm—"

"What's the matter? You don't want to talk to a woman? I happen to know you've talked to all the men in the office already. Why are you just getting around to me?"

"Ma'am, I'm trying—"

"You're a big friend of Cleary's aren't you?"

"Yeah. Tom and I go way back."

"It figures. It figures."

Now what the hell was he supposed to make of that?

"Cleary's a wimp."

Oh, yeah? Well, you're a leetle beetch.

"I'm talking to everybody who might have any information that might help us solve a serious crime."

"Well, go ahead. Ask questions. And please try to remember I've got to work for a living and I don't have all morning."

Cesar didn't think it was fair. He had Detective Griesel every day, and now he had Ms. Marianne Kelly and he didn't know what to do with either one. He retreated to his notebooks and pretended to scan pages while he tried to decide on the most effective opener. Ms. Kelly seemed to hold two positions. On one hand she wanted Cesar to know she was a hotshot executive who didn't have time to waste with low-ranking detectives. On the other hand she wanted to be taken seriously as a suspected murderer. Cesar didn't take her seriously as a hotshot executive or as a suspected murderer. All he wanted was any information she might have that he hadn't already heard. He looked up to meet her eyes, which were just slightly crossed. He had a feeling that this was the expression she used on the tennis court.

"Could you give me your version of the meeting that took place last Thursday?"

Cesar thought that was a neutral question, but Marianne clumped her chair to the floor and swung around to face her Gloria Steinem poster in dramatic disdain. She knocked over a pencil cup in the process.

"Oh, *Brother*," she groaned.

"Something wrong?" asked Cesar.

"Something wrong? You've only heard about that meeting *six* times. Is that all you're going to ask?"

"No, that's not all. But it's where we start."

Out of the corner of his eye Cesar noticed Tom in the hall. Marianne couldn't see him from her seat, and it was a good thing she couldn't. Tom was imitating her cross-eyed tennis expression.

"God, you sound just like Cleary. You guys really must have grown up together. Was he always like he is now?"

"Hard to say."

"He's such a wimp."

Cesar reached over and pulled the flimsy accordion door closed without looking at Tom.

"Hey! Leave it open!" said Marianne.

"If you don't mind, Ms. Kelly. I'd like you to feel free to talk. You were going to tell me about the meeting."

"Well, if you will just look," said Marianne pointing up, "everybody can hear everything in this place. I mean we haven't even got a ceiling."

"All right, is there a conference room?"

"Yes, but I want to stay here."

Cesar was beginning to realize that any suggestions he made would be met with a negative. He supposed it was Assertiveness Training at work.

"Fine. We'll stay here. Now would you mind telling me about the meeting?"

"Yes, I would mind. But I'll tell you," said Marianne. And she began.

Cesar listened and watched. She was not a skillful narrator. At least she wasn't as good as Bennett or Golden or Enneking or any of the others he had talked to. There was no detachment for Marianne Kelly. Everything related to her and her position as an incredibly smart female surrounded by male jerks. Not even Bob Atwood, the man who nuzzled her neck, escaped her disapproval. No one had stepped in to defend her. No one had laid his career on the line for her. She was surrounded by spineless men.

Cesar tuned out for a minute and simply looked at Marianne. Despite her cranky expression, whiney voice, and tomboy slouch, she was attractive. Her three-piece suit could not completely obliterate a very good figure. Her breasts, if not major, were significant, particularly on one so short. Her legs, tan and complex, were excellent. Cesar was careful not to be caught staring. She'd have him up before the Human Relations Commission in a flash. Why couldn't she be more . . . more like Grace Golden?

Grace Golden was rich. Marianne Kelly was not.

Cesar tuned back in. She was doing pretty well for someone who didn't want to talk. But still nothing new. Cesar began to listen to a conversation floating over the wall from one of the other offices. Two women were talking about Donna Creech.

". . . awful, but who's surprised?"

"Did you ever see him?"

"(something) huge black guy."

"Her kids are black, aren't they?"

156

"Beautiful. Really. I don't know. She was so homely."

"But what do you expect? Where was it? Out in Fairmount?"

"I know. I won't even drive through there."

"Are you listening to me?" That was Marianne. "I mean if there are other things more interesting, I've got plenty to do."

"I'm listening."

"So anyway, I was just so hacked off. I mean, you probably don't understand . . . " Marianne got back into her groove.

A familiar voice worked its way down the hall, stopping at office doors and joking. Atwood. Cesar watched Marianne. She knew he was coming from the way she watched the door. When he got to Marianne's office he slammed the folding door open.

"Good morning!" Atwood beamed at his girlfriend without noticing Cesar.

"*Atwood!* Please! I've got company." She smiled to show she wasn't really pissed off. Atwood looked around.

"Cripes! It's the cops! I can't take it! Tell him, babe. We're in it together. You got to understand, officer. It was passion!" Such a joker.

"*Atwood!*" Marianne laughed.

How could she stand the guy?

"So, tell us, Detective Franck. Is there now a multiple murderer among us? Does a mass killer walk free to terrorize junior account executives as well as cleaning ladies?" asked Atwood.

"Atwood, what are you *talking* about?"

"My dear, haven't you heard? It was all over the news yesterday."

"What was?" asked Marianne. "You *know* I was gone yesterday."

"I do know. Cincinnati was empty without you. And now it's empty without Donna Creech."

"Why? What *happened?*"

Atwood drew a finger across his throat.

"No!" Ms. Kelly gasped, but she didn't look too upset. "Somebody cut her throat? God!"

"Not literally, dear. It was another blow to the brain. Right, Detective Franck?"

Cesar barely nodded. This was one of the least likable men he had seen for months.

"Well, *tell* me! What happened?! God! Donna Creech! *Really?!*"

"I'm interrupting your third degree, sweetheart. I'll tell you at lunch. Besides, Detective Franck knows far more than I. Hot on the trail, Inspector?"

Cesar didn't even nod.

"Man of few words. Be careful, Marianne. He'll have you spilling your guts before you know what's happening to you."

"Right, Atwood. I'll be careful."

"Lunch?" asked Atwood.

"I'll see. I've got a lot to do." Marianne glared at Cesar.

"Shall I call your lawyer?" Atwood laughed.

"No need. Thanks. We're almost through, right, Detective Franck?"

"Shouldn't be too much longer, ma'am."

"Ma'am?" said Atwood. "How delightful!"

"I know," said Marianne. "Isn't it *amazing?*"

Cesar was ready to punch them both out. Equally. Without discrimination. These two deserved each other.

Atwood withdrew, still grinning.

"So, where were we?" asked Marianne.

"We were—" began Cesar.

"Oh! Tell me about Donna Creech! I knew her, you know. What happened?"

"If you don't mind, I'd like—"

"Oh, come on. Tell me! What happened?"

All right. Since you asked so nicely.

"Donna Creech was killed by a blow to the head. She died in her house. She had two kids. Nobody saw anything. We don't have any suspects. I'm not on that case."

"That's all you know?"

"What else do you want to know?"

"I don't know. What about what Atwood said about a mass murderer? I mean, what do you think?"

"I don't think we have a mass murderer," said Cesar.

"What about Irving Golden? That's got to be the same guy, doesn't it?"

"Or woman," said Cesar.

"Right. Or woman." She missed or ignored the sarcasm. "You know, we all wondered why Irving kept her. She was such a crappy cleaner. I mean the worst. Do you suppose . . . ? You know, my cousin is a social worker and she said they were always having trouble with Donna because she used to leave her kids alone when she went out with black guys. I mean, *really*. Also, a lot of people think she was Irving's source of dope."

"Marijuana?" asked Cesar.

"Right. You know, I believe that."

"Did you know that Mr. Golden used marijuana?"

"Well, he never *told* me. But everyone says he smoked it like crazy."

"That's certain?"

"God! I don't know! I told you everyone said so. I mean, a lot of people do now, you know. Even *cops*." She glared at him.

"It's still against the law," said Cesar.

Someone knocked on Marianne's wall. The folding plastic door wouldn't stand up to knuckles.

"Come in," she snapped.

Jack Squires squeezed in. He started to say something to Marianne but stopped when he saw Cesar. There was a brief moment in which he looked startled and then rattled, but then he smiled. "Sorry. Didn't know you had company. Good to see you." He stuck out a hand to Cesar who tried to stand up but gave up when he realized the cramped cubicle would not allow such courtesies. "How's the investigation coming? Any luck?" asked Squires. "Coming along," said Cesar. "What did you want, Jack?" asked Marianne. "It's not important, really, dear. Just wanted to remind you about the copy conference. Fifteen minutes, if you're free." "Right. It's up to Detective Franck here." "Don't worry. We'll wait. No problem. Good to see you again." Squires started to back out of the door. "What'd you do to your hand, Jack?" Marianne pointed to a Band-Aid on the back of Squires' thumb. "What?" Squires looked at his hand and blushed. "Oh, that. Had to change a tire. First time with the new car." Marianne clucked. "You're so mechanical." "Terribly," said Squires. "See you later. Sorry to interrupt, Detective Franck." "Nice seeing you," said Cesar. "He's such a spaz," said Marianne.

Was this woman incapable of saying nice things? What would it cost her to let up a little?

"He seems like a nice enough guy," said Cesar.

"Oh, sure, he's nice enough. *Terminally* nice. But what a spaz. I wish I could have seen him changing his tire." She laughed. Then she straightened up and put on her business face. "All right, let's get this over with. I've got a meeting."

Cesar got her started again and very quickly tuned out again. Squires was jumpy as a cat. Business problems? Domestic problems? He was probably scared to death of Marianne Kelly on top of everything. What a girl to have on your team. How do you bang up your thumb on the *back* when you change a tire?

Marianne stopped talking. She was getting wise to him.

"Go on," said Cesar. "I'm listening." To be safe, he listened.

She was explaining her theory of how Golden's assailant got in and like everyone else, her guess was the same as Cesar's. But then she went on to say that she was completely baffled as to who it could have been since everyone there except Irving was such a complete wimp. Irving wasn't a wimp, he was a bastard. Cesar asked about Bennett. Was he, too, a wimp? No, she had forgotten him. He wasn't a wimp and neither was Atwood, but since they were both "nice guys" they were not suspect.

"What about Enneking?" asked Cesar. He wasn't really interested in her theories. They would all be political. He was, however, curious about her politics.

"Mr. Mystery?" asked Marianne. "You know he's a real possibility. A real possibility. He's queer for his toys, you know. A really weird guy. I'll bet he's having an affair with his Denver Doll." She laughed at her own wit and then quickly went into a tirade about Denver Dolls. She didn't like them. Cesar heard her out and then asked her about the gathering in the parking lot after the meeting. She had been the first to leave so she couldn't confirm any other departures. Cesar noted, however, that she wanted to get off the subject. He stared at her for a minute as he tried to think why. His staring made her blush. She did seem to be hiding something. Had she been waiting around for Atwood? Atwood hadn't been able to cover for his time after the meeting, not well enough to take him out of the running.

Cesar probed a little.

"Where did you go afterward?"

"Home."

"Straight home?"

"Yes. Straight home. Why?"

"You didn't meet anybody?"

"No! What are you asking for?" She was more and more uncomfortable.

"Are you sure?" Cesar was now sure that she was holding back. It had to be Atwood. There was a certain pleasure in making her squirm. She'd been rude enough to him.

"You didn't wait for anyone?" he asked.

"What do you mean? What are you getting at? Why should I wait for anyone?" She glared at him. "Oh! I know. You've been talking to people about Bob and me, haven't you?"

She was practically in Cesar's face.

"*God*, the *nerve*! I can't believe it! You know, what I do with my time and who I see is none of your business and it's sure as hell none of Tom Cleary's business, and you can believe I'll tell him that, so don't . . . don't . . ." What he was not supposed to do he would not know. She had become incoherent.

"I'm sorry, Ms. Kelly. You've got the wrong idea. Tom Cl—"

"I don't have the wrong idea! You have the wrong idea!"

"Ms. Kelly, I haven't discussed your relationships with anyone. And Tom Cleary hasn't either, so you can relax."

"I don't believe you."

"I'm sorry, ma'am."

"Sure you are. Why were you asking whether I met anyone? Answer that." She leaned back in her chair dangerously again. Arms folded. Eyes crossed.

"Ma'am, I need to know where everybody was when Mr. Golden was killed. I need to know what they were doing. That's routine police questioning. I don't care what you were doing as long as you weren't in Mr. Golden's office. No kidding. But I do need to know."

She glared at him. He stared at her.

"I wrecked my car."

"I'm sorry," said Cesar.

"That's what I was doing."

"Okay."

"I was so pissed off I got in my new car and wrecked it on a lamp post. It's a LeCar and I just got it."

"Okay."

"There was a cop who saw the whole thing. You can look it up. It's probably on a computer somewhere."

"Okay."

"But I haven't told anybody here, and I'd appreciate it if you didn't either."

"Okay."

"I really mean that. I don't want people talking about it."

What a girl. She'd rather have people thinking she murdered somebody than banged her car up.

"I won't tell anybody."

"Thanks. Now. What else do I have to tell you?"

"I guess that's it. Unless you think of anything else that might help me."

"Right. Can I go? I've got that meeting."

They both stood up, forced to stand toe-to-toe by the size of the office. Cesar stared down at the top of her head. She was short and she did not have dandruff. There was a brief temptation to take the prickly junior executive into his arms and the temptation confused Cesar for a moment until he decided it was simply due to the proximity. He didn't usually get that close to women unless he or they meant business. Cesar backed out into the hall and she followed. "Well. It's been interesting," she said and offered her hand for a manly shake. Assertiveness at work again. She headed for her meeting.

As soon as she was gone Tom Cleary appeared in the hall. "Did you have fun?" he asked Cesar.

Cesar scowled and pushed Tom toward the lobby.

"What's the matter?" Tom was laughing. "I told you she was impossible." Cesar didn't say anything until they were in the lobby.

"You shouldn't have done that, Tom."

"I wasn't listening in. Really!"

"I don't care. That girl's crazy. If she'd have seen you in the hall she would have been all over me."

"Oh, don't be so touchy. She *didn't* see me so it's all right. You're safe. What did I tell you? She's crazy, isn't she?"

"She's confusing, that's for sure."

"She ees a leetle beetch, no?" Cesar swung around. He had forgotten Renée. She was all ears. "Christ," he muttered.

"Answer the phone, Renée," said Tom. "You want to go someplace and talk, Cesar?"

"No, thanks. I've got a lot to do."

"You don't want to know all about Marianne?"

"Not now. What kind of car does your boss drive and where does he park it? Do you know?"

"Sure. A Cutlass. Silver. Everybody parks out on the street. We don't have any parking."

"Thanks."

As Cesar left, Renée called out "au revoir." To the best of his knowledge that was the first time anyone had ever said "au revoir" to him.

Ninth Street was full of parked cars, most bearing tickets. There were three grey or silver Cutlasses, all dirty. None of the tires looked as if it were fresh from the trunk.

21

IRKED BY THE waste of time spent with Ms. Kelly, Cesar slammed himself into the duty Hornet and roared out of his parking space and into the street. Perhaps it was just as well that the skinflints in Purchasing had specified the least powerful engine available or Cesar might have injured many citizens in his flight from the scene of his irritation. As it was, the engine had sufficient power to speed him two blocks beyond the Golden Time Toy Company where he was to rendezvous with Henry before he collected himself. Although he was alone, Cesar blushed at his error and his loss of control. He doubled back and found a spot in the Golden Time parking lot. The other Hornet in the lot he assumed to be Henry's.

Loyal Leonard was not on duty. His replacement was a very short woman who seemed to take as much pride in her uniform as Leonard. She peered out from under her visor and regarded Cesar with Leonard's brand of mistrust. He accepted a visitor's tag and found his way to the executive offices.

The halls were silent. Every door to every office was open. Cesar, proceeding down the hall, saw that each occupant of each office was sitting silently and staring into the hall. Work was not being done. What was going on was listening. The stares were gazes of concentration which Cesar's passage disrupted only slightly. The eyes of the listeners flicked to the detective for no more than half a second before the shamelessly industrious eavesdropping resumed.

Cesar had been tromping rather violently. He was late to his rendezvous and he was still irritated by Ms. Kelly, but he fell under the spell of the listeners and began to pad softly. There was disagreement ahead. There was shouting. And the disturbance seemed to be in Irving Golden's office. Cesar reached the door to Rosemary Meynell's office and stepped in. Henry was there, and like all the Golden employees, Henry was entranced. He gestured violently and quickly to Cesar, ordering him to freeze and shut up. Cesar obeyed.

The voices in Irving's office were those of Frederick and Grace Golden and occasionally Rosemary Meynell. The subject was control of the company. Cesar began to understand the heavy local interest and eased quietly into one of the sofas so that he could listen in comfort. Henry stood transfixed.

Cesar probably knew more about this fight than anyone in the building except the principals. He knew that Irving had left no clear plan for his succession. Irving expected to live much longer. Cesar also knew that Grace was fully prepared to do battle and that Frederick expected to pop into his brother's chair without a fight. Cesar even knew that Grandma was supposed to hold the cards. He did not know where Rosemary Meynell stood, and he did not know the ground rules of the fight.

Within minutes he saw that there were no ground rules. Grace and Frederick were fighting as family members fight, personally and viciously. Control of Golden Time Toys would pass to the fitter of the two.

Frederick was a man in his prime. He had experience, a deep voice, and he outweighed his niece by ninety pounds. Grace was a woman coming into her prime, her voice shook when she got angry, which she was, and she had probably never gone toe to toe with anyone for really big stakes.

The world expected Frederick Golden to take the helm. Grace had no clear claim to the job. She was going on willpower and Irving's genes. Even if Cesar had not been partisan he would still have bet on Grace.

"Do you really think, Frederick," said Grace, "do you *really* think for one minute that Daddy would have put you in this chair when he never let you handle anything, *anything* of any importance?"

"'Daddy' doesn't enter into it, Grace. 'Daddy's' dead. And I don't care what he would have done, and I don't care what he thought. It was not his company. It was and is Mom's. And I am her son and I have worked my ass off for years and I have *earned* this company and if you think I'm about to hand it over to you you're as dizzy as your mother and—"

"Don't you *ever* talk about my mother like that. Do you hear me? *Ever!* You've been a perfect shit to her for years and don't think I haven't noticed. And she is *not* the issue." Grace's voice was no longer shaking.

"No? Come on, honey. I know Irene. She put you up to this, didn't she? She's afraid there might be an interruption in her charge accounts, right?"

"Oh, *Frederick*." Grace was disgusted.

"Oh, *Grace*," mimicked Frederick. "I've known your mother longer than you have. Years longer. She lives to shop. No, I take that back. She lives to shop and *lunch* and I don't know how much money your father shoveled her way to keep her—"

"I told you to shut *up* about her. She's not the issue anymore than your friend Lauren."

Henry looked at Cesar. Cesar shrugged. He didn't know who Lauren was either.

"Rosemary, would you please excuse us?" begged Frederick.

"Stay right here, Rosemary. I want you here."

"I think—" began Rosemary.

"Here!" snapped Grace.

"Lauren Mandel is none—"

"Lauren Mandel is as pertinent as my mother, Frederick. And if you think she's a secret, you're the last person in Cincinnati who does. So let's not talk about shoveling money to the charge accounts."

"Grace, you are—"

"I am just pointing out that you've got a mistress and you've had her for years and you spend money on her *as well* as your wife and I don't *blame* you, Uncle Fred. Passing for a WASP is nerve-wracking I'm sure. So you probably need some—"

"Lauren Mandel is—"

"Lauren Mandel is a very nice lady. I like her. Everybody likes Lauren. But she's not the issue, is she? Anymore than Mother is, right?"

"The issue is—" Poor Frederick. He was winded.

"The issue is who's going to run this company, right?"

"You *bet* that's the issue, Grace. Only it's not an issue, because it's not a question. I'm going to—"

"You're going to come in here and spend ten thousand dollars on oak paneling and start issuing suicidal memos like this, right?"

"Did you read that?" snapped Frederick.

"You bet I read this, Frederick, and I'd like to have you locked up for it. But I can't. I think I'll duplicate it and spread it around as an example of your sound thinking. What on *earth*—"

"Give me that—"

"Don't interrupt, Uncle Fred. I'm asking you a question. Just *what* possessed you to order cancelling the Denver Dolls? *How* could you be so stupid? Do you realize—"

"Do you realize how *disgusting* those dolls are? They are the perfect example of what's wrong with this company and what was wrong with Irving's management."

"How can you—"

"You have no *idea* what people are saying about this company. I go *out* in the world. I *hear* things and let me tell you the world thinks this is a schlock outfit. *Schlock!* And we're about to unleash these disgusting little—"

"Frederick, the world that thinks this is a schlock outfit is *your* world. It's not *the* world. It's your golf-playing, coupon-clipping chums whose grandparents made fortunes in *lard*. *Lard*, for God's sake. It's real estate and municipals now, but it was lard then and they were happy to make a fortune with it. Now how toys are worse than that is beyond me, but let me tell you I think toys are just *fine*, thank you, and I mean *our* toys and that includes the Denver Dolls which, by the way, had better hit the market sooner than ever since we're going to have to beat the Boston Babes. And speaking of the Boston Babes, I can't help wondering just *how* it is that we find ourselves catching up on a project *we* invented."

"What's *that* supposed to mean?"

"You know damned well what I mean, Uncle Fred. *Somebody* leaked about the Denver Dolls. I don't suppose you have any idea who?"

"How *dare* you, Grace! How *dare* you! If you are even suggesting that I would—"

"Wouldn't you?"

"Grace! I'm your *uncle*, I'm *family*. And you are full of—"

"Mr. Golden," Rosemary cut in at last.

"What's the matter, Rosemary? Afraid I'll say 'shit'? Have your ears gone delicate all of a sudden? I'm so sorry. I forgot. My brother never uttered such a word in his life. He was such a *gentleman*.

"Oh, Frederick," said Grace with great disgust.

"I'm so very sorry, dear. I have offended the memory of a great and noble man. My apologies to both of you. I know what *deep* esteen you both held him in."

"Frederick, that is your *brother* you're being shitty about."

"Thank you, Grace. Nice of you to remember the relationship at last. Now what was this about your uncle, the industrial spy?"

"I didn't say—"

"You didn't *need* to say, dear. But let me tell you this. I don't think that Irving, no matter how he felt about me, would *ever* have suggested that I would pull a trick like you've suggested. But then my brother was just a bully, not a viper like his daughter."

Cesar missed Grace's answer, distracted by the arrival of new eaves-droppers. Irene Golden, pale but very glamorous in a sable coat, was escorting a tiny women in plain mink. The mink woman was in her late seventies or early eighties by Cesar's reckoning. Grandma Golden? Had to be.

"Who are these guys, Irene?"

"This is a policeman, Mother Golden. He's Detective Franck, who's been such a help. You remember?"

"Oh, yeah." Grandma Golden toddled over to look up at Cesar. Even on three-inch heels she had to be under five feet tall. Tough lady—no shuffling—many diamonds. Cesar was impressed.

"Frank?" she asked Cesar. "F-R-A-N-K?"

"No, ma'am, F-R-A-N-C-K."

"Oh." She lost interest at once. "Is he a cop?" she pointed to Henry.

166

"Yes, ma'am," said Cesar. "This is Detective Chapman."

"What's going on in there?" Grandma asked Henry. Henry gaped. What could he say? But Grace and Frederick had at last realized that they were not alone and had come to the door.

"Hello, Grandma," said Grace.

"Mother," said Frederick.

Cesar stared at Grace. Doing battle made her more attractive than ever. Her face was flushed. Wisps of hair lay dampened and curled on her forehead and, although she was containing her temper for Grandma, her eyes continued to flash.

Frederick looked awful. Where Grace was flushed, he was scarlet. His hair had spiked out and his eyes were red. Cesar took a second look at Frederick's nose and found it boozy.

Grandma Golden fixed them one at a time with the same look Lillian used to nail her boy Cesar to the wall when he got out of line.

She headed into Irving's office backing her son and granddaughter to the desk. Rosemary Meynell, for once, seemed to be at a loss for words or action. She finally broke the silence.

"Would you care for some coffee, Mrs. Golden?"

"No."

"Oh. Well. Then . . ." said Rosemary.

"I want to talk to these two here who can't remember that my son was buried only yesterday, and by myself if you don't mind?"

Rosemary beat a retreat.

"You can wait out there, Irene. And you," Grandma pointed to Rosemary, "close the door. There are policemen out there."

Rosemary slid out and cleared the door without a sound. Within seconds she resumed her normal poise. Cesar straightened his back and checked his tie.

"May I get you some coffee, Mrs. Golden?"

Irene nodded and settled herself into the sofa, shrugging the sable over the back. Henry was genuinely and visibly impressed. She smiled graciously at the detective and then mentally withdrew. Her face went quite blank.

"Gentlemen, may I help you?" asked Rosemary, drawing coffee for Irene.

They had come to talk to Rosemary. They had not expected to step into a major family battle. Cesar still wanted to talk to Rosemary, and he definitely wanted to find out if Grace was going to prevail.

"I was hoping to ask you a few more questions, ma'am, but I'd be glad to wait. Would it be all right to use the conference room for a few minutes?"

Miss Meynell let a little frown play on her lips. Cesar waited. He could think of no reason for her to refuse.

"Of course. You know where it is."

Henry coughed. Cesar had failed to introduce him to Rosemary. Well, he could just wait. Cesar hustled him into the conference room and shut the door. Henry plopped down at the end seat.

"That's the death chair, Henry." Henry got up and moved around the corner. Cesar sat opposite.

"How did it go, Henry? Did you pick up anything out there?"

"Hey, wait a minute. I want to know about that stuff in there. You didn't tell me these people were like 'Denver.' They're crazy."

"What do you mean, 'Denver'?" asked Cesar.

"TV, man! The show! 'Denver'!"

He was right. Beautiful young woman fighting with big powerful uncle for control of the family fortune! But as quickly as he saw the parallel, Cesar looked for ways to destroy it. He liked Grace and he didn't like "Denver." He didn't want to be part of a television soap. But he couldn't dismiss the scene. It happened and he had heard it. And he had begun to feel the scene had something to do with his job. He had heard something that made him want to work, to think. What was it? Grandma had interrupted something.

"That's the girl you like, right?" asked Henry.

"Yeah, I like her. She's a nice girl."

"Sounds like a tough lady to me."

"Yeah. I suppose. No, she's not tough. I don't know."

"Too tough for you, Cesar."

"I don't know. What are you talking about? I'm not going out with her."

"You want to hear about Millvale?" asked Henry. He took pity on Cesar.

"Yeah. Tell me about Millvale. Tell me all about Millvale."

Henry smiled. "Millvale is a mess." He had made the best of the short time available to dig for information. His technique was not the door-to-door method. Henry didn't have to go door to door in Millvale. He had taken his own Mark IV out to the project and parked right in the middle. Within seconds people were coming to him. First the kids, then a few Bad Dudes, then the old men, and finally, after they had slipped into something more comfortable, the young ladies.

Cesar could see it all and he was envious. Had he spent four days going door to door he would not have had one-tenth of Henry's contact. Little old ladies might have taken pity on him, but that would have been the extent of it. Cesar wasn't ready to become a black policeman, but he was wise enough to see when it was helpful to be something other than a white guy with a moustache.

"So, great. Everybody talked to you. What did you *learn*, Henry."

Henry's eyes cooled for an instant. He did not like to be rushed.

"A lot of you people go through Millvale, Ceez. Did you know that?"

Us people. White people. And yes, he knew that. People went through on business. Some legitimate, but most of it was funny business. Social workers and insurance collectors went in and did their stuff and got out, but they were outnumbered by the "loan collectors" and the drug shoppers and, believe it or not, some white pimps. "Only problem is," said Henry, "you all look so much alike."

Cesar waited for Henry to enjoy his joke.

"Just kidding, Ceez. Just kidding." And he was kidding. The residents of Millvale have time to observe and they observe keenly. And since Henry was a plump, balding black man with large sweet eyes and since he drove such a lovely clean Mark IV, the residents were happy to offer their observations. There had indeed been at least two unfamiliar automobiles on Donna's street over the past couple of days. The Millvale residents remembered a maroon K Car and a grey or silver Cutlass, both four-door sedans. "White folks' cars, they said, Cesar." Henry enjoyed that.

"Did they get a look at the drivers?" asked Cesar.

"White men."

"That's it?"

"White men. Business men. One kid thought the guy in the K car might have been a cop—looked mean." Henry smiled an angel smile.

"And they were on Donna's street?"

"In her block. It's dead end, remember?"

"Yeah."

"So. What do you think?"

"What I think," said Cesar, "is that there's a couple of thousand grey or silver Cutlasses on the road in Hamilton County. They didn't happen to remember anything helpful like plates?" Henry shook his head. "But that's a help. No kidding. I was just looking at grey Cutlasses this morning."

"I think you're looking for a four-door."

"Because it's a white guy's car?"

"Well." Henry was slightly embarrassed by the stereotype, but it was probably right.

"And a maroon K Car," said Cesar.

"With a tough guy at the wheel," said Henry.

"What's a tough guy doing with a K Car?" Cesar wondered.

"Hey, gas is high. Even for tough guys."

Cesar filed the K Car away. It rang no bells. The Cutlass had a future.

"Don't get too excited," said Henry. "These guys didn't stop or anything. They didn't visit anybody."

"But," said Cesar.

"But, you know how it is. People out there know what's going on— they usually know who's in trouble, who's not. And they didn't have anybody in mind for these guys."

"So they could have been interested in Donna?"

"Could have," said Henry. "And," he bit his thumb, pausing for effect, "I talked to Donna's kids. They're nice kids. Mitch reminds me of Gregory."

That was high praise from Henry. His nephew Gregory was the apple of his eye. The last time Cesar saw Gregory he had on about two hundred buck's worth of the absolute latest and best jogging gear—a typical gift from his uncle. He seemed like a normal kid, though.

"Those kids got to get out of there," said Henry. "Millvale's a mess."

"Did they tell you anything they didn't tell me?"

"I don't know. Had they seen what happened to their rooms when you saw them?"

"No."

"Well, they were steamed up about that. Both of them. That guy got into Stacey's stuff. Broke one of her dolls."

"God, he really wanted something, didn't he?"

"Must have," said Henry. "But he could have left the kids' stuff alone. That stinks."

"Yeah. But if he knew Donna . . ."

"What?"

Something scampered across Cesar's brain, but it scampered on out the door.

"I was just thinking how Donna was. She could have hidden something in their rooms—wouldn't bother her."

"What about the kids? They would have found whatever it was. No good hiding it there."

Cesar agreed.

"But they didn't know that," said Henry.

"You have to have kids to know you can't hide things in kids' rooms."

"So we're looking for a guy with a grey Cutlass with no kids."

"White guy," reminded Henry.

There was a knock at the door. Henry opened the door to Rosemary.

"Are you Detective Chapman?" she asked.

He nodded. It pleased Cesar to see that there was a woman who could leave Henry tongue-tied. "You have a call." She pointed to Irving's phone. "Line eight."

Henry picked up, listened, grunted, wrote down a number, mashed the cut-off button, and dialed. Cesar started to ask who and why but Henry waved him down.

"Mitch? . . . Yeah, how you doing? . . . Good. What's up? Why'd you call? . . . Yeah . . . Yeah . . ." He listened awhile, then "No. No, it's a good thing you told me . . . Yeah . . . Listen, put Stacey on a minute. . . . Hi . . . No, you're not in trouble . . . No, Mitch is kidding you . . . Right . . . Right, I'll tell him . . . Put him back on . . . Hi, Mitch . . . Hey, Mitch, don't give Stacey a hard time about this, okay? . . . No . . . you don't understand . . . That's the way girls are, Mitch . . . Right . . . Okay? Be good to her . . . Right, man, look, I'll see you later . . . Sometime this week . . . Right . . . Right . . . For sure, and listen, thanks for calling. Later.''

He hung up.

"What was that all about?" asked Cesar.

"Kids. They're funny. He called to squeal on Stacey."

"What about?"

"Did she show you one of those little dolls when you were out there?"

"Yeah."

"Well, she told Mitch that she wasn't supposed to have it. She said her mamma was looking for it but Stacey told her she lost it. Now her conscience is hurting her. Mitch made her call me." Henry chuckled.

Cesar didn't laugh; he was thinking.

"Kids are something," said Henry. He looked at Cesar, disappointed that he wasn't getting a reaction. And then Henry realized that he was getting a reaction and he sat down and looked across the table at Cesar.

"Is that what he was looking for?" he asked. "That doll?"

"Maybe," said Cesar.

"Is that what you're thinking?"

"Yeah, that's what I was thinking, but I don't know why."

"It's little," said Henry. "Easy to hide. Hard to find. Explain why you'd tear up the kids' rooms."

They sat and thought, staring at each other.

"But it's crazy," said Henry finally. "What's it cost? A few bucks?"

"Four or five."

"And why? What would he want it for? It doesn't make sense."

"No," said Cesar.

"Drugs?" asked Henry. "No. Too small."

"Too small," said Cesar.

"I wonder why Donna wanted it back?"

"I dunno."

That was not completely truthful of Cesar. True, he did not *know* why she wanted it back, but he had a pretty good idea. It was probably not hers in the first place. She could have "borrowed" it from Golden Time. To do what with it? Sell it?

And then Cesar was ashamed of himself. He was thinking the worst of Donna with her not even in her grave. She was believed to be a liar and a lousy mother, but no one had called her a thief.

Maybe she just picked it up and forgot to put it back. Still, why get excited about one doll when several million were due to hit the shelves this year?

Was that why Irving died? Did he have a Denver Doll that someone wanted?

"I told Stacey she didn't have to give it back," said Henry. "Okay?"

"Sure," said Cesar. Then, "No, maybe not. Let's take a look at it, okay? I think I can get her another one. Would you go out there and work a swap?"

"Sure," Henry shrugged. "You think we need to?"

"Yeah. I do."

"Now?"

"Why not?"

"I thought we were going to spend some time with Miss Meynell," said Henry.

"We were, only I didn't know there was going to be this family fight today."

"Damn! I forgot the fight. How do you suppose that came out? Who's Granny's favorite?"

"Beats me," said Cesar. "Let's go see."

They stood, stretched, and pushed their chairs back under the conference table.

"You're going back to Millvale?" Cesar asked.

"If I have to."

"I kind of want to see that doll."

"You better get that substitute for her. I don't go without it."

Miss Meynell was "filing." The filing cabinet was right beside the closed door leading from her office into Irving's, and she was standing as close as she could get to the door. It was a pleasure to see how smoothly she shifted her attention from the discussion in Irving's office back to the "filing" as the detectives entered her office. A lesser person would have blushed.

Irene's sables remained where she had molted them. She was not in the room. Rosemary slid the file drawer home and turned to the detectives. "May I help you?"

Cesar asked for a Denver Doll. Rosemary did not want to give him a Denver Doll. She asked why and Cesar claimed police business. She was not impressed. It was her understanding that such requests required a court order to back them up. Cesar said please and again she said no. Henry did not help. The issue remained unsettled as, simultaneously, Irene Golden returned and Grandma's meeting broke up.

Grandma allowed Irene to embrace her before she spoke to Cesar and Henry.

"When are you boys gonna catch the brute that killed Irving?"

Excellent question, ma'am.

"Grandma, they're doing their best. We're lucky to have them."

Grace Golden was smiling from ear to ear. Cesar took that to mean that she had gotten Grandma's backing. Frederick didn't smile, but he wasn't crying either. Grandma must have taken care of him some way. Grandma clucked her tongue. She wanted to see magnifying glasses out and in use. She wanted a collar, a line-up, and maybe an electrocution. The two detectives continued to stand in the middle of the room doing nothing. Grandma held out her arms for her coat. Frederick scooped it up and held it for her. She didn't look at him or thank him. She just went out leaving Irene to scramble for her sable and catch up. "Will there be a meeting this afternoon, Miss Golden?" Rosemary's question meant that she had divined the same outcome as Cesar, and her smile suggested that she had, again like Cesar, been partisan. "Yes. Thank you, Rosemary. See you at four, Frederick?" She managed to convey the message that an answer of "no" was unacceptable. But she was smiling. Cesar was proud of her.

Frederick made a little bow and left.

"There's been a call from Sri Lanka, Miss Golden. I asked them to call back this afternoon. And Mr. Dryden from Fifth Third needs some help. Also—"

"Thank you, Rosemary. I'll call the bank back. Do you know what Sri Lanka wanted? It's midnight there, isn't it?"

"They're working three shifts now."

"Right."

"Miss Golden?"

"Yes, Cesar."

"We'd like to get out of your way for a while, so there's—"

"Cesar, you're never in the way. Please."

"Oh. Well, thanks. As a matter of fact, I'll probably have to come back this afternoon, but I was wondering if I could have one of the Denver Dolls. I need it."

"But, of course. You should have asked Rosemary."

"I—"

"Rosemary, I know you'll cooperate with *any* request Detective Franck makes."

"Of course, Miss Golden."

"Thank you. Thank you very much."

Rosemary pushed a button on the phone and ordered up a Denver Doll for Cesar.

"You'll have it in a minute," she said.

"What are you going to do with it?" asked Grace.

"Um. It may be material, ma'am," said Cesar.

"Damn." Grace laughed. "I've turned you into a policeman again. I'm sorry. When will you be back? Do you have to go?"

Cesar would have liked to stay. It was interesting to watch Grace as Boss. But he also wanted to listen to the Irving tapes and, if Sergeant

Evans, Lieutenant Tieves, and Detective Griesel would allow, Cesar wanted to think. He did have to go.

A lady in a blue smock, about Lillian's size and shape, stood in the doorway with Cesar's doll. She did not look oppressed. She looked extremely curious.

"It's for the gentleman," said Rosemary, indicating Cesar with a nod.

"Thanks, ma'am." Cesar slipped the doll in his pocket, said goodbye to the ladies, turned Henry by the elbow, and headed for the street.

The halls, so quiet on the way in, were buzzing. The word was out. Cesar could not overhear enough to know whether employee opinion favored the new boss. He could only detect sounds of surprise.

Of all the employees, only the security guardette seemed unaffected. She logged the detectives out as she had logged them in—grimly. Leonard's standards were upheld.

As he drove back to Central Station, Cesar thought about Lt. Tieves and his advice. Warning, really. Don't get involved with business, Cesar. You don't understand it. Don't screw things up. Leave the big guys for the big guy.

It was very nice to know that the new big guy was a woman, a woman whom Cesar knew and one who seemed to like him. Grace Golden was not going to call the Manager or the Chief and ask for someone else. She was not going to be snowed by Lt. Tieves and his movie star looks. Probably. Cesar hoped.

Action. That's what she would appreciate. And he planned to oblige.

The key to Cesar's plan of action was on the way to Millvale, riding in the right-hand seat of Henry's Lincoln. Cesar had pried the doll from her blister pack and handed her to Henry on the sidewalk outside Golden Times. Henry had solemnly placed her in the passenger seat where so many other lovely ladies had ridden. Few had been so small or so quiet. Before he closed the door Henry took a little peek down the front of her dress for Cesar's benefit. Cesar didn't notice. His mind was on the doll out in the projects.

22

BY THE TIME Henry reached Millvale, Cesar was closeted with Grace's tape recorder, the Irving tapes, a legal pad, and a young patrolman. The young patrolman was eating his lunch. Cesar had no legitimate reason to kick him and his four-way from the conference room—they were there first. Cesar used an earphone to listen to the tapes and for the first few minutes he looked as if he were involved in an illegal wiretap operation, constantly twisting around to see if Sgt. Evans had somehow gotten wind of his presence and come to take him apart. But as Sgt. Evans did not appear and as the tape became more and more interesting, Cesar ceased his guilty motions and huddled over the legal pad taking notes. He played the tape through once, rewound it, and played it again. He took fresh notes on the replay.

As Cesar rewound for the third listen, the young patrolman stood up and began cleaning up his lunch mess. For the first time since entering the room Cesar realized that the heavenly smell of Skyline Chili was doing unkind things to his stomach. He had forgotten about lunch.

Cesar looked wistfully at the little waxed paper bags as the patrolman stuffed them into the empty blue Skyline carton. This little bag had held onions. That little bag had held shredded cheese, and those two little squares of paper had probably wrapped two plump little cheese coneys. The chili carton was for a double order. Cesar's gaze shifted to the plump patrolman who had failed to offer a portion of lunch to the hardworking homicide detective. The patrolman looked at the detective.

"Something wrong?" he asked.

Cesar shook his head.

"Watcha got?" asked the patrolman, pointing his chin at the cassette player.

"Tape," said Cesar. If the guy wasn't going to share his four-way, Cesar wasn't going to share his information. The cop stuffed his papers into a garbage can where the smell could continue to torture the detective. He gave Cesar a dirty look and left the room. Cesar punched the "play" button for the third time.

This last time Cesar did not write. Instead, he checked his notes as he read. When the tape ended, Cesar took out the little earphone, coiled the wire neatly, and stowed it in the little niche the Japanese had thoughtfully provided next to the battery case. Next he tore off the sheets containing his notes and set them beside the legal pad. Referring constantly to the notes, Cesar began a list of questions which ultimately filled two pages. Each question had its roots in the notes, each had a number and each had a space of several lines where Cesar hoped to write answers. When he had completed his list of questions, Cesar folded the stack of notes and stuck it in the back of the legal pad. Then he squared up the pad with the edge of the table.

For one brief moment Cesar felt triumphant. He had by no means solved the problem of who killed Irving Golden and Donna Creech. He was not even sure that he knew why they had been murdered, although he now had a theory—or at least the frame of a theory.

His feeling of triumph was due to his success at organizing and plotting on paper and in writing the problems he had to resolve, the questions he had to answer, and his conviction that he knew where to find the answer to each question.

As quickly as he had been washed by the feeling of triumph, however, Cesar was drenched with a feeling that he had done something wrong. It was not wrong that he had worked his way closer to a solution, nor was it wrong that he had been moderately clever. What swamped him in something close to panic was the sudden knowledge that he had broken two unwritten rules. One rule was his, the other was a police rule.

The latter—one of the many unwritten rules of the Cincinnati Police and possibly of many other cities—was the ban on working and thinking alone. The rule appeared odd considering only the local practice of assigning a single detective to each case. One would expect solo solutions to be the rule, but, in fact, it was the habit and practice of most detectives to thrash their cases out at length and at all stages with their associates.

Cincinnati police did not go for solitary rambles in the woods; they went in for lengthy rambles at Frisch's, in the office, in the washrooms, and over the phone. They talked when they had cases and listened when they didn't. They shared their wisdom and they shared their stupidity and they expected their brother and sister officers to do the same. There were those who were slow to pick up on this rule. Female and black officers almost always had trouble with it, as they did with so many of the unwritten rules, but they normally caught on in time. Even Carole Griesel, who considered herself head and shoulders above the entire homicide squad and maybe the whole division when it came to brains, even Carole was falling into line. She had her own style, of course. The proper style of oral problem solving called for a low-key, matter-of-fact opening.

"So, you know, I was talking to this neighbor lady of the guy who got shot and she was trying to figure out how come he was even in the apartment 'cause she don't think he was home most days and that's probably right 'cause he works at Lunkenheimer and jeez you know I can't figure out either what he was doin'. Probably some girl. Whattaya think?"

Like that.

Only Carole Griesel was likely to come in, slam her purse on her desk, and open up with, "Serves the jerk right for coming home when he was supposed to be at work. Typical!" (She never explained "typical." It was a catchall.) "You really can't be surprised he got in some kind of trouble when he couldn't even follow work rules." And then she'd fool around with her purse and say, "If I can just get my hands on the reason *why* he came home, I'll know why the jerk got his head blown off."

Both openings allow for plenty of comment. Carole found it necessary to dump all over the responses, but they helped her to think. And that was the point. You were supposed to do your thinking outloud.

In some ways it was a good rule. Everyone got in on all the problems, and you could count on a lot of extra brainpower and experience. The drawback was that nobody wanted to look real stupid or real flashy once they learned how the game was played, so some theories and ideas never got mentioned or didn't come out until all the sensible, modest theories and ideas had proved to be worthless. Sometimes it took too long to wrap things up and sometimes things never got wrapped up.

Cesar had worked on his own. Sure, everyone kept a little back, but Cesar had kept a lot to himself. He had shared some with Henry, but that wasn't the same as sharing it with the squad. Henry still was not one of the boys. And now he, Cesar, was pretty sure he was close to the end and he was not going to be able to say, "I couldn't have done it by myself."

The other rule, the rule of his own that he broke was even more important to him: be like the other cops. He had broken that by breaking the other rule.

Cesar didn't want to be different. Not in the least. The closer he came to his understanding of the quintessential Queen City Police Officer, the happier he was. He had had to overcome a number of handicaps to reach his current state. He wasn't Catholic. He hadn't gone to Elder High School. He was Belgian instead of German. He had a goofy name. His dad wasn't a cop. But Cesar had wanted very badly to be a real Cincinnati policeman. Consciously and unconsciously he had made himself into a Catholic, Elder graduate from a line of German policeman. He walked, talked, and thought as if he were born a cop, patterning himself first on Elder graduates, then buddies in the Navy, then on the real thing. But, somewhere inside, Cesar feared detectives. Having achieved his goal, having found the life of a policeman to be as fine and good as he thought it would be, there was a constant fear that his fraud would be discovered and he would be out. He might have his pension, but he wouldn't be one of the guys.

And now he had screwed it up. He had screwed it up because he wanted to impress Grace and he wanted to show Lt. Tieves that he was smart enough to deal with businessmen.

Such was Cesar's mood that, when he heard the door open behind him he *knew* it was Sgt. Evans coming to look him up for being a Fake Regular Policeman.

But it was Henry.

"Did you get it?" asked Cesar.

Henry reached into his coat pocket and pulled out Stacey's Denver Doll. Aside from the frayed and dingy silver dress she wore, the doll was indistinguishable from her replacement. Somewhere along the line she had lost an important snap and a perky little breast was in full view. Cesar lifted the doll from Henry's palm using his thumb and forefinger.

"Did you have any trouble with Stacey?"

Henry shook his head. "She thought it was a good deal. Said hers was getting worn out."

Cesar put the doll on the table beside his list of questions. She stared over the length of the tabletop, her eyes focused on the end of the room. She looked just a little tired.

"What you going to do with her?" asked Henry.

Cesar picked her up and, avoiding her stare, removed the limp little dress. Then, grasping her torso firmly in his left fist, he pulled off her head with his right hand. She gave a little pop. He peered into her head from the bottom and then carefully shook it over the pad. Nothing fell out. He set the head down at the top of the list of questions. The long dark nylon hair would not allow the head to stand upright, so it rolled until her nose caught the tabletop.

Cesar shook the headless body. There was no rattle. Neither was it unduly heavy. He examined the faint seam line that made a line around the torso. There was no sign of tampering. Working slowly, being careful not to harm the tiny ball and socket joints, he gently pried off the limbs, one by one. The pops were fainter than that made by the head when it came off. One by one he shook the limbs, listening for rattles and then he turned each one over the paper to see if anything came out of the little holes. Nothing did.

"Looking for drugs?" asked Henry.

"I dunno," said Cesar. "No. Too small for drugs."

"Diamonds?"

"I told you, I don't know."

"Okay." Henry's feeling were getting hurt again.

"I didn't think there'd be anything, I guess. I just had to check."

"You gonna X-ray it?"

"Cesar thought for a moment. "Think I should? Take a look. You think that's been fooled with?" He handed the torso to Henry.

The sight of Henry turning the tiny limbless trunk over and over in his plump dark hand, bringing it close to his eyes, was an image that would stay with Cesar a long time. He didn't laugh.

"How do they make this?" asked Henry.

"It's molded. I guess they heat it. Injection, maybe. But look, I don't see how anybody could take it apart and then put it back so it looked new."

Henry took a last close look and then set the torso on the pad beside the head and arms. "Well, if there's nothing in there, what's anybody want with it?"

"That's what I'm trying to figure out," said Cesar.

"Give it to me," said Henry. "I'm taking it to the bomb boys. Got to see. They've got X-ray."

"Don't tell them where you got it."

"Hunh?"

"Not from me, okay?"

Henry shrugged. "Won't take long." He wouldn't tell.

When Henry left, Cesar wrote an answer beside a question. The answer was "Nothing." He was confident that the X-ray would show an empty trunk.

He lined up the limbs one by one on the table, placing the head at the end of the line. It still would not lie face up. He picked up each limb and looked closely. For what, he still did not know. He lined them up neatly again and stared at them.

When he heard the door open behind him, he swept the pieces up in one hand and covered them.

"Seen Klosterman?" asked the intruder. Cesar shook his head and the guy left. Cesar lifted his hand and looked at the head and arms and legs. Then he picked up a leg and very gently bent it at the knee. It gave. He bent it into a tight angle, straightened it, and then bent it again. It held its shape. Nothing broke, nothing snapped. He picked up an arm and flexed the elbow. Same thing. Each of the limbs did the same thing. He lined them up again, only this time the limbs were bent into 30-degree angles. Now it looked as if he had been torturing a large insect. He scooped the pieces into his left hand and wrote down another answer—"Millvale doll has joints."

Cesar wished he had another doll with him. A new one. He was going on memory, but he was pretty sure the new dolls didn't flex like this.

Again the door opened and again Cesar swept up the pieces, but it was Henry.

"That was fast."

"Yeah, well, I know someone down there."

"Figures," said Cesar. "Find anything?"

"It's empty," said Henry. "Now what?"

"Give it to me," said Cesar. Henry handed him the torso and Cesar began reassembling the Denver Doll. Five pops later she was back together but naked.

"You know," said Henry, "I don't know if that's good for kids."

"Kids love 'em," said Cesar.

"Yeah. But. She's bad, Ceez. Looks real."

"They gotta learn."

Cesar gathered the limp little dress and examined it before he put it back on the doll. No micro dots, no little messages, just dingy, silver lamé. The snaps weren't meant for adult fingers. It took Cesar much longer to get her dressed than it did to put her back together.

"You still think that's what we're looking for?" asked Henry.

"I think it's what Donna had that somebody wanted."

"How come? No dope. No diamonds. What's it worth?"

"I don't know," said Cesar. "But look." And he pointed out the articulated limbs.

"I'm looking," said Henry.

"What I'm wondering . . . see, this doll's different. The arms and legs don't bend on the new ones. Or I don't think they do. So I was wondering if this isn't some kind of model. You know, wasn't supposed to be for sale."

Henry took the doll back and fiddled with the arms and legs. Then he set it on the table and looked at it. He had posed the doll so that she was sitting on her feet.

Then he looked at Cesar, waiting for the rest of the explanation.

"Well, I was thinking," said Cesar, spinning it out to include Henry. He had already decided he was right. "Donna must have gotten this and took it home and whoever killed her was looking for it. That's why he tore up the kids' rooms. And Donna caught him at it."

"Or wouldn't give it to him," said Henry.

"Or," said Cesar, "knew something about it."

They looked at the doll. No help from her.

"She didn't even have to know anything—maybe the guy just thought she did." Now Cesar was genuinely thinking aloud. "But she was kind of smart, you know."

Henry nodded once. He had his toothpick in place.

Cesar continued, "I'll bet she figured *something* out. Guessed at something. At any rate she wanted the doll back."

"What for?"

"I dunno. Maybe . . . maybe she wanted to show it to somebody, but maybe . . . maybe she wanted to put it back."

"At the office?" asked Henry.

"I guess so. That's where she probably got it."

Henry started walking around the room. Cesar watched and tried to read behind the sunglasses. Was Henry thinking how he might be right or how he might be seriously full of shit? After a couple of circuits Henry came back and stood beside Cesar. They both looked at the Denver Doll. Thinking.

"*What* are you guys doing?"

Christ! Sergeant Evans. Master of the no-click knob turn. Cesar and Henry jumped a foot.

Sgt. Evans muscled over and looked at the doll. Cesar and Henry knew what he was doing—flipping through his fat mental rolodex for the perfect sarcastic question. Cesar opened his mouth to forestall, but Henry beat him to the punch.

"It's evidence, Sergeant. The case."

Sgt. Evans looked into Henry's mirrored glasses, seeking any hint of falsehood or mysterious black thinking. Hard to find any clues when all you see is your own face. Once again he yearned to publish the memo banning mirrored shades . . . the one Lt. Tieves filed away.

"No kidding, Sergeant," said Cesar.

"Nice," said Sgt. Evans. "I'm glad you're not kidding. Who's case? Yours?"

"His. Ours."

Sgt. Evans waited.

"We think they're related. The cases. Donna Creech and Irving Golden. They've got certain—"

"Thank you, Cesar. That's interesting. That doll looks like a hooker."

"Yeah, I guess it does. You want—"

"I want to know if you're going to be in here all afternoon, and I want to know if you have any plan to finish your budget forms. I also want to know why you think it's okay to sneak around ducking your Sergeant who has told you to tell him everything you're doing and you haven't told him nothing for forty-eight hours."

"Sure, Sergeant. I tried to call you a coup—"

"Shut up, Cesar. What does this little lady of the evening have to do with your current assignment, gentlemen? Or is that a secret?"

"I told you, Sergeant. It's evidence."

"Cesar, don't hand me any more shit. I've been keeping Lieutenant Tieves out of your way for three days now—"

Not exactly true.

"And I'm tired of making up stories to make him happy, so how about telling your old Sergeant what you're doing. Okay?"

"Sure."

And slowly and carefully, Cesar told the Sergeant about the doll and why they got it and why he thought it was interesting. Midway through the explanation Sgt. Evans, who was not terribly angry and who liked to sit down and listen as much as any other short fat man, sat down. All three stared at the little doll while Cesar talked. Finally, when he was through, Cesar looked at the Sergeant. Sgt. Evans' face was slightly pained. Cesar understood. It was not what he or anyone would call an ironclad case.

"And?" asked the Sergeant.

And Cesar had to decide whether to give up his free flight . . . to end his little excursion into the world of lone wolf problem solving. He gave up. There would be no rabbit out of a hat. He would have to tear the hat apart in front of Henry and Sgt. Evans.

"I think maybe we've got blackmail here. *Possibly.* But you know, maybe it's not blackmail but what we ought to have is somebody who *thinks* it's blackmail. See, there's this tape." And Cesar pointed to the cassette player. "You want to listen? Maybe I should explain."

"No, just play it," said the Sergeant.

"Right. It's from the meeting they had at Golden Time just before Mr. Golden got killed."

"Fine. Play it."

And Cesar played the tape at the section at the end where Irving Golden got the news about Whizbang Toys and their line of Boston Babes complete with nipples and working knees. It wasn't very long. Cesar named the speakers. Sgt. Evans and Henry listened without comment. Cesar noticed for the first time the similarity between Irving's voice and that of Sgt. Evans.

After the tape went silent, Sgt. Evans picked up the little doll and delicately opened her blouse and peeked down the front.

"No nipples," he said.

"But the knees bend," said Cesar.

"Arms, too," said Henry.

"So?"

"So I was thinking maybe someone did a little industrial espionage."

"From Whiztime?" asked the Sergeant.

"Whizbang," said Cesar. "Only they got help from somebody inside."

"You mean Mrs. Creech?"

"No. I don't think so. I think . . ."

Sgt. Evans reached for the legal pad and started reading Cesar's list of questions.

Cesar blushed, blanched, and blushed again. Sgt. Evans read through the list, looked at Cesar, stood up and asked, "You know where you're going to get the answers?"

"Sure. Yeah. I think so."

"I'll see you guys later. *Today*," said the Sergeant. And then he left the room.

Henry was amazed. He reached for the list. Cesar's hands went out to stop him, but what the hell. He let Henry read.

Henry read slowly through to the end.

It wasn't fair. Henry was going to be pissed off at Cesar for holding out on him when the only reason Cesar got overorganized and wrote things down was because he thought he was in over his head.

Well. He did think he was a little slick, too.

"Thanks for letting me in on this before the Sergeant got to it, Cesar."

Jeez. A major sulk coming on.

"Hey, Henry, I was just trying to get some ideas together."

Henry looked out the window.

Cesar crossed his arms and waited. To hell with apologizing. Henry was a big baby.

"That's pretty good," said Henry.

Son of a gun.

"Yeah, well. There's a lot of stuff I don't know."

"Better get on it, right?"

"Right."

"You want me to check on the cars?" asked Henry.

"You mind?"

"No. Won't take too long. Give me the names, will you?" And Cesar carefully spelled out the names of all the men at the meeting so Henry could check with the computer to see who drove what. Henry started to leave.

"Henry, I'm going to need more help."

"I know. Just write out my directions real clear."

"I—"

"Don't worry. Just kidding." Henry, not kidding at all, left.

Cesar straightened the table, pulled the telephone close to his legal pad, and dialed Golden Time Toys.

"Flexy knees!" he hummed to himself as he waited for an answer. "The tiny Boston Babes just love to please."

And then he picked up the Denver Doll and squeezed her legs, and just like the Boston Babes, the Denver Doll kicked her legs straight out. She felt like a live grasshopper.

23

FIFTEEN MINUTES LATER Cesar and Grace were seated in what used to be Irving's and was now Grace's office. They were alone and, since Grace had let Cesar in through the private door, only Grace knew he was there. Cesar had asked for privacy and he was getting it. She had closed the door to Rosemary's office and turned on the radio. They were talking very quietly. They sat on a sofa away from Rosemary's wall.

It didn't take Grace long to read through Cesar's list of questions and, with a few quick questions of her own, she seemed to understand thoroughly where Cesar was headed and why. For just a minute she leaned back in the sofa and closed her eyes, resting a hand on one of Cesar's. He looked down at the small smooth fingers and found them to be very attractive. He did not read anything into the gesture other than a need to hold on to another person.

That one minute passed very quickly. Grace opened her eyes, stood up, and crossed to her desk without looking at Cesar. She pulled a telephone from a shelf below the desk and dialed. Cesar watched the sixteen-button phone that Grace had ignored. No lights went on when she picked up. He wondered if Irving had any real reason to fear eavesdropping. Grace talked so quietly that he couldn't hear her over the radio. She wrote something on a pad, hung up, and brought the pad back to Cesar.

"Does that name mean anything to you?" she asked. It didn't. She explained.

One of Cesar's questions concerned the arrival of a report at the Golden residence on the night Irving was killed. It was Irving himself on the tape who had led to the question. According to Grace's maid, there *had* been a visitor for Irving that evening. If he had intended to deliver something he didn't deliver it to the maid. He did, however, leave his card.

Larry Schuster. 266-4810.

Cesar fetched the yellow pages and looked up security agencies. Sure enough, there he was. On West Eighth. Schuster Security. Commercial Security and Investigating.

Before he called Schuster, Cesar called Sgt. Evans. The Sergeant was more or less happy to tell Cesar that Mr. Schuster was indeed known to the Sergeant, that he had been in business for many years and that he was respectable as far as private investigators went.

Cesar went back to the sofa. How many more times would he be able to sit arm and arm with President Grace? Besides, they had to get their act together before they talked to Mr. Schuster.

"Dammit," said Grace. "Why didn't Daddy tell me what he was doing? Why did he have to be such a *beast* about security?"

Because, Grace, he didn't expect to get killed.

"He's *always* been like that, Cesar. He loved security. It was one of his games. Like that damned lock. He never even told Rosemary when he had some sort of spare racket going. I know that. Not that he fooled her—you don't keep Rosemary in the dark long and then he'd always screw it up. He wasn't even good at it. Like the lock again. Lost the key, for God's sake! And here's this investigator that nobody knows about with a report that nobody's even read. I wonder if he's even been paid? Should I call him? Now?"

Cesar thought she should. She straightened her back and turned back into a president.

She handled Larry Schuster with ease. Schuster didn't want to release his report to anyone but Irving Golden. That was his deal. Grace firmly reminded him that Irving would be unable to pay him now or ever. She further informed him that she was now in charge of Golden Time Toys, that she was able to pay him, that she wanted the report, and that a detective from the Cincinnati Police Division would be around shortly to pick up the report. Would that be satisfactory? It would.

Cesar waved his hand at Grace and she covered the mouthpiece.

"Ask him if he talked to your father Thursday afternoon. Oh! And ask him what kind of car he drives—what color."

She asked. Yes, he had and he drove a red Aries. Grace thanked him and hung up. She immediately pulled out a piece of Irving's writing paper and wrote a message to Mr. Schuster. She showed it to Cesar. It authorized him not only to receive the report but to read it. Cesar thanked her.

"Now what?" she asked.

The dolls. Cesar had to know about the dolls. He pulled out Stacey's bedraggled Denver Doll and showed it to Grace. She agreed that it was a prototype but that was all she knew. Prototypes were Joseph Enneking's territory. Did he want to see Enneking?

Cesar thought that over. Enneking was still on his list. If the dolls were at the heart of the troubles and if Enneking was involved, he could be scared off. Cesar wanted him around.

"I'll handle it," said Grace. "I'll make it business." Thank you.

"What else?"

Nothing else. She was handling it all.

Grace looked at her watch. "I've got a staff meeting at four. If you want to go see Schuster, I'll just have time to talk to Joe. And then . . ." She thought for a moment. "Then I'd like to see your office. Could I?"

"Sure."

"Good. I'll come straight over. Where is it?"

Larry Schuster's office was across the expressway in Queensgate. It was convenient to the Holiday Inn, I-75, a Ford dealer, and other low overhead offices. It was not convenient to any nifty lunch spots or department stores and for that reason Queensgate secretaries seemed to be perpetually sullen. Schuster's was no exception. She announced Cesar and resumed thrashing her Olivetti.

Schuster opened his door and waved Cesar in. He did look like a cop. He was in his fifties and wore doubleknits without pills and snags.

Schuster checked out Cesar's badge closely, wrote down the number, read Cesar's letter, then picked up the phone and dialed. He asked for Miss Meynell. When he got her he confirmed Grace's claim to the throne. Then and only then did he hand over a large sealed envelope to Cesar.

"How do you like homicide?" he asked, thereby showing off his contacts in the Division.

"Fine, sir." Cesar wasn't impressed. He himself had contacts in the Millvale Housing Project.

Cesar ripped open the envelope and started leafing through.

"Sit down, kid," said Schuster. Cesar sat down. "Tough about Irving, he was a nice guy."

Cesar grunted.

"That's not a final report. I wasn't done."

The report said "Golden Time Toys—Interim Report" on the front page.

"The good stuff starts on page five," said Schuster. "Do you know what was going on?"

"Not for sure. Industrial espionage, maybe?"

"Very good, Detective Franck! Very good! Only early—while they were in development. Happened a couple of times. And somebody leaked this new doll."

"But you didn't find out who," said Cesar.

"Nope."

"Any idea?"

"Read page five."

"Were you following Donna Creech around Millvale?"

"Read page five." Christ, this guy was an ex-sergeant for sure.

Cesar opened to page five. The heading was "Employee Activities" and the first group was Frederick, Donna, and Joseph Enneking. Cesar read quickly and then looked at Schuster. At the end of each person's section he had typed and underlined *Not a Current Suspect.*

"How far'd you get?" asked Schuster.

"First three. You still agree with this?" Cesar waved the report. Schuster ticked off the names.

"Frederick Golden. He's spending every spare minute with his girlfriend. I mean he's there in between meetings, on the way home, you name it. Unless he's home sleeping, he's with his friend, Mrs. Mandel. And I don't blame him. His wife's a stick. He doesn't do drugs, doesn't do horses. Stays out of bars. And he's got plenty of money anyway. Doesn't need to sell secrets.

"Donna Creech. If she's making money out of anything, it's invisible. She's got nothing to show for it. I couldn't see she was doing anything but hanging around black guys and going to discount stores. And her guys got no money. They're all dopes."

"Were you out in Millvale?" asked Cesar again.

"Of course I was out there." Schuster sounded as if Cesar were an idiot child. "That's my job, kid." He resumed his lecture. "Joe Enneking. He goes straight home every night, feeds his dogs, puts on his hangman's outfit, and goes to the Castle Club. You know it?"

Cesar knew it. Middle class (tame), heterosexual, S&M bar over in Newport.

"Read the rest," said Schuster.

Cesar read, but had to reread. He got distracted by the image of Enneking cracking the whip over in Kentucky. Enneking must have lived alone in his own castle too long.

The second group was from The Bennett Advertising Agency.

Only the first, Phillip Bennett, was *Not a Current Suspect.* According to Schuster, anytime Phillip Bennett was out of the office he was either at home or in Christ Hospital. Schuster had even checked his phone calls from both places. No calls to Whizbang. No calls to anyone other than family. That made Cesar happy.

The second and third were *Current Suspects.* Bob Atwood and Jack Squires. Schuster seemed very interested in their trips to New York as well as their spending patterns. But that didn't seem like a lot to go on as far as Cesar was concerned. He looked across the desk at Schuster.

"So, I told you, I hadn't got it figured out." The investigator wasn't embarrassed.

"Is this all you have on these two?"

"No. But Golden already knew the other stuff."

"What other stuff?"

"Atwood gambles and does coke—bums it mostly but buys every now and then. And Squires is into doctors for his family. He's also sending money out of the country."

"Why?"

"Beats me."

"And that's it?"

"Hell, no. Read on, boy."

Cesar read. The report was mostly padding, but every now and then there was a little substance. Cesar found the part on Whizbang Toys interesting. The company had recently been bought by an oil-rich Arab. "Jeez." Cesar muttered. "Arabs are going to own everything."

"And did that ever piss off Golden," Schuster laughed. "He nearly busted his desk pounding on it when he heard about that. Hated Arabs."

"On principle?" asked Cesar.

"He was Jewish, kid. What do you expect? He took it personal. Said they bought Whizbang just to wipe out Jewish-owned toy companies."

"Did they?" asked Cesar.

"How would *I* know? I just figured they needed some place to park all those dollars they take out of my pocket at the gas station. I'm not real big on conspiracies."

"But they did wind up with this new doll from Golden Time."

"Yeah."

"How'd you find that out?"

"I got contacts, kid."

"How'd you get contacts at Whizbang?" asked Cesar. Schuster looked mysterious and didn't answer. Cesar took that to mean he bribed someone.

"But you didn't find out anything more than you got here?" Cesar held up the report.

"I told you—it's an interim report. What do you expect?"

Answers. Cesar expected *answers*. This was questions. How much did Irving have to pay for a bunch of questions?

"Besides, you're looking for a killer, kid. I was looking for an industrial spy. Right?" Schuster was right. The killer might be the spy and he might not. "But I'll tell you what, kid," said Schuster. "My industrial spy is going to turn out to be your killer. What do you want to bet?"

It would have been a pleasure to disagree. Cesar didn't like Schuster very much. Schuster didn't seem to have worked too hard so far. But what work he had done seemed sound. More important, Schuster's work fit into Cesar's thinking.

Irving's last-known call was from Schuster and it was about the dolls. Not the new dolls, the models. The prototypes with the knees and arms that bent. Cesar didn't have to go back to the Irving tapes to know that whoever was selling the company's secrets would have no trouble understanding Irving's end of the phone call. Irving's reaction after the call made it perfectly clear that someone was going to be in big trouble. So someone got rid of Irving.

Cesar picked up the report and stood up.

"You know this Grace Golden?" asked Schuster.

"Yes, sir."

"Tell her I'll send my bill. Tell her I'm interested in staying on the case, all right? Give her my best regards. You know how to do that?"

Cesar started to walk out of the office.

"Ask her if she can find Irving's doll list he was supposed to give me."

Cesar stopped. "What's that?"

"He was supposed to make a list—we were trying to figure out where all the Denver Dolls got to."

"The first ones?"

"Right. The prototypes. We figured somebody whipped one over to Whizbang for a peek real early. Irving was supposed to track them down."

Cesar turned back.

"He thought he had great security," said Schuster, "but he was sloppy. He didn't get control on those dolls until they had been out for weeks. Trusted too many people."

"Do you know who had them? How many there were?" asked Cesar.

"Six. He couldn't remember. Probably everyone in that report except Donna Creech."

24

HENRY THOUGHT IT was terrifically funny. Jack Squires, Bob Atwood, Frederick Golden, and Joseph Enneking all owned grey or silver Olds Cutlasses. Golden also owned a Seville and Atwood had a Ford Country Squire, but for the others the Cutlass was the only car. Cesar pointed out the fact that the Cutlass was the most popular car on the road and that he had seen plenty of blacks in Cutlasses, but Henry still thought it was terrific. Another new white cliché.

They sat waiting for Grace in the Homicide office. It was after five. Cesar told Henry about Larry Schuster, showed him the report, then filled him in on Schuster's unwritten remarks. Henry pursed his lips when he heard about Enneking and the Castle Club. He was capable of greater prudery than Cesar at times.

While Henry took a call from one of his lovelies, Cesar mulled over the Schuster report. It was not a total bust even though it was an interim report. A bullshit interim report.

But the report was mostly questions. Like what was Squires doing sending money out of the country? And how much money was it? A lot? A little? Was he deeply in debt to his doctors? Slightly in debt? And Atwood.

Atwood thought he was Red Hot. He thought it was okay to carry on with Marianne Kelly in public. He thought it was okay to harass his wife in front of strangers. It was okay to make stupid jokes in front of detectives. And now it turns out it was okay to do coke and gamble. It was going to be just fine with Cesar if a creep like Atwood turned out to be the murderer.

"See? I told you he'd be working hard."

Cesar looked up. Grace was smiling down at him. Standing beside her was Tom Cleary. It was Tom who had spoken. What the hell did she bring Tom for? She was in love with him. That had to be it.

Grace had her father's list. Only it wasn't a list, it was a receipt. "R'c'v'd. four Pixikin prototypes fm. Golden Time Toys Sept. 9" The signature was florid and impossible to read.

"What's a Pixikin?" asked Cesar.

"That was the working name for the Denver Dolls," said Tom. "They didn't really start out to be Denver Dolls; they were just dolls. Irv . . . Mr. Golden turned them into Denver Dolls."

Grace's interview with Enneking had done the trick. As soon as she mentioned the prototypes, Joe had steered her to the receipt. Not only did he know where Irving the Security Nut hid it (behind his picture of Henry Kissinger), but he also knew why he had it.

Joe Enneking had warned Irving about the dolls. It was Joe who insisted on controlling the dolls and Joe who drew up the receipt.

"Whose signature is it?" asked Cesar. "Looks like a drunk wrote it."

Grace looked at Tom, waiting.

"It's Jack Squires'," he said at last. "But I don't think . . . I mean you have to understand . . . It's such a *mess* over there . . . At the office. I mean . . ." He stopped, confused.

"Tom, I don't think Cesar is assuming anything. Just tell him about it." Grace was getting a little impatient.

"Cesar, Jack did have the dolls. Everybody knows that. See, they were his product. He's got the doll group, so he had to have them. But they were all over the office, too. I mean lots of people had to use them."

"What for?"

"Lots of things. We took pictures of them, drew them. I even had one for a while. I was drawing inspiration for my copy. I do that with lots of things."

"You don't have to apologize," said Grace. "It *is* your job, Tom."

"So they were all over the office," Cesar prompted.

"Right. Until the new ones came."

"When was that?"

"A couple of weeks, maybe four after the originals came over."

"And?" asked Cesar.

"Well, then they all got collected into a box on one of Jack's bookshelves and they just kind of sat there collecting dust. But I know they were there for a while. I remember seeing them." He stopped and looked at Cesar and Grace. They looked at him. "And then I don't know what happened to them. Nobody needed them since we had the production models, and we didn't want to get them confused. It would have been a disaster if we had one of the old ones turn up in one of the ads. They've got different features.

"But they *were* there. At least until the Dollsarama contest. Or, rather, that's when they *weren't* there anymore. I know because Gretel Tenbosch needed some extra dolls for Evelyn's display and I sent her to Jack's office."

"And they weren't there," said Cesar.

"Right. She said she couldn't find them so I went to look for them. She's perfectly capable of losing a car in a driveway—remind me to tell you about the time she forgot her—"

"Come *on*, Tom."

"Sorry. So I went to help her look for them and they definitely weren't there."

"Did you ask Mr. Squires about them?"

"I couldn't. He was in New York with Mr. Bennett and Bob Atwood for the toy show. And by the time he got back I had forgotten about it and Evelyn had changed his Dollsarama idea so no one was interested in them."

Cesar chewed on a pencil and looked at his friend. Tom was worried about his boss, and it showed on his face. "So, what do you think?" asked Cesar.

"I don't know. I asked . . . I hope I didn't screw anything up, but I asked Jack about the dolls today. Just to see what he'd say. I just wanted to know. Is that okay?"

Cesar bit down hard on his pencil, grinding through the paint and into the wood. It wasn't okay, but there was no undoing it. "Sure," he said, "It's okay What'd he say?"

"He said they were on the shelf. I said they weren't so he came and looked for himself. He got worried because he had signed for them but I told him it wasn't any big deal and not to worry. Was that all right?"

"Fine," said Cesar.

"God, I hope he doesn't have anything to do with this. I really do. He just doesn't need this."

"He probably doesn't, Tom. I don't know who's done what. I don't even know for sure if the dolls are what we're looking for. Would you take a look at this for me?" Cesar reached into a drawer and pulled out a brown envelope. He turned the envelope upside down and Stacey's Denver Doll tumbled out onto the desk top where she lay on her back. Her little arms reached out to embrace the group.

"You found them!" cried Tom. "Where were they?"

"I just found this one. Donna Creech had it."

"Oooh!" said Tom. "*That* one."

"What do you mean?" asked Cesar.

"That's Irving's."

"Daddy's?" Grace was confused. "That's a prototype! He wouldn't give her that."

Tom laughed. "He didn't. She swiped it from right under his nose last week. At the meeting."

"You saw her do it?" asked Cesar.

"Everybody saw it except Irving. He was too mad about his coffee getting spilled to notice."

"But that *is* a prototype." Cesar wanted to be sure.

192

Tom picked it up and played with the legs. "Yep. I thought it was because of the dress, but see? Only the prototypes have these flexible knees."

"Oh!" said Grace. "I haven't told you! We got our hands on a Whizbang Boston Babe (*don't* ask me how), and Joe Enneking took it apart. They've used his mechanism. He swears it's exactly the same. You're so *smart*, Cesar."

"What's he so smart about?" asked Tom. "How come *you* know what's going on? When am *I* going to be old enough to know?"

"It's the dolls, dear. That's what it's all about! Donna had this and somebody wanted it, right, Cesar?"

"I'm not sure—"

"Of *course* you're sure! There's a doll missing."

"There's four missing, Grace."

"No, no, dear. I mean one of those four. Whizbang had to take one apart to copy it. They copied the knees."

"And the elbows. So what?"

"Cesar, was he always this dense? Somebody from *your* office had to replace that missing doll, so he tried to get this one from Donna. And he . . ." Grace had brightened with excitement when she saw the solution at hand, but now remembering that this was not just an interesting puzzle, she looked forlorn. "What a bastard," she said at last. "What an evil bastard."

They had all left Cesar. Tom and Grace were having supper with Grandma Golden up in the Regency. Henry was having supper with one of his Honey Lambs. Cesar was having supper with his budget forms and his thoughts. Supper was Fritos and coffee.

He didn't feel so smart.

How was he supposed to wrap this up? He didn't even know who he was supposed to wrap up.

Cesar pulled out the budget forms.

At 11:00 Henry came back. He was through with one Honey Lamb and ready to set up another. Cesar was asleep in his chair. The budget forms were done. Henry sent him home.

By 11:30 Cesar was at home. He ate pie in the kitchen and thought.

By 12:00 Cesar had arrived at a course of action to speed things along. Feeling slightly smarter he went to bed.

"It's entrapment, Lieutenant. Good idea, I suppose, but it's entrapment." said Sgt. Evans.

"Where's the budget, Cesar?" asked Lt. Tieves.

"Getting typed, sir."

"Done?"

"Yes, sir."

"Can we do entrapment, Lieutenant?"

"How come you're calling it entrapment, Sergeant?" asked Cesar.

"Because that's what the lawyers are going to call it and that's what the paper's going to call it."

"I just want to see if anybody drops in. That's all. Is that entrapment, Lieutenant?" asked Cesar.

"Who's typing the budget?" asked Lt. Tieves.

"Cheryl, sir."

"Tell her I want it at noon."

"Yes, sir."

"I don't know, Sergeant. Nobody's getting bribed." Lt. Tieves finally abandoned the goddamned budget.

"No."

"Kind of stagey, though."

"Sir?"

"I wish you had a little more to go on. What are you going to do if nobody drops in?"

"I've got some leads, sir. I just think I could save a little time."

"You want to do it by yourself?"

"I don't . . ."

"Take Chapman."

"Yes, sir."

"Don't screw it up, Franck," said Sgt. Evans.

"Don't screw what up, Cesar?" Detective Griesel was crazy to know what was going on.

"Som'p'n," said Cesar.

"Asshole," said Detective Griesel.

Cesar reached for the phone and called Grace Golden.

"No nipples," said Grace Golden. "It's too late to change and I want to hold costs down. We're going to beat Whizbang on price. Is that clear?"

Except for Grace, who sat in her father's chair, the assembly in the Golden Time conference room was the same as that of the previous Thursday.

"Great," said Marianne Kelly.

"It's not a matter of taste or politics, Miss Kelly. Strictly cost," said Grace. "Besides, Barbie's gotten away without them for years."

"Screwing up God knows how many ten-year-old boys," said Bob Atwood. He laughed alone.

"And we'll go with the spots the way you shot them," said Grace.

"Good. I'm sure you'll be happy with them." Phillip Bennett was visible relieved. So were Jack Squires and Tom Cleary. Evelyn Osborne was busy locating Rosemary's knee and missed the good news.

"I'm not at all sure I'll be happy with them, Mr. Bennett. I don't know why I should be. I'm certainly not happy with the agency. These may well be the last spots you do for this company. They're ragged. I don't like the color and the copy's weak. *Very* weak," She said, looking firmly at Tom. "But they're set, and I want these dolls moving early."

The telephone buzzed.

"Take that in your office, please, Rosemary. And tell the switchboard when I say 'No calls,' I do mean *No Calls*."

"Yes, Ms. Golden."

"Now, I've been talking to Sri Lanka people about these blue jeans." Grace held up a tiny pair. "I don't know how long we can stick with them."

"But we studied—"

"*Please*, Miss Kelly."

Marianne flushed and leaned back in her chair. Grace continued.

"They've turned out to be horribly expensive, even with the slave wages we're paying over there. They're simply too complicated for the size. It takes about three times as long to turn out one pair of bluejeans as . . . What *is* it, Rosemary?"

"I'm sorry, Ms. Golden. It's a Mr. Larry Schuster." From her lips Larry Schuster's name sounded like something soiled. "He insists on speaking to you."

"About what?"

"I'm sorry, he won't say. He says it's important."

"I'll take it in there."

Grace went into Rosemary's office, leaving the door open.

By unspoken agreement the people around the table kept their remarks soft enough to allow comfortable eavesdropping.

"This is Grace Golden . . . yes . . . yes, I am . . . no . . . no, Mr. Schuster, he didn't. Tell me . . . yes . . . I see. What was it for? . . . What? . . . I see . . . no."

She listened for a minute then. "I see. Yes, that's very interesting, but I don't know anything about it and I really don't now intend to spend money on . . . Mr. Schuster, I have no record of any investigation . . . all right, fine. Bring it . . . no, *you* bring the report here and I'll look at it . . . no, I'm leaving at five o'clock. I have an appointment . . . no, you can leave it with the guard at the front desk . . . he'll get it to my office . . . no, I'll read it tomorrow . . . no, send that, too . . . If it's as convincing as you say I'll contact you about payment . . . yes . . . well, that's the best I can offer . . . yes . . . goodbye."

Grace returned and sat down.

"Now, the blue jeans. Miss Kelly, I've seen your research, I understand why we chose blue jeans, but I want to know what the reaction to a miniskirt would be if . . . Mr. Bennett, are you all right?"

Phillip Bennett was gasping for breath.

"Rosemary, call the Rescue Squad!"

Grace was frightened, as were they all.

Phillip Bennett seemed to be dying.

Cesar knew it was no use. It was a dumb stunt. He was in Grace's office where he had been since before the meeting started. Grace had again let him in the back way.

He hadn't planned on a heart attack. He was going to be fired for failing to give CPR. It didn't matter that Jack Squires knew CPR better than Cesar and that he kept Bennett alive until the med techs got there. Cesar should have done something instead of staying in his hiding place. Well, he was going to stay another hour.

It was dead quiet. The room still smelled slightly of the late Irving's cigars, but there was also the slight ghost of Grace's cologne. Cesar's thoughts wandered to Grace and Tom. He was trying to imagine life with a corporation president when he heard footsteps.

5:34. Leonard with Larry Schuster's report.

Leonard walked in and set the brown envelope on the desk. He looked at Cesar as if Cesar were going to make off with the office furniture. Didn't even say hello.

"Thanks," said Cesar.

Leonard turned and headed back to his post, squeaking on his ripple soles.

Cesar left the comfort of the presidential chair to go stand in the hall. He set the door from Grace's office so it was slightly ajar. He made sure he could see the whole office.

6:00. Nothing. Absolute quiet.

6:15. More of same only Cesar had to go to the bathroom.

6:30. This was the dumbest idea he had ever had.

6:34. Cesar heard a very quiet scrape from someplace inside Grace's office. He peeked through the open space in the door as Bob Atwood emerged from the back staircase, stepped into the office, stopped, listened, looked around, crossed to the desk, picked up the brown envelope, read the return address, put it in his coat, and quietly walked back to the stairs. As Atwood went down the back stairs, Cesar eased into the office and listened to Atwood as he quietly opened the back door and stepped into the arms of Detective Henry Chapman.

196

This was a higher-up Research, Evaluation and Budget twerp than Cesar was used to dealing with. He didn't fit the image: big clunky wing tips, dumpy yellow drip-dry shirt (Cesar had two just like it in his own closet), bristly moustache. He didn't look at all like a banker or a lawyer. He didn't talk like the usual REB twerp either. He was unpleasantly frank.

"This is terrible."

Cesar blinked.

"Did you have our usual instruction in how to complete the Budget Narrative Form?"

"Yes, sir."

"That explains it."

Cesar blinked again. The REB supervisor leaned back in his chair and looked at Cesar.

"Would you want to defend this to City Council? Do you know what the City Manager would say if she read this?"

"No, sir."

"She would say, 'This is just as bad as all the other garbage everybody turned in.' And she would be right."

Cesar stared at the REB supervisor.

"So you're going to have to do it over. I'm sorry."

"What's wrong with it, sir?"

"What's wrong with it? It's baloney."

Isn't that what it's supposed to be?

"I know we've accepted baloney in the past. I also realize that we train you how to do baloney. However, last year's budget and training were prepared under the previous manager. Do you understand?"

"Sir."

"Mrs. Klein is a graduate of Smith. It is her policy that all budget documents should be written in English. Now I realize this may be seen as strange and unusual. Maybe even bizarre, but it is her policy."

"Oh."

"Oh. You *are* a chatty detective."

"Sir!"

"Aren't you the detective who cracked the Golden case?"

"I was assigned to that case, sir."

"It was very interesting. We might even get a conviction out of it. Very unusual. Anything new?"

"Some blood, sir. On an overcoat. And some cooperation from a firm in New York that was indirectly involved."

"Well, well. And you figured it all out?"

"I'm on the Homicide Squad, sir."

"I know that, Detective Franck. I can read."

"Sorry, sir."

The REB supervisor smiled at Cesar. "You're not going to tell me anything, are you?"

"Sir?"

"Would it kill you to tell me how you did it?"

Cesar stared at the bureaucrat. Could a deal be struck here? As a policeman, Cesar had become sensitive to the subtle change in atmosphere that indicated Bargaining Time. He bargained with witnesses, with suspects, with lawyers, with judges. This guy really wanted to know how Cesar had done his job and he was willing to trade something for the information. But what was the trade? The guy probably already knew about the bloodstains the dry cleaner hadn't got out of Atwood's English trench coat. That was in the papers.

If he told the bureaucrat that once he had realized that he was dealing with industrial espionage as well as murder and that the dippy little Denver Dolls were germane (a favorite word at Research, Evaluation and Budget), Cesar was able to sit down and think where he had seen or heard about flexible knees and elbows and legs that kicked when you squeezed them, would the bureaucrat absolve him from responsibility for the Homicide Squad budget?

If he told him that Bob Atwood's daughter had shown him one of the prototypes that she had swiped from her father, could the REB supervisor see to it that Carole Griesel would receive all future budget assignments?

If he told the guy that the quickest way he could think of to catch Atwood was to make him use Irving's Israeli key if he hadn't thrown it away, would the guy make his staff come to the squad room and apologize to all present for being creeps?

Above all, if he made such a deal, could he trust the guy to keep it? Was it possible to trust anyone from City Hall? Ever? Cesar thought not. He stared back at the Supervisor. Bargaining Time elapsed forever.

"Okay. Enough of that. Tell Lieutenant Tieves the reason I called you in was because buried deep in your stack of baloney I have seen some glimmering of intelligence. That is more than I have seen in ninety-nine percent of the baloney on my desk. So I'm going to borrow you for a while. I'm going to train you to be a trainer."

"Sir?"

"For the budget. You're going to be the most knowledgeable officer in the entire division as far as budget goes. I've talked to the Chief about it. You'll be responsible for editing the total Police Budget Narrative. What's the matter? Aren't you happy?"

Is this guy kidding?

"I'm kidding. Not about the assignment. You'll do that. But you don't have to be happy. You just have to do it."

The supervisor smiled.

If you have enjoyed this book and would like to receive details of other Walker mystery titles, please write to:

Mystery Editor
Walker and Company
720 Fifth Avenue
New York NY 10019